ULTRAMAN

ULTRAMAN

The Official Novel of the Series

ULTRAMAN

ULTRAMAN

The Official Novel of the Series

PAT CADIGAN

TITAN BOOKS

Ultraman: The Official Novel of the Series
Print edition ISBN: 9781803362458
E-book edition ISBN: 9781803363011

Published by Titan Books
A division of Titan Publishing Group Ltd
144 Southwark Street, London SE1 0UP
www.titanbooks.com

First edition: December 2023
10 9 8 7 6 5 4 3 2 1

A CIP catalogue record for this title is available from the British Library.

Printed and bound by CPI Group (UK) Ltd, Croydon CR0 4YY.

This one is for Roz Kaveney—brilliant mind, beautiful soul, true friend, and all-around superhero—with admiration and love

And for Jim Cappio, whose kindness and friendship has so often helped me keep on keepin' on. Trust me, Jim, you're also a superhero

And, like everything else I do, for Chris Fowler, my one true love in all the universe and always the most interesting person/superhero in the room

CHAPTER
ONE

The pursuit had gone on for longer and farther than any other in the Ultra Being's experience.

The creature he was chasing, a particularly vicious brute calling itself Bemular, wasn't the first monster to make a break for it but it was an unexpectedly adept pilot. Their starting point had been in an area of the galaxy where the stars were so numerous and so close together that total darkness was virtually unknown, and continued all the way to the ragged edge of the Milky Way. Beyond that lay the pitiless black void of intergalactic space, where even advanced sentient lifeforms could die of loneliness.

The Ultra's quarry wasn't looking to die, and certainly not like that. After the long chase, Bemular needed to find a place where it could remain hidden long enough to replenish its energy. But the odds of finding anything like that in this part of the galaxy weren't good. The interplanetary systems were fewer and farther between, and the small percentage of inhabited worlds among them weren't developed enough for Contact. The Ultras scrupulously observed galactic quarantine for the well-being of the lifeforms involved. Monsters, however, didn't care about anyone's well-being.

Scans showed the Ultra that within a planetary system orbiting an unremarkable G-star, there was a small, rocky but water-rich planet with abundant resources that could easily be extracted and converted to energy. It was the best option for a monster in a hurry. Bemular's blue Travel Sphere dived into its atmosphere and the Ultra dived right in after—and then discovered the monster's best option put him at a disadvantage.

The inhabitants of this world weren't Beings of Light— far from it. For them, most forms of radiation were harmful, even lethal. The planet's atmosphere filtered out the most dangerous kinds, which had allowed for the emergence of carbon-based life in quite a profusion of forms, from single-cell organisms and basic vegetation all the way up to individual vertebrates capable of abstract thought.

Current environmental conditions weren't ideal. It was a densely populated world and such a high concentration of discrete intelligent beings kicked up a lot of pollution, of all kinds—light and sound as well as particulate. Bemular would have no trouble surviving under those conditions but for the Ultra, it meant a sharp reduction in the amount of available energy. And Bemular was no fool—it had gone directly to the night-side of the planet, where there would be even less power to draw on. The Ultra had to redistribute the various feeds just to keep the Travel Sphere in flight.

Normally redistribution was performed at a much lower velocity, not while chasing a monster through an unfamiliar environment. The Ultra vowed that the pursuit would end here, on this small, obscure planet and, if at all possible, without endangering any of the indigenous life, including the ones gathered at the edge of an inland body of water.

The sight of Bemular's Travel Sphere stirred them all up and put them in an agitated state of avid curiosity but it was clear they had no flying vehicles among themselves. Which was very fortunate—pursuing Bemular in these conditions was hard enough without having to worry about dodging inquisitive airborne natives.

Agent Shin Hayata of the Science Special Search Party, aka the SSSP, or simply the Science Patrol, had chased his share of UFOs through the night sky. Some had turned out to be phantoms and others had been more substantial, but he'd never had so much as a near miss with any of the latter. He was just too good a pilot.

The UFO *du jour* (or *de la nuit*) looked like a great big ball of blue light and flew like something too sophisticated to obey the laws of physics. It had darted around the treetops of Ryugamori Forest for a while as if it were searching for something. Then it had reached the lake, where it now seemed to be doing some impromptu aerobatics for a group of campers on the shore.

At first, he'd thought the UFO pilot was playing with the

vessel's reflection just to show off. The campers had *ooh*ed and *aah*ed excitedly at every tricky maneuver. Hayata was just as impressed as they were, although it also made him think of something his flight instructor had told him back when he'd been a new member of the Science Patrol and still in training to fly the fancy VTOLs:

Son, there are old *pilots and there are* bold *pilots, but there are* no *old, bold pilots. Decide which one you want to be so the rest of us can file the appropriate flight plan.*

Whoever was on the stick in that glowing blue ball either hadn't heard that bit of wisdom or put no stock in it. Either way, Hayata was going to have to stay extra alert if he wanted to end his shift in one piece. He called in to Headquarters to give them a status report and smiled when he heard the voice in his headphones.

'What's up, Hayata? You sound serious.'

Some things you could always count on, he thought; the sun always rose in the east, you could always find people camping at Lake Ryugamori, and when he called in to HQ, Akiko Fuji would answer. Life was good; not easy, but then, what fun would that be?

'I've got the UFO in sight over Lake Ryugamori,' Hayata told her. 'Looks like a glowing blue spotlight and the way it moves should be impossible. It's putting on quite a show for the campers.'

'Muramatsu here, Hayata,' the captain said, joining the conversation. 'Stay with it, see if you can get some idea of its structure. It's got to be made of something more substantial than light. We'll be out to back you up shortly.'

'Copy that, Cap. Hayata out.' He chuckled to himself. All the Science Patrol agents had come across some pretty strange things in the course of the job but a UFO made of light would be a first.

Captain Toshio Muramatsu was too restless to stay behind his desk in the Operations Center. Any time civilians were in close proximity to a UFO, it made him nervous. He made sure Fuji was recording everything that came in from Hayata, then checked on how Daisuke Arashi and Mitsuhito Ide were doing with the map they'd put up on a glass-board.

Ryugamori Forest was the region's largest wooded area and very popular with campers. Lately it had also been popular with strange lights in the sky; the number of reports had increased. Some had been spurious—city-folk not used to the great outdoors, who'd never seen a falling star—but others had involved some kind of genuine phenomenon or event witnessed by three or more people, most of whom were sober.

In any case, all calls about strange or suspicious activity had to be investigated and reports filed. If a report turned out to be a false alarm, that was all right with Muramatsu—no fault, no foul, no harm done, and no tears shed. Anything else was an open case they had to keep track of. Arashi and Ide had created the glass-board map to do exactly that, color-coding each case and marking the spot of first sighting, trajectory followed, and last known location, dated and time-stamped. The way things were going, Muramatsu suspected they were going to need extra glass-boards and a lot more colors.

Fuji had suggested they use the computer but both Arashi and Ide had balked. They preferred working with something they could physically touch, write on, and move around; it gave them a better feel for directions and distances. A computer screen was entirely too small, completely unworkable. Muramatsu told Fuji he was inclined to let them be. This was one of the very few things the two men had ever agreed on.

Both men were excellent Science Patrol agents—Arashi was fearless and his ability as a sharpshooter was practically supernatural, while Ide had a genius for invention and innovation. But Arashi also had a tendency to see things in stark black and white. By contrast, Ide was younger, less certain, not as serious or as self-possessed. The way Muramatsu saw it, they needed each other.

As Communications Officer, Fuji did more than simply respond to their calls in. She had a way of getting them to communicate with each other clearly and efficiently, which Muramatsu knew from his time as an astronaut was crucial to keeping a team functioning at their peak.

And then there was Hayata, who rounded them all out. He seemed to do everything right but was never arrogant about it, always treating his teammates with respect. He was level-headed, easygoing, slow to anger, and, best of all, he had a sense of humor, which was why Muramatsu had promoted him to his second-in-command and, in

Muramatsu's absence, acting CO. Arashi, Fuji, and Ide had accepted this without complaint or any sign of resentment or jealousy.

Muramatsu was relieved that they worked together as well as they did. He had been uncertain about taking this assignment after his years as an astronaut but so far, it was going well for everyone involved. His big concern at the moment, however, was this UFO Hayata was chasing. It was just a gut feeling but in Muramatsu's experience, there were times when the gut was smarter than the brain.

Fuji turned from the communications console to look at him, apprehension large on her young face. She had a way of picking up on how he was feeling—it was probably that talent for communicating, he thought. He gave her what he hoped was a reassuring nod and she nodded back at him, but her expression was no less anxious as she turned back to the console.

Hayata flew a wide circle around the glowing blue sphere, varying his altitude to scan it from different angles. So far, however, all the readings were crazy. Either the equipment was completely out of whack or the UFO was actually made of light—very weird light, dense light that behaved like a solid, which made no sense. Not on Earth, anyway.

He wished Professor Iwamoto were available but he was away at a conference. The good doctor had co-founded the Science Patrol to investigate unusual and/or anomalous phenomena. The professor might not have been able to explain anything but Hayata would have felt better knowing he was aware of it.

Meanwhile, the UFO pilot seemed to be focused on three particular spots above the lake, flying from one to another repeatedly in a lopsided triangular pattern. Hayata scanned the areas, hoping to discover what the alien visitor was drawn to but found nothing other than mud, rocks, lichen, and fish.

Hayata shifted to what he hoped was a safe distance and flew over the water in the same pattern but there was no reaction from the UFO, no change in brightness, altitude, or speed. Either the pilot didn't see what he was doing as an overture to communication or didn't care. Hayata thought it was probably the latter. It seemed unlikely that a lifeform capable of space travel wouldn't know when another intelligent being was trying to communicate.

Backing off a little more, Hayata increased his altitude to give himself more room for evasive action, just in case the alien pilot stopped ignoring him. Was there a crew on board? he wondered. If so, they must have been small in stature and number. Unless the UFO were some kind of quantum vessel and the inside was bigger than the outside. No, that was even more unlikely, Hayata decided.

And while he was at it, how long was this thing going to hang around before the pilot went after whatever was down there? And how would he—or she, or they—do that? Send the theoretical crew down in a submarine? Or did they have some sophisticated device that would teleport things aboard?

As if on cue, the UFO descended slowly into the lake, making the water churn and foam madly.

Hayata let out a surprised laugh. Okay, he hadn't seen that coming, although he probably should have. It made sense— any vessel that could travel safely through the vacuum of space would also be waterproof as well as airtight.

He heard the campers shouting in excitement on the exterior audio channel and pointed one of his outside cameras in their direction. Someone yelled at a guy named Tom to go get that fancy camera he'd insisted on bringing with him right now, dammit, or he was gonna miss the whole thing—

Which, sadly, Tom did, after tripping over something in the dark. By the time he got back, there was nothing to see but water bubbling up at the place where the UFO had gone down. Hayata felt sorry for him. He just hoped none of them got the bright idea to dive in after the thing.

He took the VTOL up a bit higher, looking for a blue glow in the water but there was nothing. Scans told him only that there was something big sitting on the muddy bottom and it had scared away all the fish. Time to call HQ and tell them to bring out one of the subs.

As Hayata reached for the cockpit comm, there was a flash of bright red in the windscreen directly in front of him. He had just enough time to register the thing as an enormous red sphere coming at him too quickly for evasive action.

Then everything went black.

* * *

Most people have the great good fortune to live their entire lives without ever seeing a midair collision. Even fewer witness a collision involving a UFO. The lakeside campers had no thought of how unique they were, only that the burning wreckage had fallen into the forest not a hundred meters from where they stood gaping in shock.

By then two members of the Saitama Park Police were with them, responding to their report of a UFO that had fallen or deliberately sunk into the lake. For all that they were law enforcement officers, Park Police more often functioned like land-based lifeguards, rescuing lost hikers who took a wrong turn on the path less traveled, or coming to the aid of those not properly equipped for a weekend of roughing it, and making sure campfires were completely extinguished.

Taking reports of strange activity was also part of the job. The Park Police handbook had a section on how to deal with nervous souls who thought they'd 'seen something' after scaring themselves silly with ghost stories around the campfire. Any reports about UFOs went directly to the Science Patrol while the Park Police kept the eyewitnesses calm and reassured.

Officers Tanaka and Uchido had over fifteen years of experience between them. They had arrived too late to see the blue UFO sink into Lake Ryugamori but along with the campers, they had a clear, unobstructed view of the red sphere crashing into the Science Patrol VTOL.

Police and civilians both had been transfixed, frozen in shock as the aircraft came apart and dropped into the forest.

Then one of the civilians said something about looking for survivors.

Everybody in Ops jumped when the phone rang, Muramatsu included.

Arashi took the call. His complexion was ashen as he put the receiver down and said there had been *two* UFOs over Ryugamori Forest. One was blue and was now at the bottom of the lake, although some of the witnesses weren't sure whether it had fallen in accidentally or gone into the water on purpose. The other UFO was red and all the witnesses had seen it collide in midair with a Science Patrol VTOL.

The team turned to look at Muramatsu. He clamped down on his emotions, showing no reaction to what Arashi had just told them.

'This is only an initial report,' he said, looking at each of them as he spoke. 'We mobilize, get to the crash site, and find out what actually happened. Fuji, keep trying to raise Hayata. Arashi and Ide, you're with me. Let's move.'

Neither Officer Tanaka nor his partner Officer Uchido had ever dealt with an air crash but the procedures were basically the same as for any other disaster. Uchido had immediately called Fire and Rescue; thanks to the fire-suppression system built into all Science Patrol transport, the flames were already dying down. The primary task for Tanaka and Uchido was crowd control—keeping the civilians back from the wreckage, which wasn't always easy, as every crowd seemed to have a couple of people convinced that they could help. Telling onlookers they had to keep the way clear so emergency workers could reach any casualties usually worked.

But the only casualty any of them could see was a man in a Science Patrol uniform lying on the ground beside part of a broken wing bearing the Science Patrol logo. There was no blood, no horribly mangled limbs or worse, but Tanaka could tell by the slackness of his body and the unnatural angle of his neck that the man was dead.

He and Uchido were moving the campers back another few meters when they heard rustling and the sound of brittle, burned wood breaking in the undergrowth. Tanaka winced; animal predation already? All the wildlife in the area should have been scared off. As he and his partner were trying to push the campers even farther from the crash site, they all suddenly began shouting and pointing and he turned to see the body of the dead Science Patrol agent levitating.

Uchido turned on his flashlight, putting it on the brightest setting. 'You see this, too, right?' he said to Tanaka in a low voice.

'I see it,' Tanaka replied.

'You got any idea what's doing that?' Uchido asked.

'I got nothing,' Tanaka told him. 'But whatever it is, we have to keep these people away from it.'

'Hey, look—is that supposed to happen?' one of the campers said in a high, panicked voice.

Now Tanaka saw there was a red glow around the floating

body. Transparent at first, it grew brighter and more substantial until it became completely opaque and they could no longer see the man at all.

'That looks like the UFO that crashed into him,' Uchido said to Tanaka.

'Don't ask me, I still got nothing,' Tanaka replied.

'Well, whatever that is, it's not nothing,' Uchido said, keeping his flashlight on the glowing red sphere. It continued to rise until it was about ten meters above the ground, hovering in a strange silence broken only by the soft crackle of the dying fire below.

The Science Patrol and emergency services had better show up fast, Tanaka thought, before the damned thing flew away or popped like a soap bubble or plunged into the lake after the other one. Because there was no way anyone who hadn't seen this would believe a word he told them.

I'm dreaming, Hayata told himself, although he knew he wasn't. No dream had ever been this definite, this *solid*, the way reality was definite and solid. Some force, strong, irresistible, and as volatile as a live electric current had taken hold of him and was literally lifting him up. But not *just* literally—it was lifting him in a deeply personal way. His mind, his *self* was rising up—

Always seek out those things that elevate the human spirit.

The thought came in his mother's voice. She had said that many times to him, even when he was a little kid. He'd joked about how she wanted him to press the up button for the human-spirit elevator and she'd thought that was pretty funny. But she had also made sure he was exposed to fine art of all kinds—painting and sculpture, music, literature, film, classic Kabuki and Noh theater, and more.

Hayata liked to think the Science Patrol aspired to the same kind of thing—elevating the human spirit by working to increase understanding of the world and the people in it, because there was far more to all of it than just those things that could be seen and heard and touched. In fact, he was in the presence of something more right now. What held him now wasn't just a force like gravity or magnetism—it was an individual consciousness. Someone.

Who's there? Hayata asked, too curious to be frightened. *Who in the world are you?*

He sensed the other considering the question of who in this world he was, and the possibility that the answer might be different in another world or even another time. It was an idea Hayata wouldn't have given any thought to simply because here and now were parameters that didn't change in this particular context. But the presence was one whose intelligence and understanding was far greater than his own and yet somehow it saw him as a kindred spirit.

In this world and all others, I am a Being of Light from Nebula M78—an Ultra.

It hadn't been a trick question but he'd gotten a trick answer, one that explained everything for an Ultra and nothing for him. But perhaps it was the best a dead man could hope for. And he really was dead, Hayata understood that now. His life had ended in a bright red flash and he had no choice but to accept it, although it certainly wasn't like anything he'd ever imagined. Of all the things that might have come next, he would never have guessed he'd be communicating mind-to-mind with an alien from Nebula M78.

I had not expected this, either, the alien told him. *I was taking Bemular to its final resting place when it escaped. I pursued it across the galaxy to your Earth.*

There was still a tiny possibility he was dreaming, Hayata thought. If so, his subconscious had really outdone itself this time. This was so vivid, so wild, and yet so personal.

What's a Bemular? Hayata asked.

A demon-like monster who disrupts peace and harmony in the universe.

Of course it was, Hayata thought. An Ultra wouldn't go clear across the galaxy for a shoplifter.

I apologize for this, the alien added.

Hayata could feel the depth of his sincerity. Did all aliens personally apologize to people they killed, or just Beings of Light from Nebula M78?

In return, the alien continued, *I give you my life.*

You what? Wait a minute— Hayata's thoughts were spinning like pinwheels in a typhoon. *You can do that? How? What'll happen to you?*

I will merge myself with you. We will become one and together we will work for peace on Earth.

Well, that was a relief, Hayata thought, because if the alien had wanted to destroy the Earth, he sure couldn't have stopped him.

Abruptly he felt something small and light drop onto his chest near the base of his throat and he had a mental image of a cylindrical object, similar to a penlight.

This is the Beta Capsule, the alien said.

Not a capsule I've ever taken, even on prescription, Hayata replied.

Use the Beta Capsule whenever you're in trouble, the alien told him.

And when I do? Hayata asked. *What happens?*

You'll have nothing to worry about.

What was that supposed to mean? Hayata wondered. *Okay, good to know. Sounds like a very useful capsule. Thank you.*

For a moment, he could sense the power contained in the object, power that had now been extended to him, and then something touched his mind. The sensation was unmistakable even though he'd never felt it until now, because the alien was merging with him. It was invigorating and exhilarating, as if he were being remade and enhanced. The intensity became overwhelming. He was rising even higher, he was flying, he was—

The explosion came only a few minutes after they set down near the lake. It sent Ide sprawling, threw Arashi against a nearby tree, and almost knocked Muramatsu off his feet. For a few seconds in the ensuing silence, none of them dared to move.

'W-was that *another* collision?' Ide said finally. He got to his feet slowly and brushed himself off.

'Remember, there were two strange lights in the sky,' Arashi said, looking to Muramatsu.

'Right now, I don't see any lights in the sky,' Muramatsu said firmly. 'Just smoke up ahead, which I'm guessing is the crash site. Arashi, you take point, Ide, you're behind him. I've got our six.'

Ide seemed about to say something, then fell in behind Arashi. As they drew closer, they could smell burned wood and brush as well as scorched metal and oil, but that was all—there was no sickening reek that indicated the presence of human casualties.

After several meters, Arashi held up one fist to signal a stop. 'Cap, I can see people up ahead. They're all lying on the ground and I can't tell if they're—if—uh, what condition they're in.'

Muramatsu felt a terrible dropping sensation in his stomach as he moved to Arashi's side and raised his flashlight. This was every emergency worker's nightmare, to discover an air crash had killed people on the ground. Except these people all seemed to be intact, not bloodied or burned or injured in any way that he could see. A second later, he heard a soft groan and saw a young woman move, then raise herself up on one hand, pushing her hair back from her grimy but uninjured face.

The rest of them began to stir then and Muramatsu gestured for Arashi and Ide to go to them. 'Ide, call emergency services,' he said briskly. 'I want a fleet of ambulances and doctors here immediately. We have, what—at least a dozen people, possibly hurt—' He broke off as he spotted a man in a Park Police uniform pushing himself to a kneeling position.

Muramatsu rushed to him and offered his hand. 'Can you tell me what happened here—' He looked at the man's name tag. 'Officer Tanaka.'

Tanaka leaned heavily on him as he got to his feet with a dazed expression. Everyone was regaining consciousness now, all with the same disoriented look. Muramatsu caught Arashi's eye and mouthed, Keep them here. Arashi nodded and passed the message to Ide.

'I called Fire and Rescue already,' said Tanaka's partner Uchido, materializing next to Tanaka. 'As soon as it happened.'

'As soon as what happened?' Muramatsu asked tensely, then noticed Arashi staring past him. He turned to follow his gaze and saw part of a VTOL wing in the charred undergrowth. The internal fire-suppression system that had kept the forest from going up in a grand conflagration after the VTOL had crashed had also left the Science Patrol insignia clearly recognizable.

'It's Hayata's after all,' Arashi said, his voice bleak. 'No way he could have survived that.' He moved a little closer to the broken wing, shining his flashlight on the ground around it. 'But it's very strange—his body's not here.'

'We saw him,' said Officer Tanaka. His partner Uchido nodded to a murmured chorus of agreement from the civilians. 'A man—he was wearing a Science Patrol uniform.'

'In the wreckage? What did you see?' asked Ide, glancing at Muramatsu. 'Tell us everything.'

'I can tell you but I can't explain any of it,' Tanaka said. 'His body just—' He floundered for a moment. 'Rose. Went up in the air. Levitated.'

'And there was a glowing red light around him,' put in one of the civilians, to another chorus of agreement. 'It got brighter and brighter until the man disappeared into it.'

'But the light kept rising up,' Uchido said, demonstrating with one hand.

'That's impossible,' Ide said flatly.

Tanaka straightened up to his full height. 'That's what happened.'

A young woman leaned forward between him and Uchido. 'We all saw it. All of us.'

Ide shook his head. 'Impossible,' he said again.

'You can say it's impossible all you want,' Tanaka told him, his expression more than a little defiant. 'We're telling you what we saw.'

Ide opened his mouth to respond but Muramatsu put up a hand. 'How high did this red light rise?' he asked Tanaka.

'As high as some of those trees by the shore. The younger ones.' Tanaka pointed.

'What happened to it?' Muramatsu asked. 'Where did it go?'

'It exploded,' said Uchido. 'The next thing we knew, you were here.'

Ide's expression of disbelief wavered as he looked from Uchido to Tanaka and then to Muramatsu. 'We heard an explosion right after we got here. Are you saying it knocked you all out but didn't hurt you?'

Uchido spread his hands. 'Look, none of us understands what happened. For all we know it could be aliens.'

'I vote yes on aliens,' said a man standing behind Uchido, to yet another chorus of agreement.

'We don't know anything for certain,' Muramatsu said, talking over them. Where were the damned ambulances? He should have been hearing sirens by now. 'We only know something caused all of you to lose consciousness. You all seem to be all right but you need to be thoroughly examined by doctors—and that includes both of you,' he added to the Park Police. 'Until then, we need you two to make sure all of these people stay right here and remain calm, so they don't exacerbate any injuries we don't yet know about.'

'Will do,' Tanaka said. He and Uchido looked less dazed now, more alert as they spoke to the civilians in tones that were soothing but authoritative, persuading all of them to sit down again and talk quietly with each other. The sirens Muramatsu had been waiting to hear were finally audible but still farther away than he'd have liked. He told Ide to keep an eye on the group, then turned to Arashi, who was still surveying the wreckage.

'Find anything else?' he asked.

Arashi shook his head. 'It's going to be light in another hour or so, Cap. As soon as backup get here, we can organize a search for Hayata. If his body's missing, maybe he did survive and he's wandering around in the woods, half-conscious, injured, with no memory of what happened to him or where he is.' He glanced at the group. 'What do you think about them? Mass hysteria, maybe?'

'No idea,' Muramatsu said. 'Maybe Hayata can tell us, if we're lucky.'

'If he remembers,' Arashi said. 'What if he doesn't?'

'Then I'll settle for getting him back alive,' Muramatsu replied. 'Let's take it one crisis at a time.'

Hayata woke to find himself lying on a cushioned bench in the stern of a modest, well-kept speedboat. A middle-aged couple were standing over him looking anxious.

'See?' the woman said. She was a bit plump, dressed in a flowery shirt and white trousers. Her cat's-eye sunglasses had bright red frames and mirrored lenses, a combination Hayata might have thought comical under other circumstances. 'He was asleep, not in a coma.' She folded her arms the way Fuji did whenever she won an argument with Ide; Fuji always won.

'Science Patrol agents don't just fall asleep in marinas,' the man replied, also folding his arms Fuji-style. He'd flipped up the dark lenses on his aviator glasses and was peering closely at Hayata with watery eyes.

Sitting up slowly, Hayata looked around, wondering how he'd gotten to the marina, which was clear on the other side of the lake from where he'd been.

'Well, he's awake now,' the woman said. 'We can just ask him. Were you on a stakeout? Are there smugglers around here?'

Hayata pulled off his helmet and rubbed his ears, wincing. Memo to self: Always remove headgear before passing out for several hours.

'Can we offer you something?' the man asked him. 'Some

tea, perhaps?' He was already pouring a cup from a silver thermos.

'Thank you,' Hayata said, accepting the cup from him. Steam rose from the dark gold liquid; the aroma mixed with the fresh air and made him smile. These were good people, nice people, who would be kind to a stranger they found asleep in their boat rather than treating him with suspicion or hostility.

'You were on a stakeout, weren't you?' The woman sat down beside him. 'You know, I had a feeling something was going on around here.'

'Don't be ridiculous, he's with the Science Patrol,' the man said. 'He wouldn't be chasing mere smugglers, he'd be on a science stakeout.'

'Maybe he'll tell us after he wakes up a little more.' The woman patted his shoulder.

Hayata sipped the tea, feeling himself come back into focus. He remembered everything: the blue UFO sinking into the lake, the campers giving poor Tom a hard time, the glowing ball of red light rushing toward him too quickly to evade—

No, he must have evaded it somehow since he wasn't in bits and pieces scattered all over in the forest along with his VTOL—his very, very expensive VTOL—

Something had saved him. No, someone.

The memory was like a bright light going on in his head, illuminating the truth in perfect, life-quality detail: the pure, unselfish soul of the being who had merged their two lives instead of leaving this little corner of the world diminished by one. And the being had done it all by elevating the human spirit. Hayata's human spirit—

He blinked. All this had gone through his head before he'd even swallowed the next sip of tea. It was truly wonderful tea, too, the best he'd ever tasted. He drank the rest of it and handed the cup back to the man.

'Thank you, I feel much better now,' Hayata said. 'I came out here last night on an investigation. Not to stake out smugglers,' he added, smiling at the woman. 'But something just as crucial. Involving science.'

The couple looked at each other, pleased they were both right. Hayata wondered how often that happened.

'I ran into some difficulties before I could wrap things up,' he continued. 'I thank you so much for your kindness but I'm afraid now I have to ask an even bigger favor of you.'

'We're more than happy to help,' the man told him.

The woman nodded emphatically. 'Tell us what we can do.'

A few minutes later, Hayata was speeding across the lake in the boat while the couple watched after him from the dock. They'd insisted he take the thermos of tea with him.

At about the same time that Hayata was waking up in the marina, Muramatsu was coordinating emergency workers and volunteers in a search of the area immediately surrounding Lake Ryugamori. His energy was starting to flag but he refused to quit. He knew Arashi and Ide wouldn't want to give up, either, but at some point he'd have to call time on them and drag them back to HQ.

He paused to have a cup of tea and gazed glumly out over the lake. If they'd been searching for a civilian, they'd have been thinking in terms of recovering a body but no one had said anything like that yet, or at least not where he could hear it.

Fuji would be calling again soon, he knew; she'd been calling every twenty minutes. Muramatsu was thinking about how he would still have nothing to tell her when he saw the water start to foam and froth, as if it were boiling. More disturbing, however, were the blue lights flashing just below the surface.

Tanaka and Uchido were suddenly on either side of him. The paramedics had given each of them a clean bill of health but hadn't been able to persuade either man to go to the hospital for observation. Muramatsu couldn't help feeling glad they'd insisted on sticking around simply because they'd been the last people to see Hayata, even if the account they'd given was flat-out unbelievable. In any other situation, Muramatsu would have insisted the hospital put them on a seventy-two-hour psychiatric hold. But with everyone telling the same story, he couldn't just dismiss them all as crazy. Obviously, something unusual had happened here, and it was still happening.

'Last night, they said the UFO that sank into the lake was glowing blue,' Tanaka told him. 'And I'm pretty sure that's about where it went down.'

Before Muramatsu could answer, the water shot up like a fountain and something broke the surface.

His first impression was of something reptilian, with

enormous armored scales ending in sharp points. Huge, unblinking eyes appeared and Muramatsu reflexively took a step back, thinking the creature was looking directly at him. Water poured off it as it moved into the shallows until it towered forty meters over him, its malevolent gaze still fixed on him. Unable to move or speak, Muramatsu could only stare up at it as if he were frozen in place.

Baring its teeth, the monster roared and the sound hit Muramatsu with the force of a physical blow, snapping him back into sharp focus.

'Get all these people back from the lake!' he told the Park Police and drew his weapon. Arashi and Ide flanked him now, their own weapons up and ready as the three of them lined up on the shore and took aim.

The weapons were a variation on the standard law enforcement sidearm, developed by Ide for use in situations that regular police never faced. The energy beams they fired could be adjusted in strength. The two lowest settings weren't lethal to humans, although they were pretty painful even for those wearing protective gear, as Ide himself had emphatically assured the team after volunteering to be a live test target. Muramatsu had authorized their use only in extreme situations and never with lethal intent on any living creature, if at all possible. Looking at this horror now, however, made him wonder if they had enough firepower among them to do more than tickle it.

The creature let out a furious bellow and Muramatsu thought he had never heard a more vicious sound. Instead of coming all the way out to attack them, however, the beast sank below the surface of the lake again. For several moments, the water churned madly, then subsided.

'Did we get it?' Ide asked in a small voice.

'I don't think we even got its attention.' Arashi blew out a breath, gazing hard at the place where it had disappeared. 'If that's what crashed into Hayata—'

'We don't know that it did,' Muramatsu said sharply.

'Whatever you say, Cap,' Ide said, as if he were afraid Muramatsu was going to hit him.

Muramatsu felt a surge of impatience. Ide was a good agent but you had to keep him focused on the immediate present to counter his tendency to overthink, especially in a high-pressure situation.

On his other side, Arashi was looking out over the lake to the marina in the distance. 'Cap, we're gonna have to raise the alert level and evacuate everyone, starting wi—what the hell?'

Muramatsu followed his gaze and felt his blood pressure jump forty points. They'd had the whole area on alert all night, telling everyone to stay off the water. So of course, some idiot had decided this would be the perfect time to take a high-speed cruise around the lake.

Akiko Fuji's voice was nearly gone after a night of trying to raise Hayata on the radio when the console signaled an incoming communicator call.

'This is SSSP Headquarters,' she croaked, adding, 'Fuji here,' in case whoever was calling didn't recognize the voice.

'Oh, hey! How are you, Akiko?'

For a moment—not a long moment but a great, big, gargantuan, impenetrable obstacle of a moment—she thought she was imagining Hayata's voice. She had imagined hearing it all night, trying to will him to answer every time she'd said his name. But he hadn't and her imagination had buckled under reality.

Now the new reality crashed in on her and she found what was left of her voice again. 'Hayata! Where on earth are you? We've been looking for you all night—'

'Never mind that right now.' Wind buffeted his microphone and he was shouting to make himself heard over the buzz of a motor.

'Are you on a boat?' she asked, squeaking with amazement.

'Yes, I had to borrow one—long story, tell you later. Right now I need you to bring the S-16 submarine to the Y-mark point at Lake Ryugamori as quick as you can.'

'The Y-mark point—copy that,' she replied, forgetting she wanted to rip him limb from limb for scaring her and the rest of the team. 'See you soon!'

She grabbed her helmet and ran for the hangar without signing off, unaware of the joyful tears on her face even as she wiped them away.

'Who *is* that idiot?' Muramatsu demanded.

Arashi was peering through the new enhanced binoculars Ide had developed. 'Can't see, Cap, they're still too far away.'

Muramatsu turned just as a VTOL appeared above them, carrying exactly what he'd been about to tell Ide to radio in for. 'Fuji?' he said incredulously, then remembered to tap his communicator so she could hear him. 'Fuji, how did you know to bring the S-16?'

'Hayata called in and requested it,' she said, raspy but cheerful.

He couldn't possibly have heard that right, Muramatsu thought.

'Don't be ridiculous,' Ide was saying. 'Unless you can get radio calls from a ghost?'

'No ghost, it was Hayata himself,' Fuji insisted in her happy-froggy voice. 'Setting the sub down now at the Y-mark point. Everybody, stay clear.'

'Why there?' Ide asked her.

'That's where Hayata wants it.'

Ide leaned closer to Muramatsu and lowered his voice. 'Cap, I think the shock of losing Hayata is too much for her. I mean, she's a great Science Patrol agent but she's never lost a teammate before—'

'Neither have you, Ide,' Fuji said, squeaking a little. 'How are you holding up?'

On Muramatsu's other side, Arashi suddenly grabbed his arm. 'Cap! The idiot in the boat out there—that's no idiot, it's Hayata!' He pushed the binoculars at him so he could see for himself.

This wasn't a job, it was a roller coaster with no brakes, Muramatsu thought, looking at Hayata's face through the binoculars. 'Muramatsu to Hayata—where the hell have you been? We've been searching for you since we found the wreckage last night—'

'I know, and I'm really sorry about the VTOL, Cap.'

'Never mind that, just tell me how you survived,' Muramatsu said.

'He saved me,' Hayata replied.

'Who's "he"?'

'I'll get to that, Cap, but right now we have to take out Bemular.' Hayata sounded brisk and professional, as if he were talking about one of those contingencies they had to take care of immediately but was otherwise nothing out of the ordinary.

'What's a Bemular?' Muramatsu asked.

'It's the giant creature currently resting at the bottom of the lake, and it's not going to stay down there munching on fish.'

'Yes, we just saw it. It's not a pretty sight,' Muramatsu told him. 'What's it doing here, where did it come from? Does this "he" who saved your life have anything to do with it?'

'I'll explain everything later, Cap, I promise,' Hayata said, his tone becoming more urgent. 'But right now, I really need to take the sub down and surprise that thing with a torpedo while it's napping. And then, when it comes up again—'

'We'll attack from the air,' Muramatsu finished for him. 'Good plan. Did you get all that, Fuji?'

'I copy, Cap,' she croaked. 'Setting down near you in seven... six... five...'

* * *

Fuji had left the top hatch open so Hayata could transfer quickly from the boat. He didn't like the idea of just leaving the boat adrift. But as he came alongside the sub and cut the motor, it occurred to him there was a way, given the prevailing wind as well as the current in this part of the lake, to position the boat so it would drift out of harm's way into the shallows and beach itself in a spot where the owners could easily recover it.

Exactly how he knew this was unclear to him; he simply did. As he boarded the sub, he caught a glimpse of the Beta Capsule nestled in his jacket pocket.

You'll have nothing to worry about. He sure hoped that was true.

The S-16 could carry two people. In Hayata's opinion, however, that was one too many, not only because of the tight quarters but also because of the carbon-dioxide buildup, which tended to have a dulling effect on the mind. If there had to be two people aboard, Hayata had recommended to Muramatsu that one of them be asleep.

Muramatsu had told him he was probably right but he should keep that to himself until they had the budget for Ide to make the necessary improvements. Seeing as how they had just lost a VTOL, however, Hayata was certain that wasn't going to happen any time soon.

He'd never used the sub in a freshwater lake before, only in the ocean east of Japan. The big differences were temperature, movement, and visibility—the lake wasn't as cold or as turbulent, though it was much murkier. There was also a total absence of fish, which Hayata figured wasn't really all that strange—the locals probably didn't like sharing their neighborhood with a monster. Either that, or Bemular had eaten them all.

Which reminded Hayata that he'd had nothing to eat for about twelve hours or so. If he could take care of the Bemular problem quickly enough, he might make it back to HQ in time for breakfast—

A proximity alarm went off; the sensors had picked up something big nearby. Its composition registered as an odd mix of organic and inorganic material as well as some very strange substances not found in Lake Ryugamori. Or, for that matter, anywhere else on Earth.

No kidding, Hayata thought as armored scales appeared in the view screen above the helm.

'Ide to Hayata,' came a familiar voice in his headphones. 'We're airborne and ready any time you are.'

'Hayata here, stand by. I've got it in sight.'

'Commence firing when ready,' Muramatsu told him.

'Aye-aye, Cap.' Hayata flipped up the cover over the torpedo controls and hit the button marked #1.

The moment the creature surfaced again, Arashi fired a missile at it, scoring a direct hit on its left flank. Bellowing in rage, it turned to see where the shot had come from but Fuji was already bringing them around its other side. The monster spotted the VTOL but instead of going after them, it only growled before sinking down into the lake again.

'What the hell?' Arashi said. 'Is it on a tea break?'

'Hayata, this monster of yours doesn't want to come out and play,' Ide said.

'Then I'll just have to be more persuasive,' Hayata told them. 'Trying again—be ready.'

With Bemular on the move, the flurry of mud and silt somehow combined with the creature's bizarre organic/inorganic composition to confuse the sub's sensors. Hayata had to follow it just from what he could see through the thick view screen. But when the mud cleared enough to let him see properly, the monster was nowhere in sight.

Because it had two other favorite places, Hayata remembered, and he knew where they were. He just had to figure out which one Bemular would head for first.

The most likely answer came to him in the same way he'd realized how to position the borrowed boat so it would end up in the shallows. It was something to do with certain mineral composites—the alien within him could identify what they were but despite their merged state, he was unable to get any kind of feel for how he was doing it, only that it seemed natural, even normal.

'Okay, big fella,' he muttered as Bemular made a slow turn toward him. 'Ready for round two?' He fired the second torpedo, aiming it at those unblinking eyes.

The creature batted it away like a fly and came at him, its jaws wide open.

* * *

When the creature surfaced again, Fuji had the VTOL at a higher altitude, keeping it in line with the sun until the monster moved into the shallows. Then she circled around behind it and Arashi fired.

The missile made a direct hit high on its upper back and it roared in fury. As it turned toward them, they saw there was something metal in its jaws.

'Hayata!' Fuji cried as the monster spat the submarine into a patch of thorn bushes near a comfort station. The creature's gigantic, hostile eyes tracked the VTOL as it made a wide arc just beyond the reach of its forelimbs and again Muramatsu had the impression of it not simply seeing them but looking at them with something more than just animal aggression.

What the hell are you? Muramatsu asked silently.

The thing opened its mouth but instead of roaring, it sent what looked like a concentrated beam of energy at the VTOL. Fuji pulled the yoke hard to one side and they all heard a crackling noise as the beam missed them seemingly by centimeters.

'Good one, Fuji!' Ide said breathlessly.

'For someone who feels so deeply, you mean?' she said.

'I told you I'm sorry. Will you just forgive me already?' Ide said as the VTOL took another hard turn.

'Ask me later,' Fuji replied, 'when I'm not busy saving all our butts from a monster.'

'Stow that, you two,' Muramatsu said sharply. 'Where's the sub?'

'Ten o'clock.' Fuji yanked back on the yoke, taking the VTOL higher again.

Their new position gave them a clear view of the S-16 lying in the midst of some scrubby bushes and broken trees, looking like nothing so much as a toy discarded by a giant bored child. The monster roared and sent a blue ray of energy at it, setting it and everything around it on fire.

Consciousness returned with a jolt this time. Hayata found himself gazing through the thick glass of the view screen from an awkward sideways angle, watching Bemular stomping toward him, crushing trees and turning a few picnic tables into splinters, all the while thinking that the temperature in the sub had risen rather precipitously and, in fact, was still rising.

I'm next, and he won't need a can opener, Hayata thought, glancing down at the Beta Capsule safely stowed in his jacket. This definitely qualifies as being in trouble.

As soon as his hand closed on the Beta Capsule, he felt its power again, much more strongly now because it was on the verge of being unleashed, and he really wanted to do that, more than he'd ever wanted to anything else in his life. Hayata tore himself free of the safety harness, boosted himself up the ladder and popped the hatch open. As Bemular stomped toward him, jaws wide in a vicious predatory grin, Hayata raised his hand high in the air in defiance.

Use the Beta Capsule whenever you're in trouble.
    And when I do?

You'll have nothing to worry about.

Hayata's gratitude to the alien for saving his life had been laced with a certain amount of frustration for his vagueness about the Beta Capsule. Even after they had merged, he'd been unable to get a sense of what having nothing to fear would entail.

Now it was perfectly clear. He understood everything, including the fact that nothing in human nature was even slightly comparable to this. It was a wordless understanding and all the more profound for being so, allowing them to coalesce and survive as a single being, to live a life that for both of them was… more. Greater. Beyond.

Ultra.

From human man to Ultraman.

What else could you call someone forty meters tall, he thought as Bemular advanced on him, fangs bared, roaring in bestial rage.

As Fuji flew them in a circle above the area, Muramatsu stared dumbfounded at the giant red and silver figure squaring off against the monster. The creature roared its displeasure so loudly, Muramatsu was sure he felt the vibration in his seat.

The giant suddenly leaped over the burning submarine as if it were merely a tiny, dying campfire, and raised his fists, keeping them close to his face like a boxer. Except he didn't look like any boxer Muramatsu had ever seen.

Was the giant wearing a silver helmet? It was smooth and

featureless, except for the ridge that went from the crown down through the center of his face, where a nose would be. There was no faceplate—but there were eyes; they were large, white, and seemed to be lit from within. Optical enhancements? Nice; R&D had been trying to develop something that would work as binocular vision but so far, the hardware was still too heavy to deploy.

Or maybe it wasn't a helmet. But if it were, Muramatsu thought, it was the first one he'd ever seen with an actual working mouth built into it. Except something like that would be mechanical, like a marionette's, and this wasn't. The giant's mouth was expressive; he could see it as the giant surprised the monster with a flurry of punches. The creature gave another loud roar, then pounced on him.

The red and silver figure caught it and the two of them grappled furiously, struggling for dominance. Muramatsu heard Ide gasp as the monster's clawed foot flattened a comfort station into splinters.

'There could have been kids in there!' Ide said, horrified.

Muramatsu said nothing as the giant took hold of the creature's neck, pivoted sharply, and executed a move that looked an awful lot like a judo throw. Before the monster could get up again, the giant flung himself down on it and pummeled it ferociously.

With a deep, raw-throated bellow, the kaiju forced them to roll over so that the red and silver giant was on the bottom. They rolled over again, and continued to roll until they reached the water and rolled right into it with the monster on top. The giant struggled out from underneath the scaly reptilian body and moved back onto dry land, drawing the monster away from the lake. Only then did Muramatsu notice the bright blue light in the middle of the giant's chest. A weapon? A status indicator? Or some other kind of device he couldn't imagine?

The kaiju reached for the giant with its forelimbs as it lumbered toward him. The giant ducked and, staying low, rammed the creature's midsection headfirst. The monster gave an irate bellow and turned away to go back into the lake. The red and silver giant grabbed it by the tail and yanked, dragging it back to land. As the monster struggled to get away, Muramatsu saw the blue light in the center of the giant's chest turn red and begin flashing.

Damn, Hayata thought, *what the hell is that?*

The Color Timer. It came to him like something he'd always known but had somehow forgotten; his energy on this planet was limited and now it was starting to run low.

You didn't think you should've led with that *instead of 'You'll have nothing to worry about?'* Hayata's thought was a desperate wail in his head even as another part of his mind was telling him not to waste time talking to himself because the Color Timer wasn't a secret from Bemular.

'What's *that*?' Arashi said, pointing at the flashing red light.

'Must be a danger signal,' Ide said, sounding as if he knew.

'And it only went on now?' Arashi grimaced at him. 'Five minutes ago, there was no danger?'

'Hey, don't ask me,' Ide said. 'They're aliens. But it's blinking faster now and that can't be good.'

Unbidden, the image came to Muramatsu of a tiny light on his personal phone. Red meant the battery was low; when it flashed, it was about to die.

Was the red and silver giant a machine?

No, he thought, absolutely not. The giant moved like a living thing, not a construct. And aliens or not, nobody deployed a machine that big and that versatile if it couldn't run for longer than a few minutes. Would they?

He was still trying to decide when the monster aimed a beam of hard blue energy at the giant's feet, igniting the surrounding bushes. The giant jumped away from the flames, looked up at the sun, and suddenly soared high into the air.

Muramatsu's jaw dropped. Of course the giant could fly. The more important question was, could the monster?

The creature stood bawling in outrage at the diminishing red and silver figure but made no move to launch itself into the sky. Muramatsu hadn't realized he'd been holding his breath until it rushed out of him in a long, relieved sigh. No, the monster didn't fly and you only had to look at it to know that, he thought, ignoring the fact that the giant had no physical features indicative of flight, either. What the hell; aliens.

'Where'd he go?' Ide was asking. 'Anyone see him?'

For several moments, they were all at the windows,

searching the sky. 'Maybe at a higher altitude—' Arashi started.

'I see him! I see him!' Ide shouted. 'He's coming back!'

The four of them watched as the giant approached the monster from behind, coming down feetfirst on its scaly back. It squalled and raged as it hit the ground under a barrage of powerful blows. Moving quickly but without rushing, the giant held onto the monster's hindquarters as he spun around and let it go. The beast landed hard and the giant leaped on it, pounding with both fists.

'I think he's winning!' Ide crowed, shaking Arashi in excitement.

'Then I hope he really is the good guy,' Fuji said.

'Of course he's the good guy!' Ide gave her a *look*. 'He's fighting the monster, not us!'

Fuji met Muramatsu's gaze, her face uncertain. He could practically hear her worrying that the silver giant might be fighting the monster to claim its prey—except it wasn't. Muramatsu had no idea why he felt so certain about that. Maybe it was that flashing red light in the middle of the giant's chest.

Having pounded the monster into submission, the giant now picked the creature up, raised it over his head, and hurled it into the lake, where it sank without a struggle.

'Is it over?' Ide asked. But even before he'd finished speaking, Muramatsu saw lights flashing below the surface as the water churned and frothed madly.

Something dark broke the surface; in the next moment, a large round blue sphere rose up out of the water, and kept rising. Muramatsu felt himself sag; apparently the monster could fly after all.

This must end here. It will end here.

The thought came to Hayata as the reminder of a promise, although he hadn't forgotten. Something like sense memory took over. Without thinking, but utterly aware—Ultra aware—he felt his Ultra body settle into a new position that was really not new at all. Facing the blue sphere, he crouched with most of his weight on his right leg and placed his left arm as a horizontal brace to steady his right hand, now pointing straight up.

Power woke, surged within him from the deepest part of his Ultra self and rushed to the point where hand touched arm, sparking into the pure white beam that was the Spacium Beam.

'Captain, look!' Fuji said.

The blue sphere shuddered under the white light from the giant's hand and then blew apart in a noisy explosion, leaving only a fine dust that blew away in the wind.

'He did it! He got the monster and he saved us!' Ide cheered, shaking Arashi even harder as the red and silver figure soared into the sky again.

'Where's he going *now*?' Arashi wanted to know.

'When we catch up, you can ask him,' Muramatsu said briskly. 'He's headed toward the north end of the lake.'

* * *

'I don't understand,' Fuji said, squeaking hoarsely in frustration as she stood in the VTOL's open doorway. 'He's forty meters tall—that's over a hundred and thirty feet! How can he just disappear?'

Muramatsu looked around the stone expanse where they'd landed, then at the rock formations so popular with climbers and shook his head. 'I wish I knew.'

'We should try looking for something that doesn't belong,' Ide said. 'Something that seems out of place.'

'Besides us, you mean?' Arashi said wryly.

'How about that?' Fuji said suddenly, pointing at something behind him. 'I don't think that belongs.'

The other three turned to see Hayata running toward them.

Muramatsu felt his jaw drop yet again. This was nowhere near the original crash site and pretty far from where the S-16 had landed. He filed that away to puzzle over later. Right now he was too relieved to see his second-in-command alive and well.

'Are you the real Hayata?' Ide asked as they all met on a broad stretch of red-brown rock.

'Oh, Ide,' Hayata said, laughing gently. 'There's no real or fake. There's only one me.'

Rather an odd answer, Muramatsu thought. But then, Hayata had crashed twice in under twelve hours, once in a VTOL and once in a submarine on land. It was amazing he was even coherent.

'What happened to that monster?' Hayata asked them.

'An alien got rid of it for us,' Muramatsu said. It was the last thing he'd ever expected to hear himself say. Perhaps it was amazing that he was coherent himself.

Hayata sighed, his expression relieved. 'So he did come, just as he promised.'

'*That* was the alien who saved you?' Fuji looked awestruck.

'It was.' Hayata looked from Fuji to Ide, then to Arashi and finally to Muramatsu, who was about to ask him what he could tell them about this helpful alien.

But Ide spoke up first. 'You keep saying "he" and "him." What's his name?'

Hayata hesitated, glancing briefly at Muramatsu. 'I don't know. I'm not sure he has one.'

'Oh, come on,' Ide said, rolling his eyes. 'What are we supposed to call him—Mr. Nobody?'

Muramatsu suppressed the urge to laugh. Ide had no problem with a giant alien coming out of nowhere and saving them from a giant monster but couldn't wrap his mind around the notion that the alien didn't have a name. It was so apt, so utterly characteristic of him; so Ide.

'All right, you want a name?' Hayata gave a put-upon sigh. 'How about...' He made a thinking-hard face. 'Ultraman.'

'Ultra. Man.' Fuji spoke each word distinctly in her froggy croak, as if she were testing how they felt when she said them aloud.

'Right. Ultraman.' Hayata smiled at her, then turned back to Ide. 'Is Ultraman okay with you?'

Ide blinked at him, slightly taken aback. 'Well, that seems—' He hesitated. 'Nice and ultra. Ultra good!'

'But where is he now?' Fuji asked, looking around. 'Is he going back to his home planet already?'

'No, he's still here,' Hayata assured her. 'His spacecraft was damaged when he crashed into me, so he'll be sticking around for a while.' He turned to Muramatsu again and the other three did the same, as if they were all waiting for him to give an order, or maybe just tell them that, yes, everything was now okay. Muramatsu could feel how tired they all were after the all-night search followed by an encounter with a giant monster. All except Hayata, that was—he looked as if he were fresh from a good night's sleep and ready to start the day.

'Cap?' Hayata's expression was curious and Muramatsu realized he'd been staring.

He tried to cover it with a big smile. 'I was just thinking that you really are a lucky man.'

Hayata returned his smile but there was a new seriousness in his eyes. It was the look of a man who had a lot more on his mind than he'd had the day before.

'Oh, I'm more than lucky, Cap,' Hayata said. 'I'm invincible.'

CHAPTER
TWO

Oh, I'm more than lucky, Cap. I'm invincible.

In the days immediately following, the words went round and round in Hayata's head, a trapped echo that would come back to him suddenly and without warning, most often when he was trying to fall asleep. He would be teetering on the edge of slumber when all at once he'd hear his own voice in his head. Then suddenly he was wide awake, staring at the ceiling, adrift and alone in the night.

Not that he really had a problem with being alone. As Muramatsu's second-in-command, he had a room to himself instead of having to bunk in with Arashi and Ide. They both snored like buzz saws in a busy machine shop (and both denied it vigorously). The buzz-saw chorus wouldn't have helped him think.

It was just that he'd thought if anything were going to repeat on him, it would be the crash, or his conversation with the alien, or their merging, or the moment when he had burst from human form into Ultraman. He remembered everything as clearly and vividly as when it had first happened. And what did he get instead?

I'm more than lucky, Cap. I'm invincible.

A throwaway remark; he hadn't meant anything by it, more of a joke. Although as long as he could vanquish a problem in the space of three minutes without his Color Timer going dark, it was true. That was the catch, but everything had a catch, didn't it?

For the two weeks following the events at Lake Ryugamori, he was restricted to light duty. Normally he'd have been chafing under such constraints and trying to figure out how to get around them. But now he was glad to sit behind a desk, collating data, putting it through analysis, studying the results, writing reports, and hoping any incursion of monsters or aliens or monster aliens would hold off until he could acclimate to his new normal, or get it acclimated to him. Then maybe he could concentrate on something without being distracted by the subject of his invincibility.

Sometimes it wasn't just the words by themselves; sometimes they were accompanied by the mental image of how small everything looked from a vantage point forty meters higher than normal.

Maybe his mind would become more settled once he had his debrief with Muramatsu, he thought. The debrief loomed large in his mind, even larger than Bemular or Ultraman. What he'd been through was unprecedented; Hayata wasn't sure he knew how to talk about it, or that he ever would. He yearned to get the debrief over with as soon as possible while at the same time wanting to put it off indefinitely, and when he asked himself what he really wanted, the only thing that came to him was, *Oh, I'm more than lucky, Cap. I'm invincible.*

Hayata had already turned in his incident report; compared to the others he'd submitted, this one was pretty sketchy. Had he received the same thing from someone else on the team, he'd have recommended further investigation. Only in this case, they couldn't investigate any further than they already had and leaving so many questions unanswered went against Hayata's grain.

How the hell had he woken up in the stern of a private boat in the marina, all the way on the other side of the lake? Was it some kind of spatial displacement caused by merging with an alien or had the alien deliberately put him a safe distance from the monster?

Better yet, how was he supposed to manage a double life as a regular human and a giant superhero who was invincible against the threat of alien monsters, but only for three minutes?

When Muramatsu had finally called him into his office, Hayata had half expected to find a couple of higher-ups from Central Command sitting in just to hear how he'd lost both a VTOL and a submarine in one day. Instead, it was just him and Muramatsu and the captain hadn't interrogated him or demanded a moment-by-moment account of the destruction of the VTOL and the S-16. Hayata found himself staring dumbly into his commanding officer's face as the man assured him that he wasn't responsible for those losses.

The circumstances had been extreme; Hayata had done nothing wrong.

He had listened to this in silence, thinking, *No, Cap, what's bothering me is, I told you I was invincible and I don't know why. It's not exactly a lie but it's only true for three minutes, give or take a few seconds on a sunny day.*

The debrief had ended with Muramatsu telling him he would remain on desk duty for the rest of the week, after which he could resume his regular duties. Or if he felt like he needed some time off, he could take it. Hayata had left Muramatsu's office feeling a little like he'd gotten away with something without meaning to.

And now, for the safety and well-being of his team and anyone else nearby, he would have to keep getting away with it. Of course, 'nearby' was a relative term; on a scale the size of, say, the galaxy, 'nearby' would be the planet Earth. The realization made the Beta Capsule feel heavy in his pocket.

It was all that damned monster's fault, the demon-like Bemular who went around disrupting the universe's peace and harmony. The thing just had to pick Earth for a pit stop so it could disrupt the peace and harmony of Hayata's little corner of the galaxy. All Hayata had ever wanted was to do good, to elevate the human spirit in whatever small way he could, to have a distinguished career in the Science Patrol and, just by the by and purely for his own private satisfaction, to make his parents proud.

Hayata had imagined working his way up in rank in the Science Patrol and, in time, finding someone special to share his life with. He had always considered this the formula for a life well lived: meaningful work and a family. But the family part of the equation was currently out of the question until— well, there was no telling. Indefinitely, possibly for good. And now that he was thinking about it, rising up through the ranks would be equally problematical for someone with a secret forty meters tall.

So much for achieving the right balance between work and personal life, he thought as he went into the break room.

Fuji, Arashi, and Ide were sitting at a table together, squabbling good-naturedly about a movie they'd seen. He smiled; at least the topic wasn't Fuji's emotional temperament. Ide saw him first and waved him over, asking him to decide who was right. Hayata got a cold drink from the fridge cabinet and sat down with them.

Only he could know about Ultraman, Hayata thought as Fuji began explaining why she was right and Arashi and Ide were wrong. But that didn't mean he was all alone.

Some weeks later, Hayata walked into the Operations Center to find Ide standing in the middle of the room in a flamboyant pose.

'Well, hel-lo there,' Ide said to his hand in the la-di-da tones of a game show host.

'What on earth is he doing?' Hayata whispered to Fuji.

'A website contacted him after what happened at the Science Center and asked him to do a video blog,' she whispered back, giggling a little. 'A day in the life of a Science Patrol agent.'

Hayata looked from her to Ide and back again, slightly incredulous. 'And Cap's okay with this?'

Fuji nodded. 'Ide has to show him everything, of course, so he can make sure nothing confidential slips in.' She giggled some more. 'Ide's our very own budding media star.'

Hayata couldn't help laughing a little himself. 'Tell me, did they ask him for this vlog before or after he got the black eye?'

'I heard that.' Ide turned and aimed the video camera at them. 'And here are two of my associates, Fuji and Hayata. Fuji's the one on the right. Or the left?' He frowned. 'No, the right.' He moved a bit closer to where they were at the communications console. 'Does it really stand out that much?' he asked, pointing at his right eye.

'"Stand out" hardly begins to describe it,' Fuji told him.

Ide looked at Hayata with a plaintive expression. 'Really?'

'It's definitely one of the most magnificent shiners I've ever seen,' Hayata assured him with mock solemnity.

Ide looked puzzled, then turned his attention back to the video camera. 'You're probably wondering how this happened. If I tell you, you must promise to keep it between us—' He glanced over his shoulder at Hayata and Fuji. 'And not tell anyone. Especially not my friends. Deal?'

'At least he doesn't expect us to be his audience,' Fuji said. 'I've got far too much to do.'

Hayata chuckled as he took a seat at one of the Ops computers and reopened the file with the incident report he'd been working on. In fact, the report was practically finished. The version of events as Ide told them for the video blog was far more entertaining, including his description of how Arashi's snoring had kept him awake.

'It wasn't my snoring keeping you awake,' Arashi said, looking up from the map of Tokyo on his monitor. Muramatsu had managed to convince him to try working on the computer instead of glass-boards. Arashi had sulked and grumbled while he got acquainted with the software but before long, his grumbling tapered off and he was engrossed in what he was doing. 'You were dreaming you couldn't sleep, and counting sheep at the top of your lungs.' His gaze went to Hayata and Fuji. 'When the callout came, I had to shake him awake.'

'I wouldn't know,' Fuji said primly.

'Don't look at me,' Hayata said, chuckling. 'I was already at the defense base.'

'Too bad—you really should've seen Arashi wearing his slippers in full uniform,' Ide said smugly.

Arashi blew out a breath. 'Could happen to anybody. I was still half asleep when I got dressed,' he said gruffly. 'I was anxious to get to the Science Center; I had a feeling it was more alien activity.'

'Even in slippers, Arashi's a real tough guy,' Ide told the video camera.

'It turned out there was only one alien at the Science Center,' Arashi went on quietly. 'But one of them was plenty and I'm not embarrassed to admit it.'

'Nor should you be,' Hayata said. Fuji nodded in agreement and even Ide sobered for a few seconds.

* * *

Arashi shifted in his chair feeling awkward, not just because they were all looking at him but also because what had happened at the Science Center still had him spooked.

Despite its name, the Science Center had no direct connection to the Science Patrol. It had begun its existence as a research facility. As more buildings were added to the complex, the main one was redesigned and expanded, and now had exhibits, displays, and events that were open to the public. The latest renovation had added another auditorium that could stream talks from guest lecturers.

Although he hadn't been to the Science Center lately, Arashi had always liked it. That night, the first thing he'd seen on entering had been a security guard frozen in the act of reaching for the telephone on the reception desk. Whether he'd been trying to answer it or call out for help was impossible to say, but the look on the man's face was seared into Arashi's brain for all time. The poor guy had been confronted by something terrible, and Arashi couldn't help thinking that he was now stuck in that moment with no escape.

His heartbeat had kicked into a higher gear as he'd moved out of the reception area toward the stairs leading up to the mezzanine. For a few moments, he had stood motionless, straining to hear sounds of an intruder moving around but there was nothing. Drawing his sidearm, he climbed the stairs, careful not to make a sound—which, it now occurred to him, would have been a whole lot easier if he'd still been wearing his slippers.

That should have been funny; Arashi told himself to

remember it for Ide later. Maybe by then it would be so funny, the whole team would laugh till they hurt.

He had never imagined anything could make a great place like the Science Center feel creepy, and the longer he was there, the worse it felt despite the fact that he'd never been especially jumpy. Even as a kid, he'd never been afraid of the dark. Not that he was afraid now but the sight of the frozen guard had seemed like a bad omen, even though he didn't believe in omens of any kind, good or bad. Were all the other security guards like this one, waiting in the shadows to give him an extra dose of the creeps? Maybe the entire Science Center had been frozen in a single, endless creepy moment.

A ridiculous notion—or it would have been in the light of day, with the rest of his team there, too. Arashi trotted quickly up to the mezzanine, saw nothing in the shadows, and kept going.

He had almost reached the next floor when he suddenly knew there was something behind him.

Arashi whirled, raising his weapon and grasping the banister with his free hand. He only saw it for a second but it was so extremely clear that the alien was visible to him in perfect detail: the long arms ending in razor-sharp crab-like pincers, the strange V-shaped head, the round, lidless eyes, the thick limbs on its thick body.

Then it was gone.

Arashi's heart skipped a beat and began to pound faster. He turned to continue climbing the stairs just as the alien reappeared in front of him. It lifted its open claws and sent a beam of light at him.

He threw his arms up defensively to shield his face but it was as if a switch had been flipped, cutting him off from his body. His muscles hardened and came to a dead stop, along with all movement within him—the air in his lungs, the blood in his veins, his no-longer-pounding heart. As his awareness faded, he had the distinct impression the alien was laughing at him.

'It must have been awful, Arashi.'

Fuji's voice brought him back to the present and he shrugged with his standard gruff expression. 'Nothing I couldn't handle,' he said. 'I was just doing the job I signed up for—investigating strange phenomena. It's what we do. Right?'

'Right,' Fuji said staunchly, sneaking a glance at Hayata.

'It is, indeed,' Hayata said, still sorry he hadn't dropped everything at the Defense Force base and raced to the Science Center. The Defense Force base was pretty far away but in the middle of the night with no traffic, he might have made it to the Science Center quickly enough that Arashi wouldn't have had to face the alien alone.

When Hayata had first arrived at the Defense Force base, none of them had known anything about the invading force, or even that it *was* an invading force. As the officers had showed him the recording of the alien signal and its trajectory from space into the atmosphere, there was a stirring deep within himself. All at once, his awareness had increased in size and scope; what he needed to know came to him from his new best friend's memories. It was an odd sensation, recalling things he'd never actually known himself. At the same time, it wasn't that different from being briefed on something—it was just the interface that was different.

They called themselves the Baltans, these aliens. They were more advanced scientifically and technologically but—his enhanced mind hesitated, trying to find the right conceptual terms—they didn't play well with others. The Being of Light within him wasn't sure how many of them there might be, but they wouldn't have come to Earth simply to shake hands and establish diplomatic relations. That understanding had sent him rushing to the Science Center with two soldiers from the Defense Force. By the time they arrived, Fuji had called to tell him they'd lost contact with Arashi, which made him sorry that he hadn't brought half a dozen soldiers. Or better yet, all of them.

The sight of the security guard at the reception desk had given them all a nasty start. The soldiers unslung their rifles and Hayata had drawn his own weapon. What he had gleaned from his new best friend hadn't included anything about the Baltans having the capability to immobilize lifeforms they perceived as threatening. Hayata suspected that would be anyone, or more likely, everyone.

I know you're there, he said to himself silently as he and the soldiers moved cautiously out of the reception area toward the stairs. *If there's anything else I should know about these Baltans, now's the time to tell me.*

Nothing. No surprise recollections, no stray thoughts, not even the vaguest of notions.

The soldiers motioned for him to hang back as they went up the steps to the mezzanine level. For a minute or two, Hayata heard them moving around, and then nothing. All sound ceased, not tapering off or receding but stopping short. He waited while the silence stretched, and stretched, and stretched, until he finally went up the stairs himself.

The mezzanine was all murky shadows in the unbroken, eerie silence. Hayata brushed one hand against his jacket and was relieved to hear the soft whisper of his fingertips on cloth. He could still hear, noise was still possible—there just wasn't any. Because somewhere in the soundless gloom, the soldiers had been rendered inert.

Should he look for them, Hayata wondered, or try to find Arashi? No, Arashi wouldn't be on this level, he would have gone all the way up to the roof to secure the high ground before conducting a search from the top down. He started up the stairs to the next floor and discovered Arashi's intentions hadn't taken him even that far.

Hayata approached slowly, weapon in one hand and flashlight in the other. Arashi had been trying to protect his face and head; his expression was a mix of shock and indignation at whatever had had the effrontery to attack him.

Abruptly, the anomaly alarm pinned to his tie began flashing. Hayata looked down at it, momentarily confusing the device Dr. Iwamoto had invented to alert the wearer to potential peril from anomalous conditions with Ultraman's Color Timer.

He looked up to see the Baltan in front of him. It raised its arms with those strange pincers and he fired at it. The creature made an ugly guttural sound Hayata instinctively knew was laughter and vanished—

—to reappear behind him, at the foot of the stairs. Without thinking, Hayata dropped into a crouch, steadied his right hand against his left arm and fired his weapon.

The alien let out another ugly laugh and disappeared again.

Retreat. Come up with a plan.

The thought came unbidden, as clear and immediate as if he'd just heard the words spoken aloud. Hardly an ingenious strategy but it was his best option if he wanted to avoid finding himself as the other half of a matched pair with Arashi. Hayata straightened up, shining his flashlight over his teammate again.

He wanted to call the paramedics, have them take Arashi and all the others to the nearest hospital and put them in intensive care. But moving them might be dangerous, and not just to them—maybe the Baltans wouldn't allow it. The last thing he wanted to do was add more people to their collection of human statues.

Tapping his communicator, he said, 'Hayata to Headquarters: I don't know what we're dealing with here. We need to set up a perimeter and cordon off the Science Center under heavily armed guards. I'm going to call the Defense Force, wait till they arrive, brief them on the immediate situation, then return to HQ. Hayata out.'

* * *

'Nothing? Absolutely nothing?' Hayata scrolled through the overnight event logs on the monitor.

'That's right.' Fuji's tone was light but Hayata could see how tense she was. 'No alien signals anywhere. These aliens of yours either have cloaking technology generations beyond anything we have or they packed up and left the planet.' Pause. 'Which I doubt. If the aliens were gone, I don't think Arashi and the others would still be frozen.'

'Me, either,' Ide said from where he stood behind them.

'And that makes it unanimous,' Hayata said. He switched from the overnight logs to the feeds from the Science Center's security cameras. Ide had spent a few hours tweaking the video resolution so they could see more than fuzzy shadows. The whole security system had been tampered with, Ide told them, and these were the only four he could get any clear images from. Nonetheless, the footage had been illuminating. One showed the security guard in reception, two of them displayed each soldier; the last was Arashi.

'I hate seeing him like that,' Fuji murmured.

'Me, too,' Hayata said, glad she hadn't had to see him in person.

'And I hate this *waiting*,' Fuji added. 'I wish Cap would come back *now*.'

'No more than I do,' Hayata said, sympathetic.

Muramatsu had been gone since early morning, leaving Hayata in command while he sat in with the Defense Force as they decided what to do. It was the first time Hayata had been left in charge but all Muramatsu had said to him was, *You know what to do.* Just that simple statement, as if they were doing this for the thousandth time, not the first.

Fuji and Ide were still looking at him, waiting for him to come up with the solution.

'We all know what to do, don't we,' Hayata said.

Both nodded. 'I just wish we could do more,' Fuji said.

'So do I,' Hayata admitted. 'I'd like nothing better than to go over to the Science Center and rescue Arashi and everyone else. But we can't just charge in without a clue.'

'You're right,' Ide said. 'But if we could investigate more— examine Arashi and the others—'

'We can keep going over the video.' Hayata gave Ide an encouraging smile. 'Thanks to you, we can actually *see* what happened to Arashi *as* it happened, *how* it happened, and from a better angle than we have on any of the others. There's a good chance we'll spot something helpful. Fuji, full-screen Arashi's feed for us and roll it back to just before the first appearance of the alien.'

She did so and Hayata replayed it in frame-by-frame mode, watching the alien appear, wait, then disappear; he did it twice more, all the while feeling hyper-conscious of the Beta Capsule in his jacket.

'See anything new?' Ide asked him.

'I'll tell you only if you stop looming over me and sit down,' Hayata replied, chuckling a little in spite of everything.

Ide obligingly hooked the leg of a nearby chair with one foot and plumped down on it like an attentive student. Hayata replayed the first appearance of the alien, pausing the video before it vanished. 'It's hard to see but when the alien first shows up, I don't think it's really there.'

'You don't?' Fuji reversed the video and replayed the sequence to the same point. 'How?'

'Look closely,' Hayata said, 'and you'll see it doesn't just pop out of existence all at once. It starts to fade out first.' He pointed at a spot on the left side of its V-shaped head. 'You can see through it to the wall behind. *Then* it vanishes.' He replayed the sequence twice more for them.

'Sorry,' Fuji said, sitting back in her chair. 'I just can't tell.'

'Me, either,' said Ide. 'Your eyesight must be a hell of a lot better than mine. If you *are* right, what do you think it means?'

'That there's only one alien,' Hayata said. 'No matter how many you think you see, there's really just one, projecting images.'

Fuji frowned, looking from the screen to Hayata and back. 'You think it came here alone and it's trying to make us believe it's an army?'

'Oh, there's no way it came here alone,' Hayata told her. 'The rest are hiding out somewhere nearby. It wouldn't have come without plenty of backup. No alien would.'

'That monster out at Lake Ryugamori did,' Ide pointed out.

'Yeah, but it was a fugitive on the run from Ultraman,' Fuji said, speaking up before Hayata could answer. 'This one doesn't seem to be running from anyone or anything. The way it's freezing people tells me it's not trying to hide from us. It *wants* us to know it's here.'

'That's pretty damned insightful,' Ide said, looking impressed.

'For someone who feels things so deeply, you mean?' Fuji said, all innocence.

Ide sighed. 'I *did* say I was sorry. I've got ear-witnesses.'

'Children, please—no fighting on the playground.' In spite of everything, Hayata had to feign a fierce frown just to keep from laughing.

'*He* started it,' said Fuji.

'And I apologized, over and over,' Ide said. 'I really didn't think you'd hold it against me for *this* long.'

'Neither did I,' Fuji replied. 'But then I found out how much fun it is.'

'That's *enough*.' Hayata no longer felt like laughing. 'Ide, you've got to be more careful about what you say in the future. And Fuji—' He swiveled around on the chair to look at her. 'If you have to torture him even though he's sorry, do it later, when we don't have to worry about an alien freezing people.'

'Yes, boss,' they said in unison, which startled him so much, it took him a couple of seconds to find his voice.

'Okay, Fuji, why don't you monitor air traffic transmissions for unusual flight patterns or even weather fluctuations.'

'Good idea,' she said, getting up.

'And Ide, you take surface traffic, especially around the coast. Also calls to emergency services.'

'Okay,' Ide said. 'What are you going to do?'

'I'm going to keep studying this video, see if I can figure out anything else about our uninvited guest.'

'You got it, boss. Shout if you find something.' He got up, then hesitated. 'You should have seen Arashi in full uniform, wearing his slippers. It was so funny—' He looked pained. 'I hope he's gonna be all right.'

'Me, too,' Hayata said and moved his chair closer to the

desk. He reran all the security feeds from the very beginning, concentrating on the alien and doing his best not to think about how easily his teammates had called him *boss*.

Watching the alien immobilize Arashi for the umpteenth time made Hayata wonder again if he should have had him and the soldiers and security guards taken to the hospital after all. As far as he could tell, none of them were breathing. Should they have been on life-support? Or was it already too late? If it was, if they *had* all died at the moment they'd been frozen, it felt wrong to leave them there.

Arashi would have told him that he could make up for it later, after they dealt with the aliens and made sure no one else got frozen. He'd have said it gruffly, of course, but without rancor. And on the heels of that thought came a deep certainty that he'd done the right thing by leaving everyone at the Science Center untouched, although he had no idea why.

Call it a hunch, said a little voice in his mind, which was almost funny. In the past, Hayata had never been much for hunches. Not that he'd ever had many, and this wouldn't be one, either, not really. This would be something his new best friend knew and it was coming to him indirectly, the only way it could.

Hayata wondered if his new best friend had had any idea how awkward and inconvenient their merging was going to be. Not to mention weird; it was even weirder than hearing Fuji and Ide call him *boss*.

* * *

It was sunset before Muramatsu finally called in from the Defense Force base.

'Are we glad to hear from you,' Hayata said as he and Ide joined Fuji at the communications console. 'I hope you're on your way back.'

'No such luck, I'm afraid,' Muramatsu said. Hayata had never heard him sound so weary.

'Is there anything we can do, Cap?' Fuji said.

'Glad you asked, Fuji.' Now there was a hint of a smile in Muramatsu's voice. 'The Defense Force have gone round and round about what to do, reviewing the security video over and over, and they've finally come to the conclusion that there is no conclusion to come to.'

Hayata exchanged looks with the other two. 'So they still haven't decided on a course of action?'

'Oh, they've decided several things.' The weariness in Muramatsu's voice was even heavier. 'But there's no way to get a solid fix on the alien energy signature—it pops in and out of existence like the aliens at the Science Center. And we have nothing to counter that freeze weapon of theirs. Without knowing more than we do now, we might as well make wishes, not decisions. They asked me if the Science Patrol had any ideas. I told them we should try communicating with the aliens.'

'How did they react to that?' Hayata asked.

'You'd have thought I was suggesting we surrender and let the aliens do whatever they wanted. It took some time to make them understand I was saying we should find out why they're here, if they were forced to land because their spacecraft had been damaged or disabled. Or maybe they were just out of fuel.'

No wonder he was so tired, Hayata thought.

'If it actually turns out to be that simple,' Muramatsu continued, 'we might be able to help them make repairs and send them on their way without hostilities. Which, in turn might inspire them to show their gratitude for our hospitality by sharing some of their more advanced technology.' Muramatsu gave a short, humorless laugh. 'Or they could simply fly away and never look back. Either way, the result is a peaceful resolution that doesn't require the use of weapons like the Hagetaka missile, leaving everyone involved with no casualties and no hard feelings.'

'They want to use the Hagetaka?' Fuji looked as if she were going to be sick.

'They'd have used it already,' Muramatsu said grimly, 'except they don't know where to aim it. The alien energy signature doesn't last long enough and when it disappears, it's like it never existed. Even the most sensitive spy satellites can't pick up a trace. It took all day, but I finally managed to persuade them that trying to communicate with technologically advanced aliens is a far better option than rattling our sabers.'

'I agree,' Hayata said. 'So how do we go about trying to start a conversation?'

'Well.' Muramatsu let out a long, heavy breath. 'That's the question of the hour, isn't it.'

'The Fibonacci sequence!' Ide said.

Hayata and Fuji turned to stare at him, surprised.

'I'm listening,' Muramatsu said, his voice suddenly less exhausted.

'We use a laptop—no, a tablet, it'll be easier to handle—and show it a simplified representation of the Fibonacci sequence, with simple graphics, like squares. One square, two squares, three squares, then five, eight, thirteen, twenty-one, and so on. We could also have a spiral showing the golden ratio.'

'Along with pictures of sunflowers and pinecones, to show how it occurs in nature,' Fuji put in, catching Ide's enthusiasm. 'So they can see that we learn from our surroundings.'

'Can you set that up in the next twenty minutes?' Muramatsu asked, almost all the weariness gone from his voice now.

'More like fifteen, Cap,' Ide said, looking pleased.

'Get it done, and you and Hayata bring it to the Science Center,' Muramatsu told him.

'You think the alien's still there?' Ide asked.

'Despite the signal jumping all over the world, the aliens themselves haven't been sighted anywhere else, so I think it's a safe bet,' Muramatsu replied.

'I'll find a tablet for you in the electronics workshop,' Fuji said, getting up from the console. Hayata could see she wasn't happy about being left behind yet again. He followed her out of the room and caught her in the hallway.

'I'll need you to be prepared for anything here,' he told her. 'There's no telling what could happen—we might need a submarine at short notice again.'

Fuji's smile was a bit reluctant. 'If you do, I'm driving.'

* * *

'You really think this'll work?' Ide asked Hayata as they pulled up a few meters from the cordon around the Science Center. His enthusiasm had morphed into apprehension. Hayata had seen this happen before. It was one thing to have a great idea but quite another to take it off the drawing board and make it real.

'It's an excellent idea,' Hayata assured him. 'Mathematics is universal, common to all intelligent life.'

'But we don't actually know that for sure,' Ide said, making no move to release his safety belt.

'Yes, we do,' Hayata said. 'The same way we know that if you shine a light on a solid object, it will cast a shadow.'

Ide blinked at him. 'Oh.'

'Plus it's a much better idea than firing the Hagetaka first and asking questions later.' Hayata gave him a soft, buddy-punch on the arm. 'Now let's go in there and prove you're a genius.'

They got out of the car together but as they approached the cordon, Ide started lagging behind. The soldiers on duty who opened the barrier also did them the courtesy of pretending not to notice how Hayata had to drag him through.

A couple of meters from the front door, Ide dug in his heels and came to a full stop. 'Maybe now isn't a good time?' he said. 'Maybe we should wait for daylight?'

'It's okay, we've got backup.' Hayata turned him around so he could see the Hagetaka missile platform set up under floodlights in the parking lot. The soldiers on the platform waved at them and they both waved back.

'See?' Hayata said. 'You've got nothing to fear.'

You'll have nothing to worry about.

Hayata heard his new best friend's voice in his head as clearly as if he were back at Lake Ryugamori, back when he'd been dead. Looking down, he saw a glint from the Beta Capsule in his jacket.

'What is it?' Ide asked him tensely. 'Did you think of something?'

'Yes—that you're also carrying the Spider Shot,' Hayata said smoothly, gesturing at the sidearm clipped to Ide's belt. 'You know how well it works, you invented it.'

Ide started toward the front door, then stopped again. 'Remind me—the first alien I see is a decoy, a mirage. The second one is real and that's the one I should show the tablet to. Right?'

Hayata put both hands on Ide's shoulders. 'What I told you was, the first one Arashi saw was an illusion and the second one was real. It did the same thing with me and since most living things, including aliens, tend to repeat patterns of behavior, you can probably expect the same treatment. Just keep your eyes open.'

'I'll try,' Ide said, 'but I'm counting on you if things go south.'

'I think it'll take more than the Fibonacci sequence for things to go south,' Hayata said, hoping he was right.

'I guess,' Ide said. 'But I just need you to do me one more favor—'

'Yes, I'll come in with you.' Hayata opened the front door and made an after-you gesture.

Ide took a breath, squared his shoulders, and went in. Hayata followed and immediately collided with him in front of the reception desk, where he had stopped short at the sight of the immobilized security guard.

'I know, it's a lot more disturbing in person than on video.' Hayata turned Ide away from the security guard and walked him over to the stairs up to the mezzanine. 'But you're okay.'

They went up the first few steps together before Hayata stopped, leaving Ide to continue. As soon as Ide realized Hayata wasn't beside him, however, he stopped, too.

'You go up and I'll keep watch from here,' Hayata told him. 'I have to be behind you if I'm going to have your back.'

Ide nodded, squared his shoulders again, and marched up the steps.

There really was no one better than Hayata to have his back, Ide told himself, no one more dependable. Hayata had never let any of the team down in the slightest way. Later, after this was all over—tomorrow morning, three days from now, next week—he was going to feel silly for being so jumpy.

Only it wasn't next week yet, it was now and his nerves were in overdrive. There was something in the air, a feeling of something about to happen like in the last minutes before a thunderstorm. Except thunderstorms didn't happen indoors. At least, not on Earth.

But maybe it was different where the alien came from. Maybe the alien had brought an alien thunderstorm with it. Ide wished the idea seemed as silly now as it would next week.

Unless that was what was about to happen. Then it would never seem silly, ever. Dammit.

Ide looked down at his tie and discovered he'd forgotten his anomaly alert. The night was just getting better and better, he thought as he drew the Spider Shot. At the same moment, he caught a movement in the corner of his eye. No, it was ahead of him, a dark shape—

Clutching the tablet, he backed up a step, raised the Spider Shot, and then realized the dark shape he was taking aim at was his own silhouette on the tiled wall in front of him.

Unbelievable, he thought, now shaking with silent laughter. He'd actually been afraid of his own shadow. If anyone else had been there, they'd never have let him live it down. Fuji would have been merciless.

He stopped laughing but he kept on shaking. The feeling of something about to happen was more intense than ever.

Pull it together! he ordered himself as he clipped the Spider Shot back on his belt and looked down at the tablet. All he had to do was show this to the alien and it would understand, wouldn't it? Sure it would, because Hayata was right—any lifeform capable of space travel had to know the Fibonacci sequence. Mathematics was universal, underpinning every aspect of civilization—art, music, language, education, even social interactions and movements. The alien had to understand they were trying to communicate with it. Ide just hoped it wouldn't think the tablet was another weapon and freeze him.

As he took a step forward, something else occurred to him.

What if the alien understood this was an attempt to communicate and froze him anyway?

Intelligent life wouldn't be so unreasonable... would it?

Maybe not on Earth but who could say what aliens called 'reasonable'? Who knew if they even cared about being reasonable? What if on their world being reasonable was a bad thing?

What if he stopped thinking up worst-case scenarios and just got this over with?

Ide moved farther into the mezzanine, going slowly and using the tablet screen to light the way. He hadn't been able to get anything from the security cameras on this level but when he saw the frozen form of a security guard ahead of him, he wasn't surprised. Giving the man a wide berth, he tried not to look too closely at his face—tried not to look at him at all, if possible, but couldn't help himself.

The man had been terrified. He had one hand up to ward something off and his mouth was open, as if he'd been about to cry out for help. The alien had probably immobilized him before he could make a sound.

Ide wondered how the frozen body felt—hard and cold? He had a sudden, terrible mental image of the security guard falling over and shattering into a million pieces. Which was probably ridiculous—no, it was ridiculous—but he couldn't know that for sure. There was no telling what these aliens were capable of.

The something-about-to-happen feeling in the air intensified and Ide knew he wasn't alone.

It was behind him, of course; where else would it be? He didn't want to turn and look but he couldn't stop himself.

The alien regarded him with those unblinking, merciless

yellow eyes. But this would be the illusion; no point in showing it the Fibonacci sequence. He turned away and it popped into existence in front of him.

'Hello,' Ide said, holding the tablet at arm's length to show it the screen. 'Peaceful greetings. I greet you in peace. All of us greet you in peace. I don't know why I'm talking, you can't understand a word I'm saying.' He held the screen a little higher. 'Fibonacci sequence, see? One square, two squares, three squares, five squares, eight, thirteen, twenty-one—each number is the sum of the previous two. See?' Holding the screen with one hand, he pointed at it with the other. 'See?'

The alien made a deep guttural noise and suddenly a whole troop of aliens began pouring out of it, one after another in single file. All of them were transparent like ghosts or phantoms, and they marched past Ide in a seemingly endless line, without bothering to look at him. The one Ide had thought was real disappeared but the phantoms kept on coming, pouring out of thin air and disappearing into the shadows.

Another alien, not transparent, appeared on the other side of the endless marching line of phantoms. That had to be the real one, Ide thought and held out the tablet again. The substantial alien then divided in two, and the new one looked as solid as the first. Ide had no idea what to make of this latest development but it seemed safe to assume they didn't care if humans knew about the Fibonacci sequence.

And then all at once, the aliens were gone, leaving him alone in the middle of the mezzanine. Now what? Ide wondered, and then gasped as something hard poked his back. He didn't have to turn and look to know it was the alien.

The only thing he could think to do was hold up the tablet so the alien could see it over his shoulder.

In answer, it pushed him hard toward the stairs, making a guttural grunt.

'Okay, okay, I'm going,' Ide said. He'd thought it would want him to go down but to his surprise, the alien shoved him toward the flight up. It was the last thing he wanted to do; he'd been dreading having to see Arashi. Except Arashi wasn't on the stairs anymore.

His moment of relieved surprise turned to dread. This had to be worse, he thought. Whatever the aliens had done with Arashi, it couldn't have been anything good. And since living things tended to repeat patterns of behavior, he could probably expect the same thing to happen to him.

'What happened to the man who was here?' he asked as they passed the spot where Arashi had been and started up the next flight. 'What did you do with him?'

The alien answered with another hard push.

'Are you taking me to him?' Ide went on. 'What do you want from us?'

The sharp edge of the alien's claw dug into Ide's back through his uniform. That was the only answer he was going to get for now.

When they reached the top floor, the alien marched him over to the roof access. Ide saw the lock had been torn out and the door thrown wide open. He headed up the steps into the cool night air. Maybe the alien had thrown Arashi off the roof and now it was about to repeat the behavior pattern with him. Life's rich pageant, now with added aliens; just his luck.

When he reached the middle of the roof, Ide felt one last hard prod and then nothing. He turned around to find himself alone again. At least he wasn't near the edge, he thought, then stiffened as he heard footsteps approaching. The aliens had all been silent except for that crude, ugly noise, whatever it was— maybe laughter, maybe not, but definitely not the kind of sound he'd ever heard just before something good happened.

Ide's gaze fell on the tablet in his hands. Time to give up on the Fibonacci sequence, he thought. What if those bizarre yellow eyes couldn't see the tablet screen the way humans did? Didn't matter, he thought; the fact that it hadn't exhibited any interest in the tablet told him everything he needed to know.

He leaned the tablet against a structure housing part of the Science Center's ventilation system and listened to the footsteps coming closer, keeping one hand on the Spider Shot on his belt. Even if it was an alien, it was just one. Unless it was trailing an army marching single file behind it. But to his immense relief, the figure that walked out of the shadow of the utility housing and came to a stop in front of him was no alien.

'Arashi!' Ide reached for him, then stopped, afraid to touch him. For a long moment, he stayed that way with his hand centimeters from Arashi's shoulder. Then the image of the security guard on the mezzanine level popped into his head and he pulled his hand back.

'Arashi,' he said again, a bit more quietly. 'How did you— uh, get away? Are you all right? Did they—'

'You make so much noise all the time. So much excess noise,' Arashi said, his voice strangely flat. He stared straight ahead, not looking at Ide but through him. 'We've decided to save time by using this man's brain to speak to you.'

'What are you talking about?' Ide waved a hand in front of Arashi's face and saw no reaction. 'You're acting like a robot—' He cut off and drew back, then jumped as he felt a strong hand on his shoulder. Fortunately, that wasn't an alien, either.

'Why did you come to Earth?' Hayata asked.

'At last, one that disgorges sonic coherence rather than noise,' said Arashi in his flat, robotic voice. 'Our planet Baltan was rendered unlivable as a result of irreparable damage from war and industrial waste. We have been scouting for a new world to call home. Our vessel sustained damage from—' Arashi's voice paused. 'What you call a meteor. It was necessary to land here to make repairs. Your world had the proper materials, and much more. This world of yours has everything we need. It will be a good home for us. We have decided to stay.'

'You what?' Ide said, forgetting he was afraid.

Hayata put up a hand, giving him a warning look. 'That may be possible, provided you're willing to coexist peacefully among the many different cultures that make up our civilization. And provided we have room. How many of you are there?'

'Roughly 2.03 billion,' Arashi's voice replied.

'What?!' Ide looked to Hayata, wondering if he'd heard right.

'Your spacecraft can carry over two billion of you?' Hayata said, openly dubious.

'We have rendered ourselves more spatially compact. At

the moment, we are the size of—' Arashi's voice paused again while the alien found the right word in his mind. 'Bacteria. Except for one of us who remains at proportions visible to the naked eye.'

Ide turned to look at Hayata, mouthing, Just one? Really?

'Our population is already in the billions,' Hayata said. 'There isn't enough room for an additional two billion, no matter how small you are. But there are other planets besides ours in this solar system. The fourth planet is uninhabited, although it doesn't have our atmosphere. However, we might be able to help you build some kind of habitat or shelter for yourselves, underground at first—'

'We know all about Mars.' There was no change in Arashi's blank expression but Ide thought an edge of impatience had crept into his robotic tone. 'Our scans show there is nothing on Mars except—'

Ide waited but Arashi didn't go on.

'Except what?' Hayata asked.

'It's nothing we want so it's pointless to tell you,' said Arashi's flat voice. 'Now you are starting to make more noise than sound and we are tired of hearing it. This conversation is over. We shall have the Earth for ourselves.'

'And what about the people who are already here?' Ide demanded. 'Are you just going to wipe them all out—take the life of every man, woman, and child on the planet?'

'"Life"? What is that?' Arashi's robotic voice definitely took on a quizzical note. 'We encountered the concept in this human's brain but it doesn't make sense to us.'

'That explains a lot,' Ide said darkly.

Arashi turned toward him and for the first time, his eyes focused on Ide's face. Then they rolled back in his head and he collapsed.

Ide and Hayata rushed to him, putting him on his side in the recovery position. At least he was breathing normally, Ide thought as he took off his jacket, folded it, and put it under Arashi's head. Hayata was about to tell him something, then suddenly stared past him, his mouth hardening into a straight line.

Ide turned to follow Hayata's gaze and saw the alien about three meters away from them. It raised its arms, claws opening, and Ide had the impression they were weapons that had been grafted onto its body. Had the alien volunteered for it, or had it just been done to him? Ide had a feeling it was the latter. And if that was how these aliens treated their own—

Something whizzed past Ide's head and struck the alien in the chest. Hayata had thrown a shuriken at it. He crouched beside Ide with one hand on his sidearm, waiting for the alien to react. Ide drew the Spider Shot and looked up to find the alien had vanished again. Of course. That was what it did.

In the next moment, he discovered he was wrong about that, in a big way.

Didn't see that coming, Hayata thought, backing away.

The alien that loomed over the rooftop brandishing its gigantic claws had to be forty or fifty meters tall. Hayata motioned for Ide to drag Arashi out of harm's way while he drew his weapon with one hand and reached for the Beta

Capsule with the other. If there had ever been a time when he needed to have nothing to worry about—

Then he was flying across the roof, past the ventilation system, heading for the edge, only to fetch up against something hard and ungiving with such force that it stopped everything in the world. Sight and sound receded into the distance as his awareness dimmed.

Ide looked around in confusion, then finally spotted Hayata lying unconscious against the parapet like a doll thrown aside. *Not again*, he thought, flashing back to Lake Ryugamori. Did this mean Hayata was going to levitate, disappear, and then show up somewhere else entirely? Was that a sign that Ultraman was on the way? Suddenly he wasn't sure where he was or what he was doing.

He was still trying to figure it out when he heard the sound of a missile whistling through the air above him. It scored a direct hit on the giant alien's upper body.

'They did it!' Ide shouted, jumping up and down and hugging Arashi, who was feebly trying to push him away. He watched as the giant alien faltered for a few moments, then seemed to steady itself, just before another Hagetaka missile hit and knocked it down.

'They did it *again*!' Ide ran across the roof and peered over the balustrade. The giant alien was lying face down on the ground.

Arashi stumbled up beside him. 'Where did that come from?'

'Some planet called Baltan,' Ide replied. 'But it doesn't matter, it's nowhere now! It's toast! It's down for the count! It's—'

'It's getting up,' Arashi said dully.

Ide's jaw dropped. There were two giant aliens now, one a ghostly phantom still lying on the ground and one substantial and solid, pushing itself to its feet. The one on the ground faded away as the other opened its claws and two of the neighboring buildings in the complex exploded into flames.

'We've got to get out of here!' Ide shouted. He had no idea if there was enough time to escape but he dragged Arashi back across the roof again anyway. Just as they reached the stairs, Ide remembered Hayata lying near the parapet, started to turn toward him. In the same moment, there was another loud explosion and he and Arashi were flung backward.

'Hayata!' Arashi called out weakly. 'Somebody help Hayata!'

'Where?' Ide squinted through the smoke but Hayata seemed to have vanished.

Hayata woke to the sound of explosions, Ide shouting faintly in the distance, and the smell of scorched metal and concrete. The air was full of smoke, making his eyes sting and water as he sat up and felt around, trying to find the Beta Capsule. It had to be nearby; he'd just had it in his hand. He pushed himself to his feet and squinted through the thickening smoke.

Finally he spotted it on top of the parapet, as if he'd put it down for a moment while he zipped up his jacket, with no thought that he could accidentally knock it over the edge. He lunged for it and felt his fingertips hit the barrel before it disappeared over the edge.

Well, he couldn't say he hadn't seen that coming.

Hayata leaned over the parapet, hoping to see where it landed even as he knew he couldn't possibly spot something the size of a penlight from this height through the thickening smoke. But to his surprise, the Beta Capsule wasn't lost somewhere on the ground three stories out of reach. It had dropped onto a window ledge directly below him, a mere three or four meters out of reach. He could add that to the list of things he hadn't seen coming tonight; too bad it wasn't a luckier break.

You'll have nothing to worry about.

No, he certainly wouldn't, as long as Ultraman showed up before he hit the ground. Would he be able to activate the Beta Capsule quickly enough? As Muramatsu might have said, that was the question of the hour and he had only one way to answer it.

Climbing up onto the parapet, Hayata looked down at the Beta Capsule, sitting there, waiting for him to work up the nerve to jump. Only he didn't have enough time for that; he had to jump now, whether he had the nerve or not.

With a wordless yell that was part terror, part war cry, and part plea for mercy, he fell forward into empty air.

* * *

So that answered his question of the hour: He *could* activate the Beta Capsule after jumping off the Science Center roof and live to tell the tale. Or rather, *not* tell it.

Hayata thought he must have made quite a sight, becoming Ultraman in mid-fall. He could only hope there hadn't been any witnesses to appreciate it. Not that he had time to worry about that right now; the giant alien had already taken to the air. It was headed for the city, where there were many more buildings to burn and, unlike those in the Science Center complex at this time of night, they *wouldn't* be empty.

Night. You know, when it's dark. Because the sun is shining on some other part of the world.

Immediately he checked his Color Timer—still bright blue. Except when it started blinking red this time, there'd be no flying up into the sunlight for a quick energy boost. He would have to finish this as fast as he could or dawn would find Tokyo a smoking ruin with untold numbers of dead, courtesy of an alien that had no understanding of 'life'. *Fly faster*, he told himself. At least he knew which way the alien had gone—it had left a trail of scorched earth, grass fires, blown-up roadways, and burning warehouses for him to follow.

The vibration of her wrist alarm woke Senior Security Officer Mari Endo. Groggy, she checked the clock on the small table next to her bed. Damn, it hadn't been three hours since she'd clocked out. This was the disadvantage of staying in the power station's onsite quarters—you were twice as likely to get called in the middle of the night by whomever was rocking the graveyard shift.

'Ms. Endo, ma'am, are you up?' The question came from the intercom speaker, also on the bedside table. Itsuki Kokawa sounded worried but he always did; he was still new.

'Just Endo.' She sighed, sitting up and pushing her hair back from her face. 'Up, but not quite awake yet. This had better be good.'

'Uh, it's not,' Kokawa said. 'I mean, it's a good cause to wake you but I don't think it's a good thing. Something buzzed us—'

'Buzzed?' Endo looked longing at her pillow.

'Like, flew over the power station real low and real fast. It triggered the drones to launch.'

'How many?' Endo asked, wincing.

Kokawa hesitated. 'All of them.'

Now Endo was wide awake. 'Did you see anything?'

'Yes, and I've got it on video.'

'All right, so what was it?' she asked.

He hesitated again. 'It's easier if you see for yourself.'

A few minutes later, she was in uniform and sitting beside Kokawa at the main console in the surveillance suite of the Hagiwara Power Station, located just outside Tokyo. In the ten years Endo had been working security, she'd been through her share of middle-of-the-night disturbances. Some had been teenagers scaling the fence on a dare, or so they could take selfies next to the warning signs. Other times, the intruders had been vandals or thieves looking for anything they could steal or sell.

On one memorable occasion, a couple of new Defense Force recruits had been blown off course during parachute training and floated down onto some scaffolding, where they had dangled for thirty minutes before a crew could rescue them. That last had happened in the middle of the day but it had triggered the launch of half the surveillance drones. Despite the fact that Endo had had to reprogram the drones one at a time, she'd thought it was pretty funny in the moment.

But an alien with big lobster claws for hands having a punch-up with a silver and red humanoid over a hundred and thirty feet tall while streaking through the night at an impossible speed, barely missing the tops of the tallest structures in the station complex—this was definitely a first.

Kokawa paused the playback as two dozen surveillance drones streamed upward from the four corners of the complex and gave chase. 'I still don't know how to describe this for the incident report.' He looked at her with forlorn eyes. 'Do you?'

'I'll take care of the report,' she told him. 'I'll just need a statement of corroboration from you as the junior officer on duty.'

'You got it,' Kokawa said, obviously relieved. 'Do you need to see it again?' He reached for the replay-from-beginning button.

'Not yet.' She turned to look at the mural-sized monitor on the wall directly in front of the console. The monitor was showing multiple feeds from the drones currently pacing the airborne combatants from what the action algorithm determined was a safe distance. Endo hoped the algo was right. 'Hey, is there any tea left?'

'Made some fresh while I was waiting for you.' Kokawa went into the closet-sized kitchenette nearby and came back with a cup for her.

Endo thanked him, took a sip, thanked him again as she set the cup down and flipped the network comm switch with her little finger as she did. 'This is Senior Officer Mari Endo at Hagiwara Power Station Security calling Science Patrol command, reporting unknown trouble.'

'Agent Fuji here,' said a pleasant but serious female voice. 'Go ahead, Officer Endo.'

'Sending you feeds from surveillance drones deployed in real time, plus one recording made minutes ago.' In spite of everything, Endo smiled a little; she'd dealt with Fuji before and liked her.

'Copy that, Officer Endo. How many drones?' the other woman asked.

Endo gave a short laugh. 'All of them.'

'Oh.' Pause. 'How many is "all"?'

'Two dozen,' Endo replied. 'Sorry, Agent Fuji, I'm still waking up. Fortunately, my partner Kokawa has been on this from the start.' She glanced at Kokawa, who was trying to see all of the feeds at once.

'Receiving feeds now, officer,' Fuji said. 'Thank y—oh! Captain! It's him!'

Endo frowned, unsure if she was supposed to know who him was.

'I can see that,' a man said some distance from Fuji's comm mic; he sounded strangely cheerful.

'Captain Muramatsu here.' He was close to the mic now and still cheerful. Very strange, Endo thought, which probably meant things were going to get even stranger. She turned to Kokawa and motioned for him to speak.

For half a second, Kokawa looked terrified and Endo thought she'd have to kick him. 'The incident clock started as soon as the drones launched, Captain,' he blurted. 'Does the Science Patrol wish to take control? Uh, of them?' Pause. 'The dro—'

'Thank you, officer, we've got them on our grid now,' Muramatsu said, and Endo could have sworn he sounded amused. 'But we'd like you to continue monitoring the feeds with us, and to keep an eye out for anything else that might decide to join the party. We'll notify your superiors, and we'll want to debrief you later.'

'We'll remain available,' said Endo. 'And we'll keep the channel open.'

'Great. Muramatsu out.' The speaker fell silent as both he and Endo muted their comms without breaking the connection.

Kokawa turned to Endo, looking a bit lost. 'That's it?'

'Not even close,' Endo assured him.

Now he was horrified as well as terrified. 'What else is going to happen?'

'I'd tell you, but—' Endo began.

'You'd have to kill me?' Kokawa guessed in a small voice.

'No,' she said with a laugh, watching the feeds. 'I'd tell you but I don't have a clue.'

* * *

The Science Center's external security cameras had brief footage of Ultraman flying away from the complex, a very high-res shot of the soles of his feet—boots?—as he chased the alien into the night.

Muramatsu was dismayed at how quickly the alien had reached the power station. The station's own recording began not even a minute later, courtesy of its own external cameras. They had caught the approach of the alien, an airborne juggernaut zooming out of clouds of smoke billowing up from the destruction on the ground.

The perspective shifted to the lead drone, which had drawn even with the alien to transmit a medium close-up of the bizarre V-shaped head, its yellow eyes, and those giant claws. How did evolution decide to give a vertebrate claws like a lobster instead of opposable thumbs?

Abruptly, Ultraman flew into the frame from below, to curl one arm around the creature's chunky body while grabbing one of those big claws with the other. Was that the pincer claw or the crusher claw? It had been a long time since Muramatsu's last marine zoology course and what little he could remember probably wouldn't apply to aliens, or even alien lobsters. He pushed the thought away; the damnedest things went through your mind at the damnedest times.

Muramatsu used the remote control to make the lead drone's feed dominant without cutting off any of the others. Neither Ultraman nor the alien paid any attention to the flyers pacing them as they struggled with each other. The alien's movements were becoming more frantic as it tried to twist out of Ultraman's grasp.

'Can we get a better angle on that claw?' Muramatsu asked Fuji. Dutifully, she enlarged the correct feed, gasping softly when she saw how Ultraman was forcing the claw to open wider.

In the next moment, the bottom part of the claw broke off completely. Ultraman let go of the alien, flinging the broken piece away as something dark and viscous spewed from the alien's arm.

Ultraman shot away from the injured creature and began to ascend sharply. A few drones followed; tiny numbers in the lower right-hand corner of their feeds noted his speed and altitude. Despite its injury, the alien accelerated after him, climbing to the same level. Apparently for this species, losing half a claw wasn't a game-changer, or even a tide-turner. Perhaps it grew back.

Muramatsu caught a glimpse of the countless tiny lights of Tokyo's nighttime skyline as Ultraman kept on climbing. At the apex, he changed course and started back in the direction he had come, with the alien right behind him. As it began closing the distance between them, the alien opened its other claw and sent several fireballs at Ultraman, who evaded them with little effort.

The claw opened again but this time, it was aimed downward, releasing a single large fireball that rolled furiously along the ground until it hit the row of backup generators lining one edge of the power station complex.

'If anyone over there was still asleep, they're awake now,'

Muramatsu said grimly. It would take more than that to breach the underground energy stores but Muramatsu had an awful feeling the alien had the power to do it. Unless Ultraman could breach the alien first—

Ultraman suddenly dropped off the bottom of the screen and for a terrible moment, Muramatsu thought the alien had hit him with one of its fireballs, or even a plasma ball. Then the drones caught up with him and Muramatsu saw he had touched down at the other end of the complex. As he watched, Ultraman went down on one knee and positioned his arms the same way he had at Lake Ryugamori—left arm making a horizontal brace for his right hand. A beam of pure white energy flowed out from him and hit the alien dead center.

Instead of blowing apart as Muramatsu expected, the alien imploded, leaving a burnt-out husk to plummet to the ground.

'What's he doing now?' Fuji said tensely as Ultraman got to his feet and started to scan the night sky, searching for something.

'I don't know,' Muramatsu said, 'but I think the worst may be over. Have the Defense Force send out a team to recover the alien's remains. Tell them I said to hurry, before the body melts or disintegrates or vaporizes.'

The Spacium Beam had made short work of the Baltan, and his Color Timer was still a bright healthy blue, but the job wasn't done. Somewhere in the vicinity, over two billion Baltans were waiting to be loosed on what they thought was their new home. How billions of aliens the size of bacteria could hope to take the Earth for themselves without the only one visible to the naked eye was something he didn't have to know. He only knew he couldn't let them land.

Concentrating, he searched the night sky with vision that was more than vision, that could perceive more deeply and broadly than his human eyes. The aliens' energy signature had been popping up all over the world but he was sure they'd stayed close to the one they'd sent out to lay claim to the planet. That wasn't rocket science, as the saying went. Not this part, anyway.

Hayata continued to concentrate, keeping his mind calm and receptive, not only to his surroundings but also to stirrings from within himself. Even in full Ultraman form, he had yet to be completely in tune with his Ultra senses—he was still relying more on his human abilities simply out of habit, although it did seem odd to him that his Ultra powers wouldn't always activate automatically. Maybe that was how it worked for a Being of Light merged with a human who, due to circumstances of time and place, had to be in the driver's seat.

Gradually, he became aware of the Baltans' presence, although it took a little longer for his Ultra vision to synchronize with the mechanism of his human sight. But finally he was able to discern the spacecraft, a disk so thick and deep it was almost a flying bowl rather than a saucer, hovering directly above the Science Center.

Should've known, he thought; *where else would they be?*

He wondered if they knew what had happened to their advance scout. If so, what could they do about it?

Better that question went unanswered, he decided as he took hold of the edge of the disk. The aliens had underestimated the intelligence and resourcefulness of humans, no doubt because they didn't know what 'life' was. A civilization needed more than superior technology before it could call itself *advanced*.

His new best friend knew that. *Must be nice to know so much,* he thought; *maybe you could find a way to let me in on it, too?*

Keeping tight control of the spacecraft, Hayata maneuvered it ahead of himself as he flew up out of Earth's atmosphere into space. He knew what to do—he had to make sure they didn't come back. There was a quick and easy way to do that but despite their heartlessness, he refused even to consider it. These were sentient beings that didn't even know they were alive. If he put an end to them before they understood what life was, their entire existence would be meaningless.

He hurled the spacecraft as hard as he could, sending it far above the plane of the ecliptic. Now that they had repaired their vessel, they could go in search of a new home, far, far away from Earth.

And if they were lucky, they might learn what life was before theirs was over.

'Hayata?'

He looked up to find Fuji standing by the desk, her face full of concern.

'I'm sorry,' he said with a small laugh. 'I was light-years away. Did I miss something?'

'Ide wants a selfie with all of us for his video blog,' she said, smiling now.

'You're okay with that, aren't you?' Ide asked, holding up the video camera.

'Of course,' he said, laughing a little more as he and Fuji joined Ide and Arashi in the center of the room.

'We've all got to move in closer,' Ide said. 'This isn't a widescreen cinematic production. Yet.'

'Ow!' Arashi said as Hayata threw one arm around his shoulders. 'Watch it. I'm still a little sore from being an alien's hand-puppet.'

'Sorry,' said Hayata, noting that for once, there weren't any jokes about Arashi being the tough guy.

'Okay, everybody say—' Ide paused, momentarily at a loss.

'Ultraman!' Fuji said and they all laughed.

'Good one!' Ide showed them the photo. 'And now you're all free to go.'

As they broke apart, Hayata noticed that Arashi was still rubbing his shoulder and wincing.

'Do you need another painkiller?' Fuji asked him.

'Not just yet,' Arashi replied, straightening up to his full height and wincing again. 'I told you, it was nothing I couldn't handle.'

'Nothing any of us couldn't handle without Ultraman's help,' Ide said.

'True. If Ultraman had shown up a second later, I'd be

dead.' Hayata chuckled, reflecting that he was the only one who knew exactly how true that was.

'You know, Hayata,' Ide said, 'for a moment there, I thought *you* were Ultraman.'

'*Me?*' Hayata burst into hearty laughter. 'Impossible!'

'It was only for a moment,' Ide assured him. 'A very short moment. *Very* short.'

'So now that you've told everyone about the Baltans,' Hayata said, 'are you going to let them in on—' He tapped a spot just under his own eye.

'Ah, right! About this black eye of mine—' Ide cut off, looking around at everyone else. 'Excuse me, this is private, between me and my audience.' He paused the recording and left the room.

Hayata stared after him in astonishment, then turned to Arashi. 'He knows we can just look at the vlog, doesn't he?'

'Sure—and now he's made sure you will.' Arashi didn't quite crack a smile. 'Spoiler: he was counting sheep in his sleep again and fell out of his bunk. Landed face-first on my slippers.'

Hayata laughed. 'You must have some pretty tough slippers.'

'Everything about Arashi is pretty tough,' Fuji teased.

Arashi allowed himself a gruff smile. 'Better believe it.'

CHAPTER
THREE

'You know, for a minute there, I really *did* think you were Ultraman.'

In the break room, Hayata looked up from the news story on his tablet to find Ide standing over him with a tray. He smiled and motioned for the other man to join him. 'So you said. But that was last week. I'm surprised it's still on your mind.'

'I had a very good reason,' Ide added, sitting down. He had a rice ball and a cup of tea, which was his usual breakfast.

'I'm sure you did,' Hayata said, setting the tablet down on the table.

'Hey, is that the Fibonacci tablet?' Ide asked.

'It is. I found it miraculously undamaged right where you left it on the roof of the Science Center. Seeing as how I managed to crash both a VTOL and a submarine on the same day, I figure that's my quota for the decade and now

I should make an effort to preserve equipment rather than destroying it.'

Ide laughed. 'They probably would have put it on *my* tab.'

'Maybe so, but it all comes out of the same budget,' Hayata said, wondering why Ide was stalling. He was more likely to blurt things out rather than circle around them in chitchat.

'Yeah, I guess it does. Anyway—' Ide began unwrapping the cellophane on his rice ball. 'It was because Arashi said he saw you jump off the Science Center roof.'

Hayata blinked at him, genuinely startled. 'He did? He never said anything about it to me.'

'That's because he decided he hadn't *really* seen you do that,' Ide told him. 'It was right after the alien stopped using him to talk to us, and then it grew, like, fifty meters or whatever. The thing swatted you aside and then our guys fired the Hagetaka at it. Right after that, Arashi told me he saw you jump off the roof. But then later, he told me that couldn't have happened. Obviously.'

'Obviously,' Hayata agreed, relaxing a little.

'He said after the alien let him go, he was all dizzy and disoriented, and he still can't remember everything. And some of the things he does remember are in the wrong order.'

'Arashi's very sensible, even when he's barely conscious.' Hayata made a mental note to do something nice for him. Nothing too big—grand gestures embarrassed him—just something a tough guy would appreciate. Like, say, new slippers.

'Anyway, then all of a sudden, Ultraman was there and he took off after the alien,' Ide said. 'So for a minute, it kinda looked like—well, you know. Like you were Ultraman.'

Hayata nodded. 'I understand completely. The truth is, Ultraman saved me from *falling off* the roof.'

'He did?' Ide paused with his rice ball halfway to his mouth. 'What happened?'

'Well, the giant alien swatted me like a fly, just like you said,' Hayata replied. 'I flew clear across the roof and hit the parapet headfirst. Even with my helmet, it knocked me out, though not for very long, probably not even half a minute. But when I woke up, I was pretty dizzy and disoriented myself. I must have thought the parapet was a barrier I had to climb over because that's what I was trying to do. Luckily, Ultraman showed up just in time to keep me from becoming one with the ground.'

'That *was* lucky,' Ide said solemnly. 'That's got to be, like, the luckiest break ever.'

Hayata chuckled. 'Very much like that.'

'Anyway, that's why I thought you were Ultraman. For about five minutes. Maybe ten, tops. I didn't realize you had such a close call.'

'Arashi didn't think I was Ultraman, did he?'

'Not for a second,' Ide assured him. 'He said there was absolutely no way you could ever be Ultraman.' He took a sip of tea.

'Why not?' Hayata asked, genuinely curious.

'Ultraman's taller.'

Hayata burst out laughing. 'Can't argue with that logic.'

The tablet chimed with a message alert. Hayata picked it up and his cheerful expression vanished.

'What is it?' Ide asked.

'You know how the Meteorological Society sent a team of four to the observation outpost on Tatara Island?' Hayata said.

'Something happened to them?' Ide guessed.

'No one knows, they've lost contact with them. The last call they had from them cut off after a few seconds and no one's been able to raise them since. They tried a flyover with a drone but there's some sort of strong electromagnetic field covering the whole island now. It crashed the drone.'

'Nothing from satellite imaging?' Ide asked.

'Just a lot of interference in pretty colors.'

Ide finished the rice ball in a couple of bites and gulped the rest of his tea. 'I'll get down to the hangar and make sure the shielding on our VTOL's instruments is airtight, waterproof, and up-to-date.'

'And I'll let Cap know you're already on the case so we can leave as soon as possible. See you in a few.' Hayata got up and headed for Ops with the tablet under his arm.

Takeshi Matsui wasn't sure how long it had been since Hiro Kawada had left but he estimated it had been around two days. He lay just inside the mouth of a cave on the edge of where the island's jungle met its rocky, volcanic area. The air wasn't as heavily humid here and it was a little easier to breathe as he drifted in and out of consciousness, listening to the sounds the island made as it talked to itself. According to Kawada, the island talked to itself all the time and if you listened closely, you would overhear its secrets. Matsui had heard plenty since they'd arrived but so far, nothing terribly secret, or useful. That Kawada; a romantic to the end.

Being a romantic was a pleasant indulgence under normal circumstances, which was to say, when you had an intact shelter with a roof to keep the rain off and solid walls dividing outdoors from indoors. Not to mention amenities like running water, electricity, and reliable communications. But when you came home with a case full of biological samples to find the roof smashed in, the walls blown out, all those lovely amenities gone, and a giant monster lying in wait to finish you off—well, that was a total buzzkill, as Sasaki would have said.

Kawada had stubbornly insisted that, buzz or no buzz, there was nothing romantic or whimsical in the notion of the island talking to itself. Matsui hadn't had the strength to argue; the infection in his leg had left him too weak for spirited discourse, or really, any other kind. Immediately after he'd injured himself, Fujita had cleaned the wound for him, applied a topical antibiotic, and bandaged the broken skin securely. But only a couple of hours later, he'd started running a fever.

Fujita had managed to salvage a lot of their medical supplies, including the rest of the antibiotics. Unfortunately for Matsui, at least half of them were some variety of penicillin and he was allergic. But Fujita had assured him there was enough erythromycin to get him through the next three days and surely by then, help would have arrived. The Department of Meteorology and Environmental Science would send out a rescue party when they couldn't re-establish contact; they wouldn't just leave them.

The next morning—or possibly later the same day, Matsui had already been too blurry to know for sure—Fujita had said he was going back to the outpost to see if there was anything else he could salvage in the way of food or medication. It was the last Matsui and Kawada had seen of him. Matsui had asked Kawada if he'd heard the island say anything about what had become of him. Or maybe he'd only thought it and not spoken out loud, since Kawada hadn't answered.

Some unmeasured time after that, Kawada had said he was going to forage for edible vegetation to bolster their much-depleted food supply. At the time, Matsui had asked him to bring back something that *didn't* taste like kale—there was a particularly delicious variety of giant blackberry in the area. Kawada had promised to try to find something tasty. Matsui was fairly certain that something had found Kawada tasty instead.

And now there was one. Matsui knew what it meant for him but he was too tired and weak to follow that thought to its logical conclusion.

He heard a chittering noise in the distance and in spite of everything, he smiled as it came closer. That would be their little mascot Pigmon, named by Sasaki in honor of a stuffed toy she'd had as a kid, also called Pigmon. The mental image of a pint-sized Keiko Sasaki cuddling a weird creature with red fur all over its round body except for its skinny legs and forelimbs, and a face that looked like a cross between a warthog and a cartoon wolf had made him laugh out loud. Sasaki hadn't taken offense. She'd insisted the creature was more intelligent than it looked. At first, he and Kawada and

Fujita had thought it was wishful thinking on her part, but she'd been right.

Pigmon had appeared the day they had arrived at the outpost, four feet tall on its spindly legs, scratching at the door to be let in. They'd all tried to convince Sasaki to keep it outside. *If it poops on the floor and starts flinging it around like a baboon, don't ask me to help you clean it up,* Fujita had said, laughing but not joking. But the creature was as fastidious as a cat, automatically going outside to do its business. By the next morning, they were all calling it Pigmon, even Fujita. That was also when it had started bringing them those wonderful giant blackberries, permanently securing its position as their mascot.

Matsui's only misgiving was that their cute-ugly little friend might have a not-so-cute, much-bigger, and *very-much-uglier* mother out there searching for her baby. He reminded Sasaki how some campers had learned the hard way why they should never get between a mama bear and her cub, and not all of them had lived to regret their mistake. But no giant, economy-sized version of Pigmon had come to reclaim her offspring in maternal fury. The scaled horror that had destroyed the outpost belonged to an entirely different, non-red-fur-bearing species.

Matsui had trouble remembering exactly what had happened despite the fact that he'd been hale and hearty at the time. He'd cut his leg open later, while he'd been climbing up to the cave. The island had a lot of caves but Pigmon had led them to this one, which seemed to be way-off the beaten path—i.e., the beaten monster path. Or it had been. But they all knew that the longer they stayed there, the more likely it was that some scaly nightmare with great big teeth and even bigger claws would find them.

As the geologist among them, Sasaki had been the least nonplussed by the fact that Tatara Island was home to impossible beasts over a hundred feet tall, most of them armored and scaly, all of them with fangs and claws of equally outsized proportions. It was her theory that their emergence had something to do with the island's location, exactly halfway between the Zenisu Ridge and the Nankai Trough in the Philippine Sea.

The location had always had some electromagnetic anomalies, she'd told them, but recently they had intensified. Then she had gone into a detailed explanation of compressive tectonics and interoceanic thrusts produced by subduction. Matsui had told her he didn't see how any of that could have produced the nightmare that had demolished the outpost just by stepping on it.

Sasaki admitted she was fuzzy on that sort of finer detail but any place where conditions were wonky and anomalous tended to produce wonky and anomalous flora, and even wonkier and more anomalous fauna stomping through it to fight each other. For all they knew, some mutant sea creature had laid eggs in the ocean and they'd washed up on the shore where they'd mutated even more. Matsui had told her that was a pretty far-out fairy tale; Sasaki had invited him to prove it.

Matsui had noted that the previous research group, which had had to evacuate in a hurry after a couple of dormant volcanoes had woken up angry, hadn't seen any mutated or monstrous wildlife. Sasaki had pointed out the group hadn't even been there a week before they'd been forced to decamp, and that had been a year ago. A year was more than enough time for a multitude of wonky and anomalous developments.

We should have brought a biologist and a zoologist, Kawada said.

And an IT guy, added Fujita.

Why? Sasaki asked, puzzled. *An IT guy couldn't have done anything about the electromagnetic field.*

No, but we could have blamed him anyway, Fujita replied.

It should have been funny but by then they'd all stopped laughing.

The harsh, bellowing roar that roused Matsui had become as familiar to him as Pigmon's chittering, albeit far less welcome. It was the beast Kawada had called the Red King (*We named the little monster so we might as well name the big ones, too,* he'd said). Kawada said this was the Red King's open challenge for any other creatures in the vicinity to come have a go for the crown if they thought they were hard enough.

Matsui was no expert on that particular subject but he was pretty sure it didn't work that way. From what little he knew, alpha males didn't issue open challenges—they just answered those from younger ones with something to prove. Kawada shrugged, saying what was one more anomaly on an island full of them?

What worried Matsui, however, was the fact that like Pigmon, the Red King seemed to display more than standard brutish predatory instincts despite the fact that it looked like a bad-tempered dinosaur. On the other hand, maybe dinosaurs had been more intelligent than anyone thought; he didn't really know that much about them, either. He knew more about the Red King—not an enormous amount but more than he'd ever wanted to.

Now he heard an answering roar from some other monster, possibly the one Kawada had said had batwing-style flaps on its arms, or maybe the one that burrowed like a mole. Suddenly, there was a different sound, a new sound, not a monster's roar or dying screech or, heaven forbid, a mating call but something that sounded a lot like an airplane.

It seemed like forever to Matsui since he'd heard that sound. Planes didn't fly over Tatara; there was too much interference from the island's whacked-out EMF. He and the others had come by boat, which had dropped them off via dinghy. Why they hadn't insisted on keeping the dinghy was one of those great, big, glaring examples of poor planning that was painfully obvious only in hindsight.

Maybe it wasn't a plane, he thought suddenly; maybe it was a monster that could imitate the noise to lure any stray human out of hiding. That idea was as ridiculous as Sasaki's notion of giant reptiles hatching out of fish eggs on the beach. Or it would have been before he had come here. On Tatara, anything was possible and ridiculous was a luxury enjoyed by those lucky enough to be anywhere else but here.

He started to fade out again and was jarred back to full

awareness by loud, urgent chittering. Pigmon was standing over him with a thermos in its paws. Sasaki had taught it how to fetch water from the pond. She had always insisted on boiling it but after she'd disappeared, none of them had bothered to do more than strain the dirt out of it. Now that he was alone, Matsui wasn't up to doing that much. So far, drinking it au naturel hadn't had any noticeable effect on him, or at least it hadn't made him feel any worse. But then he might have been too far gone to know the difference.

Pigmon shoved the canister into his hands and made slurping noises.

'Yes, yes, I know,' he said. 'Thank you.' It was an effort to unscrew the cap and he spilled as much as he poured but he managed to gulp down a healthy mouthful, frowning at the taste, which was sharper than usual.

'I really hope that's just the natural flavor of whatever pond you drew this from,' he said to Pigmon, 'and not because the Red King peed in it.'

The little creature chittered more frantically.

'Or because you did,' he added. The chittering went up half an octave. 'Oh, relax, I'm kidding. A little black humor.' He gave a weak laugh. 'I'm going to die of sepsis but hey, I can still laugh about it.'

Pigmon chirped as well as chittered.

'That's a lovely sound. I like hearing it even if I don't know what you're trying to tell me.' Matsui sighed. 'And you don't understand a word I'm saying so I guess we're even.' He let himself sag all the way down so he was lying on his side. 'I'm going to take a little nap now,' he told Pigmon; it responded by chittering less frantically. 'Wake me if anyone drops by uninvited.'

'What the *hell* is *that*?' Ide said from where he sat behind Hayata in the VTOL.

'I don't know,' said Hayata, 'but if that's the welcoming committee, we're in for a rough time.'

In the copilot seat beside Fuji, Arashi flipped open the cover over the missile controls. 'Should I give it one in the belly, Cap?'

'Not just yet,' Muramatsu replied. 'We don't want to provoke it or any friends it might have while the research team is still out there. After we find our people and get them safely aboard, we can think about pest control.'

The creature watched the VTOL carefully as Fuji flew a wide arc around it. Similar to the thing that had landed in Lake Ryugamori, it was scaly, but this one had an elongated neck like a giraffe, fierce, beady eyes, and a snout with absurdly large fangs. The fangs were dripping with blood and worse, as it had just taken a nasty bite out of another, slightly smaller creature currently dragging itself away from it.

The second one had a head more like a T. rex and loose wing-like flaps hanging from its shoulders. The bigger one turned to keep tracking the VTOL, then noticed the one with the bat-flaps was trying to sneak away. The larger beast lunged for it, took hold of one of its forelimbs and tore it off, flap and all.

'Okay, that's disturbing,' Fuji said, moving the VTOL slightly farther out. 'Not to mention gross. Ew.'

'Copy that,' Arashi said. 'Cap, are you sure you don't want me to—'

'I'm sure,' Muramatsu said sharply. 'We aren't here as aggressors. This is a rescue mission.'

The larger creature threw the torn-off limb at the smaller one as it dragged itself away, then hurled a couple of boulders after it. Then, to the astonishment of everyone in the VTOL, it beat on its chest like a gorilla.

'Once again, I pose the question,' Ide said. 'What the hell is that?'

'Versatile,' Hayata said quietly. 'A very dangerous quality in a predator.'

'No kidding,' said Fuji in a grim little voice.

The creature was still watching them when suddenly there was an eruption of dirt behind it; earth and rocks flew upward in all directions as a third beast pushed its way up out of the ground into the open air.

'Oh my God, how many of these things are there?' Fuji said, moving the VTOL even farther out. 'Where did they come from?'

'Beats me, I'm a stranger here myself,' said Arashi with a gruff laugh. 'You're right, Cap—we'd better wait and conserve our resources till we know what we're up against. And how many.'

Having freed itself from the ground, the third creature began moving slowly on all fours around the larger one as if it were sizing it up. 'That looks like the illegitimate offspring of a triceratops and a Galápagos turtle,' Fuji said. 'Possibly with some elephant ancestry—it's got four knees.'

'That's not disturbing at all,' Ide said unhappily. 'Not a bit.'

'Let's just find the outpost and get these people out of here,' Muramatsu said.

'Got it in sight, Cap,' Fuji replied, changing course to put the monsters behind them. 'Coming up on our ten o'clock. But I don't think anyone's home. I really hope they aren't, anyway.'

To everyone's relief, there were no human remains among the outpost debris, only the ruins of lab equipment, shattered glass, and splintered fragments of furniture.

'Someone's been here since this happened,' Hayata said, picking his way around a broken sink and some smashed cabinets. 'I think they've been raiding the pantry, salvaging canned food.'

'So at least some of them must have survived,' Arashi said with gruff relief.

'As of a few days ago.' Hayata nudged a crushed can of pears with one foot. 'But now? Who knows?'

'What we do know is, they had the incredibly good luck to not be home when this happened,' Muramatsu said. 'Tatara has a fair number of natural caves, both in the jungle areas and the volcanic region. Surely they must have taken shelter in one.' He frowned, looking around at the devastation. 'Arashi, you, Fuji, and Ide search the jungle area to the west of the outpost and work your way south and east. Hayata and

I will take the volcanic region to the east and move south and west.' He pulled a paper map out of his jacket and unfolded it as everyone gathered around him.

'There's a cluster of small lakes and ponds about two kilometers south of where we are now,' he went on. Hayata held one end of the map so Muramatsu could point to them. 'We'll meet up there in an hour and decide what to do, depending on what we find. If you run into trouble, don't bother with the radio—you'll just get a lot of interference. Send up a flare—' He nodded at the flare gun on Ide's belt. 'We'll come running. Or vice versa.'

'What if you send up a flare at the same time we do?' Ide asked.

'Then we'll all just have to do the best we can,' Muramatsu said. 'But let's hope we find everybody alive and in reasonably good shape and we all make it home in one piece.'

'This belonged to Kawada,' Arashi said, holding a crumpled piece of silvery metal he'd picked out of a tangle of undergrowth.

'How do you know?' Ide said. 'I can't even tell what it is. Or was.'

Fuji made her way over to where Arashi stood next to a tree festooned with thick, flowering vines to take a closer look at the blossoms as well as whatever he had in his hand.

'It used to be a beer stein,' Arashi said. 'From some of his students at Cambridge.' He showed Fuji the engraving on one side.

'A good luck present for the trip,' Fuji said, pointing at another part of the inscription that was still readable.

'I hope he had better luck than his stein,' Ide said and held up a piece of shredded, bloodstained cloth. 'I don't know whose this was but I'd say it probably doesn't bode well, either.'

Even from a few meters away, Fuji could see the soft texture of the material. It was similar to a blouse hanging in her closet but she couldn't bring herself to say so out loud. Ide pulled a plastic evidence bag out of his jacket, shook it open, and stuffed the cloth into it. Arashi tossed the stein at him so he could put that in as well; it sailed past Ide and disappeared into a thick tangle of brush.

'Good one,' Ide said sourly. He had to hunt a little before he found the stein and added it to the bag. 'Is that your first time trying to throw something?'

Arashi gave a short, gruff laugh. 'Is that your millionth time trying to catch something?'

'Stop it, you two,' Fuji said quietly.

They looked at her with contrite expressions before turning back to make faces at each other. Fuji pretended not to notice as she moved slowly around the tree, using the barrel of her flashlight to push the tangled undergrowth aside.

Under other circumstances—very different circumstances —she'd have enjoyed exploring the so-called jungle, which was more of a rainforest, as it had a canopy that was rather dense in spots. It was all those vines, Fuji thought, straightening up and squinting into the shadows above her. The way they were tangled in the tree branches made it hard to tell exactly how they were growing, whether they had spread from one tree to the next or they were parasites, consuming the trees from the top down.

The blossoms resembled orchids, although the petals were much thicker and they were all patterned like snakeskin. Maybe this was where snakes came from on Tatara Island— they grew on trees to avoid getting trampled by monsters. If so, this would be one of Mother Nature's more unusual workarounds. Not to mention preposterous.

Still, she should take a few cuttings back to the lab, Fuji thought, and see what happened when they cultivated them. Maybe they'd let her have a sample for her desk. Then she'd have her very own potted-plant snake. Wouldn't *that* scare the hell out of an ikebana instructor.

As she started to move around to the other side of the tree, she discovered she had stepped into a tangle of vines on the ground. Odd, she thought; that hadn't been there before, had it? She raised her foot to step out of it only to find one of the vines was winding itself around her ankle and swiftly moving upward. Reflexively, she tried to pull away and it yanked her off-balance.

'Help!' she yelled, falling backward. Something too strong and supple to be a human arm caught her around the waist and lifted her off the ground.

'*Help!*' she yelled again, louder. She struggled to get at the weapon on her belt but it was covered by the vine wrapped around her from just under her armpits down to her thighs. Desperate, she clawed at the coils and felt her nails break against their smooth, impervious surface.

Fuji caught sight of Ide, saw him draw his weapon and

start toward her. Abruptly, he tumbled forward in a clumsy somersault as a thick vine hauled him up off the ground by his ankle. His sidearm and evidence bag went flying in opposite directions.

Arashi was standing immobile, looking from Fuji to Ide and back again, over and over, short-circuited by a sudden inability to decide whom he should help first. Fuji felt the coils around her tightening and knew that in less than a minute, she would be beyond help, and so would Ide.

'Arashi!' they screamed in unison.

The sound broke his paralysis and for a bare fraction of a second, he looked embarrassed. He drew his Spider Shot, set it on incendiary and aimed at a point two feet above Fuji.

The vine charred, smoked, then burst into flames. Fuji hit the ground, scrambled to her feet and shoved the now limp vine remnants off her body while putting as much distance between herself and the tree as possible.

But to her surprise, none of the vines were hanging as low as before on any of the trees. All the vines were retracting as she watched, drawing themselves up and out of reach. She caught a quick last glimpse of the charred end of the vine that had attacked her disappearing into the leaves and branches overhead.

Ide dropped with a thud. 'Ow, dammit!' he yelled. 'That's my head I just fell on!'

'Don't be such a big baby!' Fuji mock-scolded, running to the spot where she'd seen Ide's weapon fall; she found it cradled in a thorn bush. 'You didn't hear *me* whining when I fell, did you?'

'*You* didn't fall on your *head*,' Ide huffed.

'Exactly—*you* landed on something soft.' She handed him his weapon.

'Very funny,' Ide said sourly, returning his sidearm to his belt.

'You're welcome,' Fuji replied, smiling brightly. She turned to see that Arashi had recovered his gruff composure as well as Ide's evidence bag. He tossed it to Ide, then turned to mouth *Thank you* at her.

'You think we could move on now?' Ide said crossly. 'I'd like to get farther away from these man-eating vines. Preferably miles—lots and lots of miles.'

'I'm pretty sure they don't like us any more than we like them,' Arashi said, looking around at the trees where the vines were all still visibly drawing back. But to where, Fuji wondered, still careful not to get too close to the trees.

Hayata and Muramatsu had come across one cave and a sort of wide alcove in a rock formation but neither showed any trace of having been occupied even briefly by humans or, for that matter, anything else.

'Cap, I don't think any of the observation team came this way,' Hayata said. 'And there's no good reason why they would. No fresh water, for one thing, and definitely no food.'

Muramatsu looked around, pausing in front of a rock wall with multicolored striations that went from the ground all the way to the top.

'They may not have had much choice about which way

they went,' he said. 'If something was chasing them—and it would have been something big—' He cut off as the stone under their feet began to tremble and they heard the sound of rocks falling. At first, Muramatsu was afraid the wall of stone was crumbling, then spotted the place in front of them where the ground was heaving upward, breaking apart as something big and covered with spikes forced its way to the surface.

'This way!' Muramatsu yelled to Hayata. They ran toward a stony outcropping near the edge of the wall as rocks and dirt hailed down around them, and crouched under the stone. After a bit, the ground tremors eased off but barrages of rock and soil kept coming in irregular bursts, punctuated by the sound of a beast bellowing to assert its dominance.

Lowering their helmet visors to protect their eyes, Muramatsu and Hayata peered over the edge of the outcropping. The creature's tail was swinging from side to side, sending boulders and dirt flying in all directions.

'Is that the same burrowing creature we saw earlier?' Hayata said.

'At this point, I'm not sure it really matters,' Muramatsu said, as he took a concussion grenade out of the hold-all slung across his body and passed it to Hayata.

'Maybe it doesn't,' Hayata said. 'I'd just like to know how many more of these things are running around here. Also, how many different kinds. It's like we're in a free-range monster zoo or game preserve or something.' He looked down at the grenade. 'Got any more of these?'

'Only one,' Muramatsu said. 'We left the rest on the VTOL. So we've got to make them count. See if you can get that thing to come a little closer so we can give it the old one-two punch.'

'I'll try but no guarantees it'll work. Either way, we'd better be ready to run.' Hayata stood up. 'Hey, ugly!'

The creature swung its head around at the sound of his voice, then turned and lumbered toward him with a speed that its clumsy-looking body should not have been capable of, loudly bellowing its displeasure. Hayata held up the grenade, looking at Muramatsu questioningly and then nearly fell as the ground began to crumble under his feet. He stepped quickly to his left, waving his arms to try to keep the monster's attention on himself and away from Muramatsu while the latter held his position.

Hayata caught sight of another stone ledge and scrambled under it as the monster advanced on him, tearing up the soil with its long claws, sending more rocks and dirt flying. It had almost reached Hayata's hiding place when Muramatsu saw his second-in-command pop up from behind the ledge and hurl the grenade. The creature turned suddenly, whipped its tail around, and slammed it into Hayata. In the same moment, the grenade exploded.

Muramatsu watched in horror as Hayata cartwheeled down a rocky embankment to land on an expanse of dark granite. Desperation surged in him as he stood up to throw his own grenade at the monster; he caught a quick glimpse of it flying toward the thing's open jaws before he ducked. The second explosion shook the ground and sent yet more rocks and dirt showering down around him. Seconds later, he heard the creature give another shriek.

Muramatsu's heart sank; he must have failed to throw the grenade into the thing's mouth. So much for the idea of blowing it to bits, he thought. Then it bellowed again in a way that was more of a drawn-out groan and he peeked over the stone to see what was going on.

The creature was still in one piece, but not in good shape. It lay on its side scratching weakly at the ground, instinctively wanting to burrow into it. The concussions had done the job after all and pulverized its insides.

Muramatsu turned to look at Hayata still lying motionless on the rock below and saw no blood. Purely by chance, the creature had knocked Hayata away at just the right moment, sparing him the full force of the explosion. Hoping this meant Hayata's lucky streak was still in force, Muramatsu began making his way down to him. But the memory of his senior agent flying off the ledge spread-eagle was far from reassuring.

Arashi, Fuji, and Ide froze at the sound of the first explosion; the second one made them all jump.

'Cap and Hayata must be in trouble,' Ide said. He scanned the sky. 'But why didn't they send up a flare?'

'I guess they handled it?' Fuji said, hopeful in spite of how her heart was pounding.

'Unless the local wildlife have explosives,' Arashi added.

'Stranger things have happened,' Ide said. 'Nobody knows that better than we do.'

Arashi wasn't listening—he was staring past Ide at

something moving around in the bushes several meters ahead of them.

'We've got company,' he said in a low voice, drawing his weapon as he made his way toward it. Fuji and Ide followed, their own weapons in hand. After a bit, they came to the edge of a small pond and stopped. The bushes on the other side were shaking even more vigorously.

It was as if something wanted to make sure it got their attention, Fuji thought, which wasn't the way most things on this island made their presence known. All the creatures they'd seen so far took the direct, in-your-face approach. So maybe this wasn't a monster... unless it was a sneaky one? But then, *sneaky* wasn't really characteristic of monsters anywhere.

Something parted the branches and leaves then and she saw what looked like red fur, a funny-looking snout, and a pair of wide, darting eyes. Beside her, Arashi set his Spider Shot on stun and fired. The creature broke cover, giving them all a quick view of a face that seemed to Fuji like a cross between a wolf and a warthog before it turned and ran.

'I can't believe you missed!' Ide said as they made their way around the pond to where the little red beast had been. 'Where did it go?'

'Dunno but it left a little something behind,' Fuji said, freeing a khaki-colored hat from a thorn bush. On the front was the logo of the Meteorological Society; inside, the name MATSUI was hand-printed in indelible ink.

'I don't think that's an accident,' Arashi said. 'I think that creature put it here for us to find.'

'Seriously?' Ide grimaced in disbelief. 'That could have been here for days.'

'Doesn't look that way to me,' Arashi said. 'And I *didn't* miss. I just wanted to flush it out, not kill it.'

'Didn't look that way to me!' Ide called after him as he and Fuji plunged through the bush behind him.

To Fuji's surprise, the creature wasn't as far ahead of them as she'd expected. Was it letting them catch up? 'Arashi, please be careful!' she said, a little breathless. The humidity was really starting to get to her now. 'It's small but it's a wild animal at the very least—maybe it wanted to flush *us* out. Or what if it's a baby? Do you *really* want to meet its mother?'

Arashi slowed down a little as the creature began chittering and chirping. It led them out of denser forest into a clearing full of tall grass and large stones. 'I guess this is where the island's two personalities come face to face—rainforest versus the volcanic region,' Fuji said, still breathless despite the marked drop in humidity.

'Good thinking,' Ide panted. He was bent over with his hands on his knees. 'Do you see our little red monster friend anywhere?'

'Over there.' Arashi pointed. The creature was bouncing up and down at the base of a rock wall, chittering and chirping louder than ever.

'It must be the Tatara Island track-and-field star.' Ide straightened up, still panting. 'And in this humidity.'

'Hey, around here, you gotta be quick if you want to survive long enough to complain about the weather,' Arashi said. He took a step forward but Fuji caught his arm.

'Look up there!' She pointed at the top of the wall where a cave opening was partly visible amid the flowering plants that had pushed their way through the cracks between the rocks in a riot of red, yellow, and green. It was easy to see how the profusion of brightly colored blossoms would distract a casual observer from the still form of the man lying at the mouth of the cave.

Fuji was the first to reach him. He didn't stir when she touched him and for a moment, she was afraid they were too late. But then she saw his chest rise and fall.

'Help me sit him up,' she said to Ide. 'But slowly, carefully.'

As the two of them got him upright, his eyelids twitched, then fluttered open.

'It's okay, we're with the Science Patrol and we're here to rescue you,' Arashi assured the man as he flinched and drew back. 'You're Takeshi Matsui, aren't you?'

The man gazed up at them, still apprehensive. 'Did you find Kawada?'

The three Science Patrol members exchanged looks.

'How about Fujita?' the man asked. 'Or Sasaki?'

Arashi hesitated. 'I'm afraid not. Sorry.'

The man bowed his head sadly. 'I'm not surprised. I knew it was too much to hope for, but I hoped anyway.' He took a breath. 'I don't know how long it's been since I last saw Kawada. He went out to forage for food and...' He coughed weakly. 'When he didn't come back, I figured that was it, end of the line. No one would ever find me.'

'We might not have if it hadn't been for your funny little

red friend,' Fuji said, turning to look at the creature, still chittering and jumping up and down.

'Ah, yes, I see you've met Pigmon.' He smiled weakly and told them how the little monster had become their mascot. 'He's why I'm still alive—he's been bringing me food and water. He's more intelligent than he looks.'

Fuji was about to respond when they all heard a screeching bellow and the sound of large rocks falling and breaking apart. 'Oh my God, is that the burrowing monster?'

'No, I know that sound,' Matsui said, his voice heavy. 'For a while, I was sure it was going to be the last thing I ever heard.'

'Get him inside the cave,' Arashi said to Ide and Fuji as he drew his weapon and crouched behind a pile of large stones at the far end of the ledge. From there, he had a good view of the ridge above them.

'Tell him to get back from there,' Matsui said to Fuji. 'We don't want that thing to see him—'

Dirt and broken boulders sprayed down on Arashi and then the long-necked monster that had greeted the Science Patrol when they'd first arrived appeared between the two escarpments. It gave a loud, triumphant-sounding squall and kicked some more rocks and dirt in their direction.

Arashi glanced over his shoulder at Fuji, Ide, and Matsui. 'Get farther into the cave!'

'No, don't!' Matsui said. 'We have to stay near the mouth. The caves on this island tend to collapse without warning— all the underground burrowing. Besides, the Red King's already seen you—'

Fuji blinked at him. 'The *what*?'

'Kawada's name for him,' Matsui said. 'Because he seems to be the big boss around here and he spends a lot of time proving it.' He took a shaky breath. 'That creature's also a lot smarter than he looks. They all are, I think.'

'How do you mean?' Fuji asked him.

Matsui gave a single, grim laugh. 'You'll see.'

The monster let out another long, gravelly screech and kicked up a few more rocks. Fuji saw Arashi set his Spider Shot on incendiary and take aim.

Instead of coming at them in open attack, however, the creature bellowed at them again, then did a series of bouncing knee-bends, pumping its arms and screeching in rhythm. Fuji looked at Ide; he seemed as baffled and frightened as she was.

Then they heard the little red monster screeching below them in imitation of the big one, obviously mocking it. Fuji burst into astonished laughter. Matsui had been right; these creatures really were more intelligent than any of them had thought. They did more than just maraud around the island fighting each other for brute dominance, there was a sort of social order—

Her laughter cut off sharply as a boulder twice the size of a basketball hit the little creature, knocking it down. Reflexively she started to get up and run to it but Ide pulled her back.

'*Don't*,' Matsui said, putting his hand on her arm. 'You'll only get yourself killed, and the rest of us with you.'

She could have broken free of his grip without even trying; Ide would have required more effort but she was sure she could take him, too, except she knew Matsui was right. Fuji turned away as another large rock landed on the little monster, followed by a third.

'That's why Kawada called him the Red King,' Matsui said in a low, sad voice. 'He's deliberately cruel.'

The monster continued flinging rocks at the inert red form until it was practically buried under them, roaring in triumph each time.

'Hey, guys, I've got an idea,' Arashi called to them.

'Take care of him,' Ide told Fuji and went to Arashi.

Fuji felt a flash of anger but she made sure that Matsui was sitting securely just inside the cave opening before she joined Arashi and Ide behind the rocks. Ide opened his mouth to protest, saw the look on her face, and thought better of it.

'How many flares do we have?' Arashi was saying to Ide.

'Two. I was going to fire one—'

Arashi nodded. 'Do that. Then give it to me.'

'They must have found someone,' Hayata said, looking up at the flare in the sky.

He and Muramatsu had climbed to within a couple of meters of the top of the embankment when they'd heard the whistling noise and then the sharp report of a flare exploding. Three clouds of smoke, one purple, one yellow, and one green, soared high above them while the flare itself only showed faintly in the bright sunlight.

'You should go to them, Cap,' he added. 'I can make it the rest of the way myself.'

Muramatsu frowned, shaking his head. 'I'm not leaving you.'

'I'm all right,' Hayata replied. 'I'll bet they need your help more than I do.'

'We don't know that—'

'They sent up a flare,' Hayata said, talking over him. 'That probably means they didn't just find someone, something must have found them, too. Please, Cap, go. I can get the rest of the way up on my own. If I couldn't, I would say so.'

Muramatsu hesitated, seemed about to argue, then shook his head again. 'If you can't go any farther after you get to the top, find some place where you can keep out of sight and wait for us to come for you. By the way, you dropped your penlight. Just requisition a new one when we get back.'

Hayata watched as Muramatsu climbed the rest of the way quickly, wondering why the man thought he'd have cared that much about losing a penlight, of all things. He watched until Muramatsu disappeared over the top, then waited for a count of ten, in case the captain changed his mind and came back to retrieve his penlight for him.

Finally, he thought, almost limp with relief as he reached into his jacket. For a while, he'd thought he might have to break cover with his CO. He hadn't wanted to put that burden on Muramatsu but sacrificing his teammates' lives for the sake of keeping a secret was out of the question. And now—

There was nothing in his pocket.

Hayata felt a dropping sensation in the pit of his stomach.

There was no telling when he'd lost the Beta Capsule, much less where. For all he knew, it had fallen out of his pocket in the VTOL, on one of Fuji's hard g-force swerves. Or even worse, back at HQ.

No, it hadn't, he was sure of that if nothing else because he remembered glimpsing it just before Muramatsu had split them into two teams—

You dropped your penlight.

He winced. It couldn't really be that simple… could it? Steadying himself against the side of the embankment, he looked down at the flat stretch of rock where he had come to, carefully scanning every crack and crevice. Maybe it was down there, but the Beta Capsule could just as easily have tumbled out of his jacket on his way down the incline, he thought, right after the burrowing monster bashed him with its tail.

No—if it had, Muramatsu would have picked it up for him. And accidentally turned himself into Ultra Muramatsu? But even as Hayata thought it, he knew it wouldn't activate for anyone who wasn't merged with a Being of Light. That was probably the closest thing to good news he was going to get right now. What he really needed was to get his hands on the Beta Capsule ten minutes ago. Why did this keep happening to him, he wondered as he started the climb down. Maybe he needed a special holster for it. Or he could just put a zipper on the pocket.

But he couldn't think about holsters or zippers right now; his teammates were in trouble that was no doubt getting worse with every passing second, and the seconds were passing, passing, passing, racing ahead of him while he made his way down this embankment. When he finally did get to the bottom, he had to force himself to search methodically rather than running around on the rock in a blind panic.

After what seemed like hours but couldn't have been more than a minute, he finally caught a glimpse of a familiar pale green cylinder and rushed to pick it up... only to find it had fallen into a small recess between one slab of granite and another slightly smaller rock. The hole was too narrow for any part of his arm past his elbow, and approximately five centimeters deeper than he could reach.

Hayata took off his jacket, rolled up his sleeve, and tried again. The only difference was in how much deeper the rocks gouged his arm. But he could stand it, he told himself, a little scraped flesh was nothing, it would heal. Getting chomped by a monster was a whole lot worse; no healing from that. Gritting his teeth, he strained, trying to make his arm longer by sheer force of will. His fingertips brushed something smooth, not rock, and he thought it was his imagination.

In the next moment, he was pulling his arm out of the hole with the Beta Capsule in his fist. His skin was torn as well as scraped, bleeding freely and already stinging like mad. But it didn't restrict his range of movement; he had no trouble raising his arm high in the air.

'Now Cap and Hayata know where we are,' Ide said, handing Arashi the flare gun. 'What's the rest of your big idea?'

Arashi aimed both the flare gun and his Spider Shot at

the Red King's head. 'Okay, you two—set your Spiders on lightning strike. The target is that ugly-assed face and we all fire on three. You think you can hit that?'

Ide frowned. 'Wouldn't incendiary be better?'

'Lightning strike delivers a harder impact with more concentrated energy,' Arashi said. 'Get ready and like I told you, fire on three.'

'Copy that,' Fuji said, trying to sound more confident than she felt. That long neck wasn't much like a giraffe's at all; the monster's head wobbled around a lot. She had no doubt that Arashi would hit it but while both she and Ide regularly scored well above the minimum needed for weapons qualification, Arashi's skill was in a class by itself. He simply did not miss.

So this time, you *don't miss, either,* she told herself, steadying her arms on the rock in front of her.

'Ready?' Arashi said. 'One… two… *three!*'

The monster screamed in pain and outrage as its head and most of its neck were engulfed by a fireball.

Fall down, dammit! Fuji thought at it. *Fall down and die!*

But it didn't fall, it just went on screaming and beating at its head with its forelimbs. When the smoke cleared, its head was still on its neck—a bit scorched but intact. And mad as hell.

'Oh, man—I thought that would put it down for sure,' Arashi said, momentarily forgetting he was a tough guy.

'Me, too,' Ide said sympathetically.

Arashi glanced at him. 'No, you didn't.'

'Well, okay, I wasn't as certain as you were,' Ide admitted. 'But I thought that would hurt it more than it did.'

'When Cap and Hayata get here, we'll have more firepower,' Fuji said. 'We can take another shot.'

The Red King repeated its little ritual again—three knee-bends, punctuated by arm motions and bellows.

'What do you think it's trying to tell us with that?' Ide asked.

'"I'm gonna kill you real bad." Unquote,' Arashi replied sourly. 'It's a rough translation but it'll do.'

'Maybe it's something else,' Ide said. 'Maybe it's telling us its name in monster language. Or it's a mating call.'

'*That* would be a whole lot worse,' Arashi said as the monster picked up another large broken rock and hurled it down on the pile the little creature was buried under.

'Why does it keep doing that?' Ide said. 'It's not like the poor little guy can get any deader.'

'Maybe by helping humans, the little one broke a major monster taboo,' Arashi said.

'"Major Monster Taboo" sounds like a punk band. Just saying…' Ide added in response to the looks Arashi and Fuji gave him.

Abruptly, the Red King turned away from them, picked up a broken chunk of rock and hurled it toward the stonier area of the clearing, causing a minor fall of smaller rocks that seemed to threaten to become something more before petering out. The rock bounced through the clearing and fetched up against a cluster of thorn bushes. They rattled and Fuji caught a glimpse of a familiar insignia on a white helmet.

'It's Cap!' she said excitedly to Ide and Arashi, pointing.

'I can't see—is Hayata with him?' Arashi wanted to know.

'I don't see him,' she replied. 'Maybe they had to split up.' She got to her feet and waved at Muramatsu with both arms.

'Okay, that's enough,' Ide said, pulling her back down behind the rocks.

'I wanted to make sure he saw me,' she said, trying to peer around him.

'Everything with eyes saw you,' Arashi said darkly, tilting his head at the monster.

It went into its weird knee-bending routine again, then snatched up another boulder as it watched Muramatsu running toward the rock wall. Raising the rock over its head and bellowing in fury it prepared to send it flying toward the man. Fuji started to scream a warning at Muramatsu and then heard the monster's roar go up half an octave before it cut off with a grunt as a giant red and silver figure landed on it with both feet.

'How did he *know*? How did he know we needed help?' Ide yelled in delight. He gave Arashi a jubilant shake, then grabbed Fuji up in a bear hug, lifting her off her feet and swinging her around so the tips of her boots scraped the rock they'd been hiding behind. She almost gave in to tears of joy but Ide would never have let her live it down. 'How did he know we needed him?'

'Because he's Ultraman,' she gasped when Ide let her go.

'He certainly is,' Arashi agreed gruffly.

Stuck the landing, Hayata thought, almost enjoying the way it felt to drive both feet into the long-necked monster's back before it could heave another large chunk of stone in Muramatsu's direction.

The creature stumbled forward into a jagged crag with a loud, almost comical grunt. It struggled to turn around to see what would have the gall to do such a thing, lost its footing, and fell heavily onto its back.

For a long moment, it just stared and Hayata saw disbelief in its brutish eyes; apparently it had never encountered a creature its own size that wasn't also a reptilian horror. The creature managed to get back up on its hind legs, screech-bellowed at him, and then beat its chest.

You're not from around here, are you? Hayata thought at it, wondering if it could have fallen from the same family tree as Bemular. They were pretty much the same size but this creature had stronger forelimbs and thicker hindquarters that reminded him of a kangaroo, although it didn't jump. And that long neck made its head look too small for its body. Same lovely disposition, though, he thought as the beast rushed him.

He stepped aside, giving the creature a hard shove as it went past and sent it headfirst into a pile of boulders. This was almost too easy.

Don't think like that. Never think like that. It could kill you.

The admonition popped into his head like a stray thought but with more weight, as if it were something important that he'd forgotten. Another message from his new best friend; he felt a wave of impatience pass over him. Dammit, why couldn't the Ultra have told him more before they'd merged?

He'd have to gripe later; right now, the monster was getting up again.

Remembering the gory sight that had greeted them on their arrival, Fuji tried to brace herself as she watched the long-necked Red King push itself to its feet. It let loose with another of its ferocious roars. For answer, Ultraman straightened up to his full forty meters of height and beat his chest.

How did Ultraman know about *that*, Fuji wondered, when he'd been nowhere in sight when they'd arrived?

Because he's Ultraman. Her own words came back to her as the Red King picked up another boulder. That was the monster's big go-to move, throwing boulders—simple but highly effective, especially against puny, regular-sized humans or really, anything else smaller than itself.

It was raising the boulder over its head when Ultraman slid into a crouch, positioning his left arm horizontally and his other hand upright. Brilliant white energy streamed from his right hand, struck the boulder, and blew it into powder. The Red King bellowed in outrage and started to reach for the giant red and silver figure that had barged in and spoiled its fun. But the latter moved first, grabbing its scaly neck just under its jaw with both hands. The monster let out a choked squall as Ultraman lifted it off the ground, spun around twice, and let go.

The Red King hit a pile of rocks on its back and slid down onto its side. Growling loudly, the monster made to get up but appeared to be having trouble.

'I bet it's never been evenly matched before,' Fuji said.

'I don't think it is now,' Arashi said, 'and it couldn't happen to a more deserving kaiju.'

When Hayata saw the monster struggling to get up, he didn't hesitate. Lunging at the thing, he grabbed its neck with both hands again, went down on one knee, and yanked the creature over his shoulder.

As he did, he felt something at the junction of its head and neck give with a wet *pop!*, inaudible but very loud under his hands and all the more revolting for it. Knowing he was about to triumph was eclipsed by a new understanding, of how easily he could become monstrous.

Lying at his feet, the creature shuddered and gave a raw-throated groan as it tried to raise its forelimbs, then looked toward the clearing before it stilled. Wondering what it had been looking at, Hayata followed its gaze and saw boulders and broken chunks of rock in a haphazard pile on top of a red furry something not quite the size of a full-grown human.

He became aware of his teammates then, shouting and cheering for him, and below them, Ide saying that Hayata had missed all the excitement *again*.

Yeah, that's the untold heartbreak shared by secret identities the world over, from Clark Kent to Shin Hayata, he told Ide silently as he launched himself into the sky. *Somehow we only show up after the party's over.*

* * *

As weakened as Matsui was by his ordeal, he refused to board the VTOL without giving the rest of the observation team a symbolic burial along with a formal one for the little red mascot. None of the Science Patrol was inclined to argue.

'I suspect we'll never recover anything of my colleagues' remains,' he said as they stood around the grave-markers on a pleasant grassy hill not far from the VTOL. 'Still, we chose to come here.'

'Yes, but you didn't know the place would be overrun with monsters,' Fuji said gently.

'Doesn't matter,' Matsui said. 'We came here of our own accord, fully aware that it was unknown territory with equally unknown dangers. Pigmon didn't bring us here and he didn't have to help us. He'd probably still be alive if he hadn't.'

'We don't know that,' Fuji said.

'*I* do,' Matsui said. 'And because of him, I think I'm also leaving here a better man than I was when I arrived.' Pause. 'Maybe even a step or two closer to enlightenment.'

'Me, too,' Ide blurted.

The rest of the Science Patrol turned to look at him in surprise.

'What?' he said, looking a little wounded. 'Don't all of you?'

'I believe I would like to lie down now,' Matsui said politely, saving everyone from having to answer. Arashi and Ide helped him to the VTOL and the others followed.

Hayata and Muramatsu hung back a little, letting everyone else board ahead of them.

'Something on your mind?' Muramatsu asked as Hayata took one last look back.

'Where did all those creatures come from, Cap?' Hayata said. 'How did they get here? There's nothing like them anywhere else on Earth and I'm not sure there ever has been.'

'Well, that's something else we don't know for certain,' Muramatsu said.

'The question of the hour?' Hayata asked him with a faint smile.

'The question of *this* hour, perhaps,' Muramatsu said. 'But with twenty-four hours in a day, there will always be more questions than we can answer.'

He gestured for Hayata to board ahead of him and took one last look back before he followed, unaware of Hayata also taking one last look back at him.

CHAPTER
FOUR

'Is it me,' said Ide over breakfast with Fuji and Hayata in the break room, 'or, lately, are we more like the Monster Patrol than the Science Patrol?'

Fuji laughed a little. 'What's the matter—did Tatara Island give you nightmares about kaiju?'

'Don't be ridiculous,' Ide said. 'We were only there a few hours, not marooned for as long as the meteorology team.'

'And it was a month ago,' Hayata pointed out, giving Fuji a surreptitious wink.

'Three and a half weeks, actually.' Ide finished his first rice ball and began unwrapping a second. 'I don't remember having any nightmares, although Arashi did complain a few times that I was still counting sheep in my sleep.'

'If anything, I'd say kaiju make you hungry.' Hayata chuckled.

'You may be right,' Ide said. 'I feel like I need to be extra fortified for the day, just in case. Although what I really need is a vacation. Maybe to an island, like Arashi.'

'That's no vacation,' Fuji said. 'He's not lying on a beach drinking cocktails, he's with a bunch of academics from Hanshin University who are looking for fossils and rare plants to exhibit at the International Expo.'

'Johnson Island is uninhabited,' Hayata added. 'So if Arashi did want cocktails, he'd have had to bring his own. But I doubt he had room in his luggage for even a small bottle of sake. Dr. Nakaya told him to pack light.'

Fuji frowned. 'Are they expecting to find *that* many fossils?'

Hayata shrugged. 'I guess they figure it being uninhabited means a lot of it is untouched, so fossil hunters haven't dug up all the good stuff yet.'

'I still wish I could have gone.' Ide looked wistful. 'Even if it's not a vacation, it's a change of scene and sometimes that's just as good.'

'I know what you mean,' Hayata said with a sympathetic smile. 'But if I were going for a change of scene, I wouldn't choose another island. Not so soon after Tatara, anyway.'

'Me, either,' said Fuji. 'Where would *you* go, Hayata?'

Hayata's face took on a faraway expression as he rocked back in his chair. 'I'd head for the center of the galaxy and look at all the different stars. Maybe check out a nebula, see what that's like.'

'Seriously?' Fuji asked, blinking at him. Ide looked equally incredulous.

'Of course not.' Hayata laughed. 'I'd have to bring my

own *air* as well as my own cocktails. I'd just like to go to somewhere I've never been to before, some place completely new to me, like North or South America. Or the Science Patrol headquarters in Paris. I've never been there, either.'

'*Definitely* Paris for me,' Fuji said.

'For the shopping?' Ide said with a mischievous twinkle in his eye. 'Shopping's a big thing with you girls, isn't it?'

Fuji shook her head. 'The first thing I'd do is go to the top of the Eiffel Tower.'

'You're such a *tourist*,' Ide said.

Fuji wasn't offended. 'There's nothing wrong with being a tourist. But for your information, the Eiffel Tower happens to be three hundred and thirty meters tall.'

'So you're not afraid of heights,' Ide said.

'So if a kaiju attacked Paris while I was there, I'd be well out of reach.'

Ide and Hayata laughed as she finished her tea and got up to take her tray to the kitchen.

Ide's question about their being the Monster Patrol came back to Hayata as he read an email from the Science Patrol's Youth Outreach program forwarded to the team by Public Relations. The team all took turns reading and responding to the messages and today it was his. Most of the emails were from kids who wanted to join the Science Patrol when they grew up; Fuji actually had a fan club who admired her for how she excelled in a STEM career without ever having a bad hair day.

Today, there was only one message, from one of their regulars. A boy named Osamu had been sending them drawings of monsters ever since their encounter with Bemular at Lake Ryugamori. The kid was nine or ten and very bright, though Hayata had the impression that he was also young for his age. Which wasn't such a bad thing, in his opinion, considering how so many kids seemed to grow up too fast.

Today's monster was quite a creation, a beast with an oddly shaped head that ended in two sharp horns on either side, and a third horn on its snout, like a rhinoceros. It stood upright on muscular hind legs and its forelimbs were more humanoid than reptilian, ending in five-fingered hands with opposable thumbs and, of course, very large, sharp-looking claws. There was also a tail that seemed to be almost as long as its body.

As always, Osamu had included a note:

> Greetings to Captain Muramatsu, Agent Hayata, Agent Arashi, Agent Fuji, and Agent Ide from your monster expert in Osaka! Nothing much is happening here right now, except I'm getting ready to go to the International Expo, opening soon—but not soon enough for me! I wish it were today!
>
> My teacher told our class that a bunch of important Hanshin University professors went on an expedition to Johnson Island to find a monster to display at the Expo! Well, they said they're looking for fossils and strange plants we don't have here but I don't think they'd really go all that way just to get a few rocks and plants! After all, they

asked Agent Arashi to go with them and I bet it's because they want someone who can fight any monsters they might run into, right?

Hayata smiled; Arashi's reputation as a tough guy had gone viral.

Anyway, I saw the pictures online that Dr. Nakaya asked artists to draw imagining what some of the prehistoric monsters looked like but I wanted to draw the Gomorasaurus in its native habitat. The teacher gave me three gold stars for it! My mom says it would be better if I got three gold stars on my math schoolwork but anybody can do math! Drawing monsters is a lot harder! I hope you like it!

'This must be the latest monster du jour from our little friend in Osaka,' Fuji said, looking over Hayata's shoulder at the computer screen. 'Quite the artist, isn't he?'

'I think he's very imaginative,' Ide said from his own desk, where he was reviewing the overnight incident logs. 'I wouldn't be surprised if he grows up to be an inventor. Like— well, someone you know.'

'Or a mad scientist?' teased Fuji. 'Also like someone we know?'

'Maybe the university researchers should have taken him along as well as Arashi.' Hayata chuckled, gazing at the drawing on the screen. He could envision Ultraman facing off against those horns.

Or was that a premonition? Hayata had never put much stock in premonitions any more than he had in hunches. On the other hand, since Ultraman's arrival, he knew there were much stranger things at large in the world.

Arashi paged through the book Professor Nakaya had given him. It was the end of the fourth day on Johnson Island and he had started to think that his being there was at best a waste of his time.

Professor Nakaya had asked for him because of his proficiency with weapons and his ability to hit virtually anything he aimed at. As yet, however, they hadn't come across anything that had called for even a warning shot. Johnson Island was pretty enough but even if the Science Patrol hadn't been to Tatara Island only a few weeks earlier, it wasn't a place Arashi would have chosen to go. His preferred destinations had electricity, indoor plumbing, Wi-Fi, and a variety of things to do, including a vibrant nightlife.

This place was paradise for botanists, florists, entomologists, and bird-watchers, but, sadly, a big disappointment for fossil hunters. Professor Nakaya had found only a few since they'd arrived; to Arashi, they looked like nothing more than lumpy bits of rock.

Regardless, he had appreciated the professor requesting him specifically and he couldn't deny he had enjoyed seeing himself identified in the group photos on the news websites as *Daisuke Arashi, Science Patrol sharpshooter*. Not that he'd ever really wanted to be famous; it simply felt good to be recognized for his skill. (Fuji referred to that as *being validated*, which sounded like something out of a self-help manual, maybe one titled *7 Days to Better Self-Esteem*, which he'd seen on Ide's desk. Ide had claimed he had no idea where it came from. Arashi had been sure Fuji had given it to him until she'd confided that Ide's mother had sent it, then made him swear he'd never let Ide know he knew.)

After four relatively uneventful days of wandering around covered with mosquito repellent in the great and very humid outdoors, Arashi had started to wonder if Professor Nakaya had asked for him simply because the Science Patrol cachet made the expedition seem like a more significant undertaking, and thus more newsworthy, which would benefit the university. At the same time, however, he knew Captain Muramatsu wouldn't have agreed to loan him out just so a university could look good.

'You've been staring at that picture for a while now.'

Arashi looked up to see Professor Nakaya standing over him with two cups of tea. The professor handed one to him, then took a seat on the other side of the table.

'Is that because it reminds you of something you and your colleagues encountered?' the professor asked.

'No,' Arashi said, feeling slightly embarrassed. 'But it *is* quite a monster.'

The professor nodded. 'It's called a Gomorasaurus. And it's not mythological. There's fossil evidence for its existence, about one hundred and fifty million years ago.' He was about to go on when they heard a new sound, a bestial noise somewhere between a shriek and a roar. It came from some

145

distance away but it was close enough to raise every tiny hair on the back of Arashi's neck.

'What was *that*?' Nakaya asked, his complexion turning a bit ashen.

'Something big,' Arashi said. 'We'd better tell everyone to stay in camp tonight.'

Nakaya gave a small, nervous laugh. 'After hearing that? I don't think we'll need to.'

Arashi finished his tea in one long gulp and got up, hand on his sidearm. 'I'm going to check on everyone anyway, do a head count and make sure everyone's present and accounted for. Just in case someone's too curious for their own good.'

Nakaya caught his arm as he started to leave the tent. 'Thank you.'

The sincerity in the professor's voice made Arashi glad he was there, and not just because he felt validated.

As Professor Nakaya had predicted, no one had been inclined to leave the safety of the camp that night. Arashi had expected most if not all of them to greet the morning bleary-eyed from lack of sleep and feeling a lot less intrepid than they had on arrival.

In the light of day, however, they had all recovered their academic aplomb and were eager to continue the search for the exotic, the rare, and, in Nakaya's words, 'the hitherto undiscovered.' It was the first time Arashi had ever heard someone actually use the word hitherto and under other circumstances, he might not have been able to keep from laughing out loud. But in this context, it seemed completely appropriate.

'Professor, you do realize that even though you don't hear it now, whatever made that noise last night is still on the island,' Arashi said as Nakaya organized the various-sized containers in his sample case.

'Of course I do.' Nakaya's eyes were a bit bloodshot but he was quite cheerful, even energetic. He slipped on a photographer's vest with many pockets, tucking a roll of small plastic bags into one of them. 'But I'm pretty sure whatever animal made that noise is nocturnal.'

'Maybe,' Arashi said. 'But—'

'Nocturnal animals don't hunt during the day,' the professor went on. 'And it wasn't really that close, so I believe we can explore the area without worrying about encroaching on its territory.'

'Do you have any idea what kind of animal it is?' Arashi asked him.

Frowning, Nakaya tucked a magnifying glass into his left breast pocket. 'No. And neither do you.'

'Which means we don't know the extent of its territory or, for that matter, if it really is nocturnal,' Arashi pointed out.

'And as I recall, when I asked you what it was, you said, "Something big." Do you know how big?'

'Bigger than we are,' Arashi said and was gratified to see it gave Nakaya pause. 'Professor, you're making my point for me.'

But apparently Nakaya was feeling too indomitable or at least too well-rested to be discouraged. 'We don't increase our knowledge and widen the scope of human endeavor by cowering in our tents because we're afraid of some creature we've only heard once, at night.'

Arashi took a breath and let it out, telling himself to be patient. 'I'm not going to be able to convince you to be more careful, am I?'

Now Nakaya's expression was apologetic. 'I'm really not trying to make your life more difficult, and I didn't ask Captain Muramatsu to loan you to us so we could ignore your guidance. But you're not here just as our bodyguard—if that was all I wanted, I'd have asked for some Defense Force soldiers. The Science Patrol understands what we're doing out here, that we've come to advance our scientific knowledge, not just wander through the jungle and shoot anything that looks or sounds scary. We consider you one of us. You're a scientist who just happens to be armed.'

'That's very flattering,' Arashi began. 'But—'

'Brain power—the geeks will inherit the Earth, right?!' Nakaya put on a fingerless glove and raised his fist in a salute.

Arashi laughed politely as the professor unzipped the tent flap and stepped outside, greeting the other academics waiting for him with the same salute; they responded with cheers. Hayata should have come with them, Arashi thought, checking the level of charge on his Spider Shot; Hayata was better at getting people to listen when he talked. He'd have had his work cut out for him with this bunch but Arashi was pretty sure Hayata would have gotten through to Nakaya before he had left the tent. Maybe even before they'd left Japan.

* * *

Thirty minutes into the first excursion of the morning, someone began yelling frantically for help. Arashi did a quick head count and discovered they were shy one academic, a botanist named Hiro Shimizu.

'Everyone, follow me—nobody go on alone!' Arashi ordered them as he went back the way they had come, weapon in hand.

He didn't have to go far—after backtracking about fifty meters and hacking through some brush, he came to a small clearing where Professor Shimizu was struggling with a thick vine that had wrapped itself tightly around him. Dammit, Arashi thought, was every island in the Pacific infested with carnivorous vines?

'Ow! It hurts *a lot*, get it *off* me!' the professor shouted, struggling in the thick green snakelike coils. He was an older, slightly built man who spent most of his time in the university greenhouse, where all the flora were far more well-behaved.

Arashi returned his machete to its sheath and unclipped the Spider Shot from his belt. Setting it on concentrated narrow beam incendiary, he aimed it roughly half a meter higher than the professor's head and fired. The vine broke apart, withdrawing as quickly as a snake into the treetops as the professor dropped to the ground.

'Ow! My ribs! That *really* hurts!' Shimizu yelled, still wrapped up in thick green coils. Arashi tore them away from him, noting that unlike the ones on Tatara, these flowers looked more innocuous, more like oversized pansies in bright red and yellow rather than the snakeskin-patterned orchids. Nakaya materialized at Arashi's side, intercepting Shimizu before he could throw himself on Arashi in a grateful hug.

'Will you please yell at this guy for going off on his own?' Arashi said, exasperated. 'I'd do it except I'm armed.' He glared, trying to look dangerous.

'No problem. I've got this,' Nakaya said over his shoulder, walking the botanist back to the rest of the group.

'I hope so,' Arashi muttered under his breath, returning his weapon to his belt. He looked around; not a hanging vine in sight. Somebody really needed to study these things, he thought. They were far too active for plant life.

Arashi clapped his hands loudly to get everyone's attention. 'Folks, let's take a break right here so I can explain *again* why you all need to stay together and not go off to pick flowers alone. I don't think these vines'll bother us any more right now but just to be on the safe side, let's gather here in the center of the clearing, away from the trees. And don't go picking *any* flowers without talking to me first.'

'I just got a text message from Arashi,' Fuji said, swiveling around in her chair at the communications console.

Ide looked up from his computer. 'Yeah? What's he say?'

'He says, and I quote: "Why is it that highly intelligent people aren't always very bright?"' She laughed a little. 'I guess he's having a harder time wrangling all those academics than he thought he would.'

'He can handle it,' Ide said. 'He's a tough guy.'

'And it's good practice for when he becomes a father,' Muramatsu added with a knowing look. 'Ide, run down to the hangar and get our largest cargo carrier ready for flight.'

Ide's eyebrows went up. 'Are we going to Johnson Island?'

'I don't know yet,' Muramatsu replied. 'But it won't hurt to be ready, just in case.'

An hour later, the jungle gave way to a field of long yellowing grass spread out below a high cliff. The same kind of grass hung over the top of the cliff like a fringe above a rough face of stone. It looked to Arashi as if a large chunk of land had broken off; something told him it was a relatively recent occurrence.

As if on cue, one of the academics said, 'I'd like to get some rock samples from that cliff, then break for lunch. Who's with me?'

'*No*,' Arashi said, raising his voice to be heard over the group's responses and they all turned to him in surprise. 'That cliff doesn't look stable to me. We'll do better if we follow a route that takes us along the edge of the jungle, *away* from the cliff. There are plenty of other things to take samples from.'

For a moment the academics stared at him with identical serious expressions. Then, to Arashi's astonishment, they turned back to each other and began *discussing* it.

Arashi closed his eyes, thinking he should have called in sick the day he'd gotten the assignment. In the next moment, he heard the ominous sound of rocks falling and opened his eyes to see the cliff-face was starting to crumble.

'Get back!' he shouted, herding the group back toward the jungle, or trying to. They weren't exactly resisting as they shouted and pointed but they didn't seem to understand it was unwise to be anywhere near falling rocks. He was about to order them all to march back to base camp at double-time when Nakaya grabbed his shoulders and forced him to turn around.

At first, Arashi could only see two enormous eyes glaring out from a hole in the cliff and he thought the stone itself was alive. Then a sharp horn knocked away more of the rock and he saw the strange angular head.

The creature was very close to the picture in Nakaya's book, although there were some differences. The horns were actually part of a hard shell that encased its head like a natural protective helmet. The third horn on the end of its snout curved a bit more sharply than in the illustration; below its chin was a fourth that curved down, like a giant beak. Arashi watched as the creature knocked away the rest of the rock in front of it, tearing at it with the claws on its muscular forelimbs as well as those on its mole-like feet. When it finally emerged, it gave the same bellowing roar they'd heard the previous night, as if it were announcing itself.

The group froze, clutching each other. 'It's him!' Nakaya breathed, sounding positively awestruck. 'It's him! It's Gomora!'

'And now we're all gonna *die*! It's gonna *eat* us!' someone else sobbed.

But instead of scooping up a pawful of academics and stuffing them into its jaws, the monster ignored them completely. It trundled over to a patch of grass dotted with rocks, lay down, and began twisting and wiggling, making Arashi think of a bear scratching its back.

'He's almost exactly how I pictured him,' Nakaya said, waxing even more rhapsodic.

'Uh-huh.' Arashi looked at Nakaya sidelong. 'And just so you know, it's definitely not nocturnal.'

'I don't care.' Nakaya sighed in ecstasy. 'Nocturnal or diurnal, I want it alive.'

'You *what*?' Arashi was incredulous.

'You heard me. I want to take it back to Japan alive. For the Expo,' he added. 'No one's ever captured a *living* prehistoric animal. We'll make history!'

'We'll *be* history!' Arashi said.

The professor paid no attention. 'I wonder what it was doing in the cliff.'

'It burrowed into it,' Arashi snapped. 'It's a burrower, you can tell by the claws.'

'Then we've got to capture it before it burrows away to some other part of the island.' Nakaya produced a dart gun from one of his vest pockets. 'I've got some cartridges with a strong sedative—' He patted his pockets, came up with a large vial of blue liquid, loaded it into the dart gun, and held it out to Arashi. 'The university gave me this in case I met a wild boar or something and you couldn't help me right away. If you'll do the honors? Since you're the sharpshooter.'

'That's no boar!' Arashi snatched the dart gun from him. 'This little expedition of yours isn't equipped to transport anything so large. We're not taking anything anywhere till I talk to my CO.'

'Fine with me—you're the Science Patrol!' Nakaya said expansively. 'You'll think of something. You always do.'

'You're kidding,' Hayata said.

'I wish I were.' Muramatsu sighed. He had called Hayata, Fuji, and Ide into his office after Arashi had contacted him on the sat-phone to tell him about Professor Nakaya's plans. 'But while Arashi was updating me on Nakaya's grand scheme, Nakaya was talking to his people at the university.'

'And they called you?' Fuji asked, looking sympathetic.

'Oh, yeah, but not just them,' Muramatsu said. 'A lot of their VIP friends and allies called me, too, including a number of people on the International Expo board. Nakaya sent them photos and a video.'

'Which are now all over the web?' Ide guessed.

Muramatsu nodded. 'The video was taken by one of the biologists. She's been blogging about their experiences.'

'Talk about a spoiler,' Ide said with a short laugh. 'Now there's no big reveal for the Expo.'

'They felt it was better to publicize what they'd found, to build up people's anticipation,' said Muramatsu. 'And it's a good way to put more pressure on us to transport it here. Central Command says we have to either make it happen or prove beyond a shadow of a doubt that it can't be done.'

Hayata shook his head. 'Have they considered the risks?'

'That's our job,' Muramatsu said. 'We're the Science Patrol—we'll think of something, we always do.'

'Right,' Hayata said with a wry smile. 'I think I heard that somewhere.'

Muramatsu chuckled. 'I've been talking to people in the Hanshin University School of Engineering about how to transport a live wild animal forty meters tall and weighing twenty thousand pounds from Johnson Island to Japan.'

'Did they have any ideas?' Fuji asked.

'Several.' Muramatsu smiled with half his mouth. 'Including one or two that could work. But we don't have anything that can carry that kind of weight, so we'll have to borrow a heavy-lift helicopter from the Defense Force. Along with a pilot and crew.'

'Good,' Fuji said with an exaggerated sigh of relief. 'I'd rather not take that on.'

'Why not?' Ide said, looking surprised. 'You're a good enough helicopter pilot.'

'Because carrying something that big is more like air show stunt flying,' Fuji said. 'I don't have enough experience. When I'm on the stick, I want to be absolutely sure of what I'm doing. I won't just cross my fingers and hope for the best—I can't.'

Hayata chuckled a little. 'Old pilots and bold pilots.'

'Exactly,' said Fuji, smiling at him. 'I'm opting for old.' She turned to Muramatsu. 'Cap, this will be incredibly dangerous.'

'I know,' Muramatsu said, 'but a lot of VIPs think it's worth it. The helicopter is already on the way to Johnson Island. Transport is scheduled for first thing tomorrow morning so we'll have to get there before dawn. Unless you want to stay there tonight?'

Nobody did.

'Are you sure the net's big enough?' Arashi asked for what could have been the thousandth time.

'I'm sure,' Hayata said patiently as they watched two men from the Defense Force laying it out over the grass. The broken cliff gaped down on them in the early morning light. 'The hard part will be maneuvering this Gomosaurus—'

'Gomorasaurus,' Professor Nakaya corrected him, smiling good-naturedly.

'Right.' Hayata nodded, trying not to show impatience. 'The hard part will be maneuvering the creature so that when we hit it with the tranqs, it falls in the center of the net. Or close to it.'

'It's absolutely vital that you get this right,' Nakaya said, still smiling but looking a bit apprehensive now as well. 'The university is counting on us to deliver and so is the Expo.'

Hayata stole a glance at Arashi; he had shifted position so that he was standing behind the professor and glaring angrily at his back. After a few seconds, Hayata managed to catch his eye; Arashi realized and assumed a neutral expression as he ambled away from the conversation, arms folded and his gaze on the ground.

Sticking his hands in his pockets, Hayata followed him until Arashi came to a stop out of earshot of Nakaya, who was talking even more earnestly to Muramatsu.

'If you're not sure about this operation,' Hayata said in a low, quiet voice, 'you're not alone.'

'It just isn't right,' Arashi said.

'Well, it's certainly dangerous,' Hayata said. 'But Nakaya's got the university all fired up and the Expo people are champing at the bit, so we have to try.'

'We should've refused. This is—' Arashi floundered for a moment, then shook his head. 'It's just *not right*.'

'How do you mean?' Hayata asked.

Arashi shook his head. 'Doesn't matter, we're doing it. So we'd better not do it wrong for everyone's sake. Including the Gomorasaurus's.' He paused to look back at Nakaya and Muramatsu; the professor was in high gear now and Muramatsu was starting to look besieged. 'When this is all over, I'm going to tell Cap that I'm not ever doing anything like this again. If that means I have to resign, then so be it.'

'Hey, let's not get ahead of ourselves.' Hayata covered his consternation with a small laugh. 'You can't refuse to do something again if you haven't done it yet.' He put a hand on Arashi's shoulder. 'Like Cap says, one crisis at a time, okay?'

'What's up?' Ide was suddenly beside them, looking from Hayata to Arashi and back again with unabashed curiosity.

'We're just trying to figure out how to maneuver Nakaya's Gomorasaurus so that it's at the center of the net when we put it to sleep,' Hayata told him. 'Since it's not like we can just roll it over.'

'I'm pretty sure I know how to do that,' Ide said as he fished his phone out of his jacket pocket. He pressed a button and they heard the creature's bellow. 'This is from the video one of the academics made. But keep listening.' A few seconds later, they heard the Red King's raw-throated roar followed by Pigmon's chittering, and then several high-pitched screeches.

'I got the next two sound files from Matsui,' Ide told them. 'And that last one, believe it or not, is a peacock. I'm going to set the whole recording on repeat and leave it in the center of the net. When it hears its own call, it'll probably think it's got a friend or a long-lost twin or something, and when it hears the others, it'll want to find out who's trespassing on its turf.' He looked at each of them. 'What do you think? Pretty good, right?'

'Clever,' Arashi said, looking a little less grumpy. 'Although you'll probably have to get a new phone after the Gomorasaurus falls asleep on yours. And there's a chance it might already have a friend or a long-lost twin and they'll both come running. Or we'll attract some other gigantic Whatever-o-saurus with fangs twice as big and an even worse temper. Then what do we do?'

'Send out for another heavy-lifter,' Ide said. 'Or two.' He glanced at Muramatsu, who was still stoically withstanding Nakaya's increasingly intense info dump. 'All I have to do now is get a word in edgewise. Wish me luck.'

Hayata and Arashi gazed after him as he approached Muramatsu. 'It really is a good idea,' Hayata said. 'Although there's also a chance that hearing the Red King will scare it off.'

Now Arashi smiled faintly. 'We can only hope.'

* * *

The recordings drew the Gomorasaurus (and, fortunately, nothing else) back to the area by the cliff within thirty minutes, which pleased everyone except Arashi. He looked angry again as he took aim from behind a thorn bush and for a moment, Hayata wasn't sure he'd go through with it. But he sent the first dart directly into the flesh just under the creature's left eye.

It looked startled for a moment, then puzzled. Arashi put the next dart a few centimeters below the first and the creature staggered, going down on one knee and braying in protest. The third dart went directly into its mouth, lodging in the flesh of its cheek. It brayed again as its eyes closed and it went face down in the center of the net.

'Wonderful!' Professor Nakaya pounced on Arashi, patting him on the back. 'I estimate it'll be out for six hours. That should give us plenty of time to get it to the Expo holding area. I've got to call the Expo board and let them know we're on the way…' He went on talking to no one in particular as he headed for the camp.

'He'd better hope six hours is long enough,' Arashi said gruffly to Hayata and Muramatsu. 'Because there aren't any more tranqs.'

'I wish I'd known that,' Muramatsu said uneasily. 'We would have brought more with us.' He tapped his communicator. 'Cue the chopper.'

The heavy-lift helicopter was a chunky military airship, round-nosed and slab-sided, made to carry cargo that was outsized, massive, or just generally hard to handle, into or out of remote areas and/or difficult terrain. The cargo in question was almost never alive, although the Defense Force pilot told them that she and her two crew members had once transported a sleeping rhinoceros. Hayata wondered what they thought when they saw the snoring monster on the ground.

The two soldiers who rappelled down from the helicopter as it hovered overhead hadn't looked particularly apprehensive, although they made a point of double- and triple-checking all the connections, especially the net seals, before they attached it to the cargo hook and signaled the pilot to bring them back up again.

'Based on weather conditions and the creature's weight, they're figuring on a five-hour flight time,' Muramatsu said as the helicopter slowly lifted its burden off the ground. The monster in the net never stirred.

'So far, so good, I guess,' Hayata said. 'We might actually get away with this.'

Muramatsu gave a single short laugh. 'Whether we do or not, I can promise you this is a one-off, once-in-a-lifetime, never-to-be-repeated feat of daring.'

'Copy *that*,' Hayata said, with feeling.

'And keep an eye on Arashi for me,' Muramatsu added, lowering his voice. 'This whole thing doesn't sit well with him.'

'You want me to have a word?' Hayata asked.

Muramatsu shook his head. 'Tough guys don't talk, but he doesn't want to be alone. He doesn't actually know that, though, so be discreet.'

* * *

All the academics had left the island by the time the Gomorasaurus was airborne except for Nakaya, who insisted on traveling with the Science Patrol. Arashi showed no feeling about his presence one way or the other, although Hayata suspected he wished the man had opted to travel in the helicopter, as Ide had.

For most of the trip, Fuji kept the VTOL at the same level and speed as the heavy-lifter. Ide contacted them with regular updates, but since there was nothing much to report, these mostly consisted of his geeking out about this or that shiny bit of Defense Force tech. They entered Japanese airspace thirty minutes ahead of schedule and Muramatsu told Fuji to fly ahead to the Expo LZ, where they would wait for the helicopter and its snoring cargo. They were still on the way when Ide contacted them.

'We've got a big problem,' he said, not bothering with the standard comm protocol. 'Our friend in the net is awake.'

'That's impossible!' Nakaya said. 'Those tranquilizer darts should've—'

'Maybe the bracing ocean air is stronger than tranqs,' Ide said, talking over him. 'But now it's wide awake and it doesn't like flying. It doesn't like it *a lot*. The pilot says she's gonna turn around and get us back over water—'

There was a burst of static. Muramatsu ordered Fuji to turn the VTOL around and head back toward the helicopter while Hayata kept trying to raise Ide. Just as she completed the turn, Ide's voice came through again.

'Sorry, but now we have a bigger problem,' Ide said. 'The Gomorasaurus is gone.'

'What do you mean, *gone*?' Nakaya shouted. 'Gone where? Gone *how*?'

'It tore its way out of the net and fell,' Ide said. 'Over *land*.'

Fuji contacted the helicopter pilot for the exact coordinates of where the monster had dropped and changed course again.

'Cap, the good news is, the Gomorasaur or whatever it is fell in open country—no houses or businesses,' she said. 'The bad news is, the area is only a short hop to the edge of the Osaka suburbs.'

One of the helicopter crew broke in. 'We issued an alert advising local authorities to evacuate the area and we've got our people on the way. But that's assuming this bad boy survived the fall. It might not have.'

'Could we really be that lucky?' Fuji said.

'No,' Arashi said flatly. 'Not today.'

When Osamu saw the monster fall from the sky, he felt as if the universe had decided to reward him for being a monster expert by sending him one he could look at up close. And even better, his friends Ken, Tomoyuki, and Akira were there to see it with him.

For a while, the boys had been playing in the construction area where all the big earth-movers were parked when no one was using them. Then Osamu had suggested they should go farther up the access road, which ran past the foreman's trailer. The land there was still undeveloped, with all kinds of hills and ridges, much better for playing Men on Mars or Alien Invasion or Explorers in Monster Land, which was Osamu's favorite, not only because he invented all the monsters but also because he got to become Ultraman and save everybody.

His friends had been teasing him again about his fascination with monsters (although not the same way as some of the other kids at school, who could get pretty mean about it). There were monsters in movies and TV shows and video games but everybody knew they were pretend. Any real monsters were all far away, like other wild, exotic animals. They weren't going to show up in Osaka.

At school that morning, he had come in with a photo he'd printed out from the Hanshin University website, of something called a Gomorasaurus, taken by one of the professors currently on the Johnson Island expedition. Some of his classmates said it was fake news, but the teacher had told them it wasn't—the professor was a real person and Johnson Island was a real place.

According to the news—the real news, she said—the Science Patrol had arranged for the creature to be flown to Japan for the International Expo. That meant it wouldn't be long before they could all see for themselves whether it was a real monster or just a big lizard or possibly even an actual dinosaur so elusive that it had existed for millions of years without anyone knowing. Wouldn't it be great to find out?

But now Osamu and his friends would be the first people in the whole country to see for themselves. The boys had gotten only a quick look at the creature as it dropped out of the sky and landed behind a stony ridge, throwing up a cloud of dust and dirt. But what little they'd seen looked just like the photo.

The prospect of getting so close to a real monster, however, wasn't everybody's idea of a good time. When Osamu said he was going to take some pictures of it to email to the Science Patrol, Tomoyuki and Akira decided this was one of those rare occasions when it was okay to admit they were chicken. They jumped on their bikes and pedaled back down the access road as fast as they could.

'They're such babies,' Osamu said to Ken. 'Next time they tease me about monsters, I'm gonna ask them if they're still too scared to look at a real one in person.'

Ken had mixed feelings about the situation himself but as Osamu's best friend, he couldn't run off and leave him to see a monster all alone. 'I bet it's dead,' he said hopefully as he followed Osamu up a steep incline toward the place where the monster had landed. 'It fell from the sky, it musta got smashed to pieces.'

'No way,' Osamu said with unshakable certainty. 'You can't kill monsters that easy.'

Near the top of the incline, they had to half climb, half slide a little way down to the stony ridge jutting out from the side. The ridge was wide enough to walk on but only just. They had to go single file whenever they played Explorers in Monster Land. Fortunately, there was a boulder right in the middle that was big enough to hide behind, which Osamu's father had said had been left by a glacier when it had receded millions of years ago. (Osamu was sure the boulder was actually a petrified monster egg, although he hadn't shared that idea with anyone else, not even Ken.)

Now as they peered at the creature from behind the boulder, Osamu realized from the way Ken was clutching his arm that his friend was scared for real, and he was starting to kinda, sorta feel that way, too. The monster really was big, all over. The horn on its nose was bigger than a man; the one just below it was smaller but only a little bit—

Abruptly, the long thick tail shivered, rose up, then slammed down hard enough that Osamu and Ken could feel the vibration from where they were.

'It's alive!' Ken whispered.

'Well, yeah,' Osamu said, trying to sound more knowing than scared. 'I told you, you can't kill a monster that easy.'

Then its eyes opened and its gigantic head slowly lifted as the thing looked around. Osamu worked his phone out of his back pocket and started taking pictures.

'Don't do that!' Ken whispered, hearing the camera-click sound. 'I think it heard you!'

The enormous horned head turned slowly from one side to the other as the monster made a low growling noise.

'I think it heard you!' Osamu whispered back. He took two more pictures, then switched to video as the creature began to struggle slowly to its feet. This was better than all the monster movies, TV shows, and video games in the world all put together, Osamu thought, as the Gomorasaurus finally stood up.

'Oh, for crying out loud—how did you two get here?'

Osamu turned to see a man in a Science Patrol uniform coming along the ridge toward him and Ken with a weapon in one hand. 'I know you!' he said excitedly. 'You're Senior Agent Shin Hayata! I've seen your picture on the Science Patrol website!'

'Never mind that, you kids can't be here, it's too dangerous!' The man re-attached the weapon to his belt, then made Osamu and Ken go ahead of him back up to the incline.

'We want to see you capture the monster!' Osamu said, fearless now. The Science Patrol could beat anything, even monsters. He was sure of it.

'Absolutely not!' The man tapped something on his lapel. 'This is Hayata, hold your fire, I've got two kids here practically in the kill zone.' Pause. 'No, I'm not kidding, Ide. Our guys must have missed them. Don't ask me how, they must have been playing out here before the Defense Force set up the perimeter. I'm going to send them down the access road to the construction staging area. Call the local police and get someone to meet them there and drive them home.'

Hayata was about to say something else when there was a sudden loud bellowing roar followed by a high-pitched screechy sound, a bit like an elephant trumpeting. He glanced over his shoulder at the monster then turned to Osamu and Ken. 'I want you both to run down to the dirt road, and keep running all the way back to the place where all those big earth-movers are parked. Got that?'

'Yes, sir,' Osamu said, saluting; Ken nodded without a word.

'You don't look back and you don't stop till you see the police car, okay? Tell the officer where you live and when you get home, stay there. Okay?'

'Okay, but that's boring,' Osamu said. 'We'd rather see you capture the monster.'

'Too bad,' the man told him. 'Now get going! Run!'

Osamu stopped at the bottom of the incline to look back but Agent Hayata had disappeared. He made a move as if to climb back up and see where he'd gone but Ken was pulling him away, insisting that they had to go.

Hayata waited until the boys were almost all the way down the incline, then made his way back onto the ridge and tapped his communicator again as he drew his weapon. 'Hayata to Muramatsu—the kids are clear.'

'Copy that. Civilians are clear,' Muramatsu acknowledged. 'Science Patrol and Defense Force—commence firing!'

The creature all but disappeared in a storm of flashing energy beams, clouds of smoke, and explosions that didn't quite drown out its screams of fury. Hayata was unaware that he was firing his own weapon in Ultraman's stance for the Spacium Beam until he heard Muramatsu's voice in his headphones saying, 'Cease fire!'

Smoke and dust hung in the air in a way that seemed to amplify the sudden silence. Weapon still in hand, Hayata stayed where he was, listening for any noises a dying monster might make, a groan or a wail or a whimper, but there was nothing.

It's not there anymore, said a small voice in his mind and he felt a brief surge of relief. The combination of Science Patrol weapons and Defense Force armaments had obliterated it. It might have been overkill except for how close it was to a populated area.

He heard Nakaya's voice in his comm. 'There's nothing left of it!'

'There's plenty left,' Arashi said in a cold voice. 'All of it.'

'That pile of dirt means it burrowed underground,' Muramatsu added. 'And there's no telling where it's going to pop up again. Or when.'

Hayata turned to look toward the Osaka suburb. The houses and apartment buildings were so far away they were barely visible from where he stood but for a monster the size of Ultraman, they were probably well within burrowing range.

'Excuse me, Cap,' Fuji said, 'but I think we can make a pretty good guess about where it'll show up.'

Everyone, Defense Force soldiers as well as her teammates, turned to look at her with curiosity (and, she noted, a little surprise).

'How so?' Muramatsu asked.

Fuji hesitated, suddenly self-conscious with so many eyes on her. But this was too important; she'd just have to get over it. 'Well, it's used to tunneling freely through plain old soil. But in populated areas, there are all kinds of things in the ground—the sewer system, water pipes, cables, underground storage facilities. Those'll be like barriers and it'll most likely turn away toward clearer ground, don't you think?'

'With those claws and fangs, it won't have much trouble ripping through any of that stuff,' Ide said dismissively.

'But it's a hell of a lot easier if it doesn't have to,' Arashi said, giving Fuji a gruff look of approval. 'It'll definitely want to take the path of least resistance first.' He turned to Muramatsu. 'Cap, I recommend we get some observation drones in the air ASAP.'

'Just gave the order,' said the ranking Defense Force officer onsite, a middle-aged woman whose name tag said Ishioka. She turned to look at Fuji, obviously impressed. 'Good thinking, Agent Fuji,' she told her, and there was a chorus agreement from her squad.

Heat rushed into Fuji's face; at the same time, she couldn't help smiling and hid it by turning away and pretending to check her weapon's level of charge.

'Let's regroup at the Osaka Science Patrol facility,' Muramatsu said. 'We need to work out strategies and a Plan B for each one, as well as a Plan B for the Plan Bs.' He raised his voice slightly. 'Hayata, did you get all that?'

'I copied everything and I think Fuji's a genius,' replied Hayata. 'The problem is, we can't count on the Gomorasaurus being as smart as she is. If we back it into the wrong corner, it'll just rip through whatever's in its way. We've got to try to drive it toward undeveloped land. I'll meet you at the facility after I make sure those kids didn't double-back for a front row seat at the monster show. Or bring their friends.'

* * *

Osamu told the police officer who met them at the construction site that he and Ken were brothers. Ken went along with it, although he obviously hadn't liked lying to a policeman. Both of his parents were at work and would be none the wiser about their adventure. Osamu's parents both worked, too, but his mother had the day off. Just seeing him come home in a police car would upset her and if she heard the whole story, Osamu was sure she'd ground him for *months*.

The policeman hadn't wanted to simply drop them off and if he'd known there was no one home at Ken's apartment, he might have called Ken's parents at work. Then they'd have both been grounded for months. But an urgent call came in just as they pulled up in front of the building and the policeman settled for watching them go inside and start up the stairs before driving away. As soon as he was gone, Osamu told Ken he wanted to go back to the construction site to play.

'It's just across the field,' he said, jerking his head at the lumpy expanse of grass and brush.

Ken looked dubious. 'The Science Patrol guy said to stay close to home.'

'It is close to home,' Osamu said, unperturbed. 'We can see our apartment buildings from there.'

'Only mine, not yours,' Ken said.

'That's just because mine is behind yours,' Osamu said. 'But I can see one of the satellite dishes on the roof of my building, so that counts as the whole thing.'

'You can?' Ken said, following him across the field toward the construction site.

'Sure,' Osamu said. 'I'll show you. You have to squint, though. First one there is Ultraman!' He broke into a run.

Ultra Osamu had vanquished half a dozen monsters when the boys felt the earth vibrating under their feet.

'Is it an earthquake?' Ken said, his voice high and anxious as he looked around.

'No, it's more like the subway,' Osamu said.

'The subway doesn't come this far out,' Ken replied, even more anxious. 'And even if it did, it wouldn't do that.' He pointed and Osamu turned to see dirt blowing up out of the ground like a geyser.

In the next moment, they heard the familiar sound of loud bellowing and that screeching noise like an elephant trumpeting. The boys took cover behind a nearby backhoe and watched as two sharp horns broke through the ground from below, followed by a pair of huge, angry-looking eyes.

'Do you think it's following us?' Ken whispered, clutching Osamu's arm tightly.

'I don't know,' Osamu said, clutching Ken just as tightly.

'What do we do?' Ken's eyes were starting to well up, which meant he was really, really scared.

'You run home and warn everybody,' Osamu said. 'I'm gonna keep an eye on it and see what it does next.'

'No, you come, too—'

'If I do, we won't know where it is.' Osamu pushed him away.

'The Science Patrol will—there's a drone! Look!'

Osamu turned to see one of the construction site surveillance drones flying around the monster's head like a somewhat oversized mechanical bee confronting a trespasser in its garden. As it swooped down to get a closer look, the monster finally noticed it, slapped it out of the air with one big paw, and stomped on it.

'*Go!*' Osamu hollered.

As Ken ran for his life, Osamu turned back to see the creature lumbering slowly toward him, kicking aside the big yellow construction vehicles as if they were toys it was tired of playing with.

Should've gone with Ken, he thought. He took a step toward the field, then retreated behind the backhoe again. If he ran across the field now, the monster would see him, throw him down, and stomp on him like the drone.

Osamu turned and ran in the other direction until he came to a shallow ditch with a pipe at the bottom. Without hesitating, he jumped in and held very still. The monster bellowed and trumpeted as it stomped around, and Osamu could feel the earth around him shaking at every step. It was so close; he'd never meant to get this close—

Abruptly, there was a new sound, of something in flight. He'd never heard it in person but he recognized it. It was the same as in the online videos, only louder. Forgetting he was terrified, he jumped to his feet, almost falling over the pipe, raised one arm, and shouted, 'Ultraman!'

* * *

Searching for some sign of the Gomorasaurus meant using up part of his alter ego's limited time at full strength, but Hayata knew he couldn't just wait and hope he'd be able to slip away unnoticed when the creature finally surfaced again. Fuji seemed to have been right about the thing not wanting to burrow through subterranean clutter, but only up to a point. The kaiju could avoid underground structures simply by burrowing deeper, into clear ground below them. But maybe it wouldn't bother; like Ide had said, a monstrous creature like this wasn't going to let some underground pipes and cables keep it from going anywhere it wanted.

Once Hayata was airborne, his heightened sensory perception picked up the creature's underground movements in a way that seemed to combine vision, hearing, and touch yet wasn't any of those things. The closer the beast got to the surface, the more strongly Hayata could sense it but at the same time, interference from various electromagnetic fields made it difficult to pinpoint the creature's exact location. When it had surfaced at the construction site, he had still been some distance away but he managed to get to it before it found the two foolish little boys playing among the heavy machinery.

When he arrived, one of the boys had left and the other was crouching in a ditch. To see Ultraman fight the monster, of course. In spite of everything, Hayata couldn't really fault him; he'd have done the same thing at that age himself.

Now he went into a long, steep dive, accelerating so that when he finally hit the monster, the impact carried both of them away from the boy. But the moment he struck the

Gomorasaurus, the world disappeared in a blinding flash. As the proverbial body in motion, he had hit the fabled immovable object and that immovable object had won without even trying. His vision cleared just as the creature kicked him away with frightening ease.

Ultraman was *so strong*, Osamu thought; the way he landed on the Gomorasaurus and knocked it down was better than any TV show (especially since there were no commercials). Now Ultraman was going to teach it some manners—

Only the Gomorasaurus suddenly heaved Ultraman off so he went tumbling backward—butt over teakettle, his mom would have said, Osamu thought, his face puckered with worry. He held his breath as Ultraman and the monster jumped to their feet at the same time, and the Gomorasaurus rushed at Ultraman.

But of course Ultraman was ready for that. He grabbed the sharp-looking horns on either side of the Gomorasaurus's head, turned, and threw the monster right over his shoulder. The Gomorasaurus landed harder, hard enough that Osamu felt the ground shake.

Immediately, the monster rolled over, sprang up, and, to Osamu's surprise, had a grandiose monster tantrum, waving its arms, roaring and trumpeting. Then it lowered its head and sort of charged Ultraman in a clumsy sideways movement.

Ultraman reached for its horns and the Gomorasaurus brought its head up sharply, throwing Ultraman into the air. Osamu clapped his hands over his mouth to keep from crying out as the Gomorasaurus *jumped* on Ultraman with both feet, trying to mash him into the ground.

'Come on, Ultraman,' Osamu whispered, watching the red and silver figure struggle under the monster's weight. He finally managed to twist around and push the Gomorasaurus off himself. As he started to get up, the creature suddenly whirled, slamming its tail into him and knocking him into a clumsy sideways tumble. The Gomorasaurus spun again, whipping its tail around for another blow. Ultraman dodged it easily but as he did, Osamu saw a light green and white object go flying away from him to land in the dirt right beside the ditch where he was hiding.

Quickly, he snatched it up. It looked something like his geography teacher's laser pointer, except it was too big, and it was the wrong shape for a phone—unless it was a Dictaphone? His dad had one of those. There was a button on the side but when he pressed it, nothing happened.

He looked up to see Ultraman knock the Gomorasaurus down with a flying kick to its chest. The monster tried to scramble up and get away but Ultraman jumped on it and grabbed it by the horns. The two giants grappled with each other, rolling back and forth on the ground until Ultraman got to his feet and, still gripping the monster's horns, forced it to stand up with him.

The bright blue light in the center of Ultraman's chest suddenly turned red and began to flash. Osamu didn't know exactly why—no one did—but he didn't think it was good.

The Gomorasaurus fell backward, dragging Ultraman with it and throwing him over its head. Quickly, it turned and slammed its long thick tail into him, then whirled to bring its tail around again, barely missing Ultraman as he somersaulted away. It tried the same thing twice more but Ultraman dodged each swing, then slipped behind the creature, grabbed one of its horns, and tried to get his arm around its neck.

The monster twisted away and whipped its tail into Ultraman again, then swung it back the other way for another blow, and it kept doing it, battering him with its tail from one side and then the other, over and over until the red and silver figure was face down in the dirt.

Roaring and trumpeting, the Gomorasaurus stepped heavily on Ultraman's back, lumbered away a few meters, dropped to the ground, and began digging in a frenzy.

With an effort, Ultraman raised himself up on his knees and put his left arm across his chest to steady his right hand against it. Osamu's heart leaped—was he going to see Ultraman use one of his Ultra powers?

Nope, not today.

By the time Ultraman was ready, the tip of the Gomorasaurus's tail was disappearing into the hole it had dug. And all the while, the red light on Ultraman's chest was flashing faster and faster.

Don't give up, Osamu begged him silently, watching him get slowly to his feet. He didn't look very steady and for a moment, Osamu was afraid he was going to fall down. If he did, Osamu thought, his own heart would stop. But Ultraman stayed on his feet, raised both arms, and launched himself into the air.

Osamu stared after him until the last glint of his silver boots disappeared. As he turned away, his gaze fell on the object in his hands. He'd forgotten all about it even though he'd been clutching it like a lifeline. He could hear voices in the distance getting closer; one of them was his mother's.

He dropped into a crouch in the loose dirt, staring at the object he was holding.

Now what?

CHAPTER

FIVE

Hayata knew he wasn't going to make it any farther than the parking lot next to the last apartment building on a street two blocks away. Putting his palms together, he aimed his fingers at the far end of the lot. A moment later, he was standing in an empty parking space, breathless, his heart pounding as if he'd sprinted two kilometers flat out. For a few seconds, he bent over with his hands on his knees and concentrated on slowing his heartbeat, silently promising himself that he wouldn't cut it so close again.

After a bit, he straightened up and looked around. The parking lot was mostly empty; since it was a weekday, everyone would be at work. Or almost everyone, he thought, scanning the windows of the building beside the lot. He couldn't see any curious onlookers but that didn't mean there weren't any—he'd just have to wait and see if there were any reports of a magic, now-you-don't-see-him-now-you-do

Science Patrol agent taking up a parking space without a car. But first, he had to get to Osaka headquarters. He contacted Fuji, who sent a Defense Force jeep out for him.

Still crouching in the ditch, Osamu heard his mother calling for him, her voice frantic; Ken must have gone to her first. It sounded like she had mobilized all the neighbors to come with her, or at least everybody on their floor. Normally Osamu would have run to her immediately to tell her he was all right but he wasn't sure what to do about this strange device Ultraman had dropped.

There was no doubt in his mind that it was Ultraman's personal property. Monsters didn't have stuff like this, unless they were robot-monsters and this one definitely wasn't. Although it probably could have beaten a robot-monster; it had beaten Ultraman.

Not for good, though—no monster could beat Ultraman for good. Like all superheroes, Ultraman had a secret weapon and this must be it, Osamu thought, gazing at the object in his hands. Maybe it was one of those skinny flashlights, what his mom called a penlight, although he didn't see anything that looked like a lightbulb or an LED.

He tried pressing the button on the side again but nothing happened. Maybe the batteries were flat but he didn't see anything that could have been a compartment for triple-As. Or maybe Ultraman had a special secret smart-pocket that kept it charged. Whatever it was, he had to get it back to Ultraman as soon as possible. Only how was he supposed to do that when his mother was going to ground him for *months*?

He'd just have to figure it out, Osamu thought as he climbed out of the ditch. His mother spotted him instantly, before he had a chance to call out to her. She descended on him, wrapping him up in her arms and kissing him repeatedly while the neighbors looked on, some smiling, others giving him disapproving looks for being the kind of boy that would scare his poor mother.

Ken was there, too, and Osamu could see he was sorry about all the fuss his mother was making. With good reason—the first thing his mother was going to do after they got home was call Ken's mother and tell her the whole story. Then Ken would be grounded for months, too, and they'd be lucky if they could even talk to each other on the computer.

'You've been told a million times this isn't a playground,' Osamu's mother was saying, and her voice had acquired an angry edge. There was going to be less hugging and more scolding now. Osamu opened his mouth to tell her about Ultraman but she was still talking.

'What's this?' she asked, looking at Ultraman's secret weapon. 'You shouldn't play with a flashlight in the daytime, you'll drain the batteries and we're going to need all our flashlights and more—the power in our building's gone out and who knows when it'll come back on. You should give that to me.' She held out her hand.

'No, it's okay, I'll put it away.' Osamu slid it into his front pocket. 'See?'

'Come on, then.' She took him by the arm and marched

him back across the field with everyone else following, chattering among themselves.

Ken managed to catch up with him on his other side. 'What happened to the monster?' he asked.

'You kids,' said a man walking close behind. 'It's all monsters with you.'

'It was a monster,' Ken said hotly.

'You kids,' the man said again and laughed. 'You've got monsters on the brain.'

Ken turned back to Osamu. 'Where did it go?'

Osamu shrugged awkwardly. 'It went underground again so it could be anywhere. Under our building. Or yours, even.'

Ken looked around, frightened. 'You think that's why the power went out? Because it's down there ripping through all the electric cables and stuff?'

'I don't know,' Osamu said. 'Right now, I have to find someone from the Science Patrol.'

'How?' Ken asked him. 'We're both gonna be grounded forever.'

'I'll figure something out,' Osamu said, trying to sound more confident than he felt.

The scene at Osaka HQ was complete chaos. The head of the Defense Force was coordinating drones and teams of human spotters flying over the city. A number of places had lost power, mostly private residences in the suburbs, although a few office buildings and buildings closer in had also gone dark. Nonetheless, there had been no sign of the Gomorasaurus.

Fuji had been mapping the power outages in an attempt to track the creature and found that it seemed to be sticking mainly to the eastern area of the city. The head of the Defense Force was in a heated three-way discussion with city officials and Muramatsu about evacuating that part of Osaka.

In between arguments, Muramatsu had Fuji contacting various laboratories to see about obtaining more, preferably stronger tranquilizers, while Ide was adapting a Science Patrol micro-transmitter to boost its signal, making it powerful enough to pass through many layers of earth, concrete, and steel. He was trying to finish before the next time the creature surfaced so it could be tagged and tracked.

Hayata had expected Muramatsu would want to know where the hell he'd been and why he hadn't shown up before now. But when Muramatsu's gaze finally fell on him, he discovered his absence wasn't the question of the hour.

'I want you to check the armory here,' Muramatsu said, taking him aside, out of the scrum in the center of the room. 'We store certain classified weapons in the sub-basement.'

Hayata's eyebrows strained upward toward his hairline. 'If you're talking about the pulse weapons—well, are you sure, Cap?'

Muramatsu's face was solemn. 'I don't think we have a choice.'

'It's just that the potential for, uh, collateral damage—'

Now Muramatsu's expression hardened. 'I never liked that term, "collateral damage." It's entirely too sanitary. How much "collateral damage"'—he made air quotes—'would you say that creature out there can produce?'

'I agree with you,' Hayata said unhappily. 'Which is why I think we ought to evacuate everyone in the eastern part of the city.'

'Uh-huh. So they all go into the streets while that monster's underground,' Muramatsu said. 'What do you suppose it'll do when it detects surface vibrations from hundreds, even thousands of people on the move? I'd say that'd be like ringing the dinner bell.'

'Excuse me, Captain.' Fuji appeared beside them. 'I'm afraid animal tranquilizer has suddenly become Osaka's rarest commodity. There are some large animal veterinarians who have some on hand but not nearly enough for anything even half the size of the Gomorasaurus. I've got a few labs cooking more for us but the earliest any of it'll be ready is something like four hours.'

Muramatsu gave a single, humorless laugh. 'Remind me to add that to our active inventory when this is all over,' he said.

'Will do, boss. I've got calls in to Nara and Kyoto to see if anyone there can supply us.' Fuji was about to say something else when someone across the room called her name and she hurried away.

'Captain!' Ide materialized on Muramatsu's other side with a metal case in his hands. 'I've got the new, improved micro-transmitter. This signal is so strong, we could track it from orbit.'

'Let's hope it doesn't come to that,' Muramatsu said. 'Find Arashi for me. Hayata, the weapons in the sub-basement— *now*.'

* * *

'Maybe it's more badly injured than we thought,' said Ide. He was sitting in the backseat of a Defense Force jeep beside Arashi. The lights on the stock of the plasma rifle lying across his lap glowed amber to show it was on standby, which was the closest thing it had to a safety setting. Going from standby to active was just a matter of squeezing the trigger.

'I'm not so sure that monster *can* be injured,' Arashi said. 'I didn't notice it limping.'

'No, think about it,' Ide went on. 'It fell from a helicopter. Then we shot the hell out of it before it burrowed underground—if it's got any internal injuries from the fall, that would probably make them worse. For all we know, it dug itself a cozy hole, then crawled into it and died.' He turned to Hayata, sitting in the front passenger seat. 'It could have, right?'

'Sure, that's probably what happened,' Arashi said in a flat expressionless voice. 'Now we can all go home.' He looked at the chronometer on his wrist.

Ide laughed. 'You got somewhere else to be? Or a hot date?'

'No,' Arashi said, 'I just want to see how long it takes the monster to respond to your cue.'

In the next moment, a loud Defense Force siren went off and a soldier jumped into the driver's seat. 'Air surveillance says it's come farther into the city and it's mad as hell.' He glanced at Ide and Arashi who were both obviously spooked. 'You guys okay?'

'They're fine.' Hayata chuckled. 'They're just struggling

with the twin phenomena of synchronicity and coincidence occurring outside the quantum level.'

'Oh, is that all?' the driver said, giving him a sidelong glance. 'As long as it's nothing serious.' He executed a tight U-turn, then stamped on the accelerator.

'Don't you ever do that again,' Ide said to Arashi, hanging onto the roll bar.

'You did it, not me,' Arashi said, hugging his plasma rifle to his chest.

'Nakaoe Park will never be the same,' said the jeep driver as he pulled up behind an armored vehicle a block away. 'Our guys are evacuating the adjacent buildings and setting up on rooftops for a three-sixty onslaught. I sure hope those plasma weapons of yours can do the job on this thing. You knock it down, we'll do everything we can to make sure there's nothing left.'

Hayata caught sight of Arashi's stony face. Arashi noticed him noticing and assumed a more neutral expression. 'I'll be giving the order to fire,' Hayata told the soldier. 'You guys good with that?'

The soldier nodded. 'Lieutenant Kotani says you're the monster experts. We follow your lead for this one.'

Hayata nodded and headed toward the bellowing roar and the sound of glass breaking and metal crashing with Ide and Arashi.

'I don't know if they're gonna be able to get everyone out of those buildings,' Ide said when they were out of earshot.

'I was listening in on their channel. People don't want to just drop everything and go, they want to pack bags.'

'Then we're going to have to keep its attention on us,' Hayata said. 'Arashi, you ready to tag it?'

Arashi unhooked the dart gun from his belt and held it up. 'All right, but that hide is too thick to penetrate—the tracker'll just bounce off. I'll have to put this right in the thing's mouth.'

'Unless we can stop it here,' Ide put in, sounding almost cheerful. 'Then it won't matter.'

'We can't count on being able to do that, even with plasma rifles,' Hayata said. 'The Gomorasaurus still has a lot of fight left in it. We haven't worn it down enough yet—'

Abruptly, a stream of civilians emerged from a side street along with a few Defense Force soldiers who were herding them away from Nakaoe Park and the sound of splintering wood and brutish bellowing.

'It tore out all the trees!' a woman hollered at them as a soldier hustled her past. 'With its tail!'

They turned the next corner and Hayata suddenly dived for the ground, yanking Ide and Arashi down with him as the Gomorasaurus's tail whipped through the air just above them. It slammed into the cars parked at the curb, sending them flying into the nearby storefronts.

'Jeez!' Ide said. 'It's a killer at both ends!'

'No kidding,' Hayata said, thinking Ultraman would agree. 'We've got to get it to turn around. Let's give it a butt-load of plasma and see how it likes that. Science Patrol only, fire on three. Ready?'

Lying side by side on their bellies, they all took aim at the base of the creature's tail and Hayata counted it out in a slower counterpoint to his pounding heart. 'One… two… three!'

To Hayata's surprise, the area around the Gomorasaurus's tail burst into flames. 'Keep firing!' Hayata yelled as the thing turned around, screaming at them in fury. Arashi had the dart gun in his other hand and sent the micro-transmitter into its wide-open jaws. The creature didn't seem to notice. Not surprising, Hayata thought; when your ass was on fire, you probably wouldn't notice you'd eaten a bug.

'Everyone, fire!' Hayata said over the open comm channel.

The creature's screams were drowned out by automatic weapons, explosive rounds, and grenades. It started to turn, preparing for another sweep with its tail. Instead, the tail broke off and flopped into the street, where it began squirming and writhing along the pavement, moving away from the creature.

Hayata's jaw dropped. 'Is anyone else seeing this?' he said over the open comm channel.

An RPG whistled through the air and hit the tail dead center; when the smoke cleared, it was lying broken and motionless in a crater in the street.

'Not anymore,' said a voice in his headphones.

'Copy that and thank you,' Hayata said, momentarily stunned.

The creature kept twitching its stump back and forth and obviously couldn't understand why nothing happened when it did. Bellowing, it lumbered away from what had once been a skate-path onto a grassy area littered with splintered tree trunks and began to claw at the ground, its movements more frenzied than before.

Hayata gave the order to cease fire as its hind legs disappeared into the ground in a wild spray of dirt, but advised everyone to stand by in case it turned around and came back.

'It won't,' Arashi said. 'It's on the run now. This time, we really did hurt it.'

'Bad enough to kill it?' Ide asked.

'Nah, it can still burrow,' Arashi said. 'But when it surfaces, it won't be able to move as well as before. Without its tail, it'll be off-balance, for one thing. And for another, from the way it was twitching that stump, I'd say it doesn't even know it's gone.'

Ide looked past him to the still-smoking crater with the tail. 'What's with that thing, anyway?'

'Some lizards can lose their tails to get away from a predator,' Arashi said. 'Then grow them back.'

Ide looked horrified. 'Relax,' Hayata told him. 'I don't think the Gomorasaurus is one of them. But when we take the tail back to the lab for dissection, they'll probably find a rudimentary brain in it.'

Now Ide's face was aghast.

'It's a characteristic of especially large creatures, like dinosaurs,' Hayata went on. 'Their central nervous systems were spread out over such a wide area, their motor controls actually had to have relays.'

'That's so weird. And kinda gross,' Ide added as he took

out his phone. He tapped the screen, then showed it to Hayata and Arashi. 'At least the micro-transmitter's working. See how it's moving east? If it keeps on going the way it is, I know what its next stop is gonna be.'

'Me, too.' Hayata tapped his communicator. 'Hayata to Captain Muramatsu. We need to mobilize everything we've got to Osaka Castle now.'

'Because it's looking for green space,' Ide said, hanging onto the jeep roll bar with both hands as the jeep raced toward Osaka Castle.

'How would it know?' Arashi asked. 'It's underground.'

'I'm not sure exactly,' Ide said, 'but just guessing, I'd say it's something about the soil—how it smells or feels, or even how vibrations from the surface come through to it. Johnson Island's nothing but green space and I think it keeps digging because it's trying to burrow its way back there. The nearest big expanse of mostly green space is the fifteen acres around Osaka Castle.'

Arashi considered it. 'That actually makes sense.'

'You don't have to sound so surprised,' Ide said.

'But eventually fifteen puny little acres are gonna feel pretty cramped,' Arashi went on. 'Especially if its tail grows back.'

The jeep driver looked at Hayata, alarmed. 'Oh, jeez— the tail grows back?' he said.

'Probably not,' Hayata assured him quickly. He tapped his communicator. 'Are you getting all this, Cap?'

'Every word,' Muramatsu replied on the general comm channel. 'Local police have already cleared out the tourists and set up a perimeter. So for the moment at least, we won't have any civilians in jeopardy.'

As it turned out, he was almost right. But then, Osamu didn't consider himself a civilian.

'That *can't* be a Science Patrol video!' Osamu's mother Rieko said, aghast at the sight of the monster's writhing, dismembered tail on Osamu's laptop screen. She'd spotted it as soon as she had come into his room to tell him the power was back on. 'They wouldn't put something so gory online!'

'I don't know,' Osamu said, trying to sound innocent. 'Maybe they did.'

'No, they would *never* post something like that where *children* could see it,' she declared and used the touchpad to close the window. 'Why did you get so close to that monster? What were you *thinking*?'

Osamu started to protest, then saw the look on her face and decided not to push his luck.

'I wasn't *that* close,' he said in a small voice, conscious of Ultraman's secret weapon in his pocket and afraid his mother was going to make him hand it over. 'And when I saw it, it still had its tail.'

'I won't have you watching such awful, violent things.'

'But, Mom, it's not a movie, it's real—'

'I don't care. No more dismembered monster parts or you'll lose your computer privileges—I mean it.' She

191

crouched beside his chair so they were eye to eye and her voice softened. 'Just because it's real doesn't mean you should see it. I wish *I* hadn't seen it. I'm going to have bad dreams for a week.'

Osamu decided not to tell her he'd thought the tail looked kind of funny.

'Honey, terrible things happen every day. Just because they're real doesn't mean it's okay for children to see them and have those pictures in their heads.' She was about to go on when they heard his father coming in. 'No more dismembered monster tails,' she said firmly, then went to greet his father, who was already describing how the office had closed early but it had taken him longer than usual to get home because the Defense Force had blocked off so many streets that all the buses were on diversion.

Osamu took Ultraman's secret weapon out of his pocket and looked it over. He still wasn't sure what it was made of—it was as light as plastic but there weren't any seams or scratches on the surface and when he tapped his thumbnail against it, it didn't make a noise.

Pressing the button on the side still didn't do anything. He'd tried holding the button down for ten seconds, then clicking it rapidly like a ballpoint pen—still nothing. Tapping it on the desk, running it under water in the bathroom, warming it between his hands had no effect on it, either.

But when he put it on his windowsill in the sunlight, he found himself remembering how Ultraman had fought the monster. It was so vivid, it was more like he was watching a movie in his head. Unfortunately, the movie was of the monster hitting Ultraman over and over with its tail while he struggled to get up. It made him more certain than ever that he needed to find Ultraman and give this thing back to him.

His mother and father had settled down in the living room in front of the new TV. This one was enormous with ultra-high definition, and they wouldn't let him hook his video game system up to it. They'd said it might damage the screen but Osamu knew it was really because they couldn't figure out how to switch back to TV mode. He had offered to show them—the new TV wasn't as complicated as their old one—but his father had told him to be content with using his computer monitor. That was all right but it would have been so cool to play Rampage in Space on something almost as big as a movie screen.

'Oh my God!' his mother cried out from the living room. 'I just made Osamu turn that off!'

'It looks fake to me,' his father said with a disdainful laugh. 'I don't buy it for a second.'

'But you can see the Defense Force soldiers and the Science Patrol!' said his mother.

'Obviously somebody spliced in a fake video with special effects. Don't be so gullible, Rieko.'

Osamu smiled to himself. His father was skeptical of anything he hadn't seen with his own eyes, what Ken referred to as 'a hard sell'; Ken's own father was the same way.

His gaze fell on Ultraman's secret weapon again, still in his hands. The news had said the Science Patrol and the

Defense Force were heading for Osaka Castle, to defend it and try to keep the monster from destroying a five-hundred-year-old landmark. Osamu was sure Ultraman would be going there, too. But without his secret weapon, the monster might beat him again. He *had* to get this back to Ultraman, it was his duty. The only way he could do that, however, was by sneaking out.

Osamu had never sneaked out of the house, ever, and he had always let his parents know where he was going. Sneaking out was almost like running away, only… well, sneakier. In his whole life, he had never imagined doing such a thing, never imagined that he would ever have a good reason to even consider it. It felt *wrong*.

But what if Ultraman couldn't save Osaka Castle without his secret weapon? How would he feel if one of Japan's most important historical places was destroyed just because he'd been too much of a baby to do what he knew was right?

Ultraman was depending on him. Osaka Castle and the people of Japan were depending on him. None of them knew it but that didn't matter. Unless he did his duty and got Ultraman's secret weapon back to him, he'd never be able to call himself a good guy and then he'd never be able to join the Science Patrol, because they only took good guys.

Osamu stood up, put the secret weapon back in his pocket, and tiptoed out of his room. His parents were still arguing about the monster-tail video and never heard him slip out. He made it all the way to the bike rack outside the front door of the building before his heart started pounding. His hands were shaking so badly it took him two tries to work the combination lock. But once he started pedaling, he was full of energy, more excited than scared.

He'd never ridden his bike as far as Osaka Castle—not even half that far!—but he had no doubt he'd make it. All he had to do was keep to side streets and alleys, and he could go off-road, too, even though his bike wasn't a BMX.

This would be the biggest adventure of his life. Also the most dangerous but in spite of that, he was going to enjoy every moment. Because when it was all over, his parents were going to ground him for *years*.

The Defense Force Heavy Weapons Unit had already arrived when the jeep carrying Hayata, Arashi, and Ide reached the perimeter set up around Osaka Castle. The soldiers waved them through and Hayata's heart broke a little as they zipped along the walkways normally filled with tourists, now empty. The carefully kept grounds hadn't fared well from the passage of tanks and armored vehicles. Hayata didn't want to think about the damage the Gomorasaurus could do, and not just to the landscaping.

The jeep driver stopped near the eastern end of the South Outer Moat and turned to Hayata. 'You sure this monster's going to come up here? Or are you just guessing?'

Hayata grimaced. 'We can't be absolutely sure of anything but it seems more probable than anything else.'

'But it could bypass Osaka Castle for a bigger "green space." East of here, there's a whole lot more of it—Hiraoka Park, Narukawa Azareus Park, orchards—' He pulled his phone out of his pocket and showed them an onscreen map.

'I doubt it can burrow that far without coming up at least once, probably more,' Hayata said. 'We didn't cripple it but we did hurt it badly enough that it isn't quite as strong as it used to be.'

'You think you can hurt it even more—enough to put it down before it goes any farther?' the driver asked.

'That's the plan.' Hayata glanced at Arashi and Ide. 'Insofar as there *is* one.'

'I don't suppose you can guess *where* it's going to come up,' said the driver.

'Your guess is as good as—' Hayata cut off, feeling the vibrations in the ground under the jeep. He looked at Arashi and Ide again; the expressions on their faces said they felt it, too. All three hopped out of the jeep, holding their plasma rifles at the ready.

'Can you feel what direction?' Ide said.

Hayata was about to tell him he couldn't when a geyser of dirt blasted upward in the Plum Grove, about a hundred meters from where they stood.

'I believe it's over there,' Arashi said, deadpan.

'You should get out of here,' Hayata told the driver, who didn't hesitate to do so. 'We line up along the Inner Moat. Ide, you stay at this end, I'll go up to where it starts to curve, and Arashi, you're in the middle. We do whatever we can to discourage this thing from stomping five hundred years of history into splinters. Stay on comms.' He sprinted away to the sound of armored vehicles rolling into position all around the creature. Reaching the bend, he spotted tanks in the area between the North Outer Moat and the East Outer Moat, aiming their cannons as they maneuvered.

One of them was obviously targeting the stump where the tail had been, or trying to. Hayata hoped a few more gunners had the same idea. Continuously hitting the open wound was probably the only way they were going to keep it off-balance long enough to kill it, or at least immobilize it, although the cruelty of the tactic wasn't lost on Hayata.

For what seemed like the thousandth time, he took a quick look at the pocket inside his jacket, just in case the missing Beta Capsule had miraculously returned without his noticing. Nope, still empty. As if he didn't know better than to hope for miracles, he thought. Just his being alive was plenty miraculous, and becoming Ultraman was even more so. But losing the Beta Capsule *again*? Not so much. In fact, that was pretty mundane, like a pen or a glove falling out of his pocket.

Only this time, it hadn't been *his* pocket. His alter ego was on the hook for this one. It had to have happened during the fight with the Gomorasaurus. For all he knew, it was why the creature had kicked his butt so thoroughly. Going back to search for it, however, was impossible—unless, of course, he wanted to tell Muramatsu what was going on.

Sorry, Cap, but this isn't really dereliction of duty. What happened was, I, uh, misplaced my special, uh, well, it looks like a penlight but the truth is, it turns me into Ultraman and I just need some time to find it. But don't you worry, as soon as I do, I'll come right back—fly right back—and you'll have nothing to worry about. That Gomorasaurus is toast.

Yeah, very plausible. Muramatsu would never think of sending him to a psych ward, he'd give him a commendation and maybe even a medal.

The screeching roar of the monster under the deafening bombardment by the Defense Force tanks jarred him out of his thoughts. The Beta Capsule was gone. Ultraman wasn't available, he wouldn't be able to make it to this party. Shin Hayata had to sub for him today and either he was up to the job or he wasn't.

He checked his plasma rifle; the charge stood at 85 per cent. That would also have to be good enough. Hayata made sure it was on maximum, then raised it to his shoulder, trying for one of its nasty enormous eyes.

Turn around.

The thought came unbidden from somewhere deep within him and with such startling clarity that he did so automatically. A little boy was standing in the middle of Gokuraku-bashi Bridge, calling out to him. He couldn't hear a thing the kid was saying but he recognized what he had in his chubby little fist.

It was like Hayata had wings on his feet—Osamu had never seen anyone move so fast except in sci-fi movies. The man scooped him up and carried him back into the empty parking lot on the other side of the moat.

'Ultraman dropped this!' Osamu shouted over the din of weapons fire, holding the secret weapon out to him.

'He sure did.' Agent Hayata was looking at him like he'd

done the best thing ever as he took it and tucked it into his jacket. 'How did you know to bring it to me?'

Osamu shrugged. 'I knew the Science Patrol could give it back to him.'

'I meant, how did you know to—' Hayata cut off. 'Never mind. You're a very brave boy, a real hero, to come all this way but you can't stay here, it's not safe. I have a new mission for you—run as fast as you can to the Kyobashi-guchi Entrance. Do you know where I mean?' Osamu nodded. 'The soldiers there will make sure you get home safely. Promise me you'll do that right now, without stopping or looking back!'

'Promise!' said Osamu. 'But—'

Hayata turned him around gently but firmly so he was facing away from the bellowing monster. 'Run *now* and *don't stop!* And *don't look back!*'

Osamu did as he was told, dutifully not looking back in case Hayata was watching. It wasn't until he reached the Higo Stone that real fear suddenly swept over him for the first time. It was like now that he'd finished the most important task of his entire life, he had been switched back to the regular world, a place where little kids didn't get to be heroes. When the soldiers rushed over to him demanding to know how he'd gotten there, all he could do was burst into tears.

They put him in an ambulance outside the perimeter, where a paramedic, or maybe it was a doctor, examined him and told him sternly that he was a very, very foolish boy and his parents were probably out of their minds with worry. She'd asked for their names but he'd been crying too hard to answer. Although he did finally find the nerve to look back, just in time to see Ultraman arrive, which dried his tears immediately.

Okay, Hayata thought, watching the boy pelt away from him, maybe miracles *did* happen, albeit in a complicated way, like origami. He'd never been able to get the hang of it himself but Fuji had a cousin who could turn paper into the most incredible things—swans, horses, flowers, dragons, even a samurai. He wondered as he raised his hand with the Beta Capsule if she'd tried to fold Ultraman yet.

This time his transformation came with a flood of images—the boy picking up the Beta Capsule, carrying it away, not telling anyone else about it, then deciding to bring it to him so he could give it back to Ultraman; sneaking out of his house for the very first time in his life, his long bike ride to Osaka Castle, making his way past the perimeter, and finally finding him. For a little kid, it was nothing short of superhuman.

And now it was up to Ultraman to make sure it hadn't all been for nothing.

'It's *him*!' Ide shouted into Arashi's ear as the Defense Force continued their barrage of the Gomorasaurus.

Irritated, Arashi was about to tell him to go back to his position when he heard it, too, above all the weapons firing, the sound of something strong, fearless, and invincible coming to help them.

'He always knows!' Ide crowed happily as he stopped shaking Arashi and hugged him instead.

'Yeah, he sure does,' Arashi said, plucking Ide's hands off himself before he could start shaking him again, the way he always did when Ultraman showed up. He touched his comm unit. 'Hayata, what's your twenty?'

No answer. Arashi beckoned for Ide to follow him as he headed for the spot where Hayata was supposed to be. They had gone only a few meters when the clouds of smoke became too much. Coughing, they retreated several steps just as the horned monster appeared, roaring in fury.

Despite the creature's rage, Arashi could see its movements were weaker and a bit clumsier than before. Blood loss and shock from losing a limb were taking their toll but the thing was still plenty dangerous. It staggered under the Defense Force onslaught but managed to stay upright, stepping over the Inner Moat as if it were a puddle, heading for the Osaka tiered tower.

Ultraman landed squarely on the Gomorasaurus's back and knocked it to the ground. In his earphones, Arashi heard Muramatsu give the order to cease fire; immediately, the weapons fell silent. The Gomorasaurus paid no attention, didn't even look at Ultraman as it stood up and lumbered toward the tower, more interested in getting at it than fighting. Probably because the tower didn't fight back, Arashi thought, watching the monster rake its claws from the top tier all the way down, cutting a wide swathe through five hundred years of history.

Ultraman seized the Gomorasaurus with both hands but

somehow it twisted out of his grip, turned its back to him, and began twitching its stump from side to side. Even now it didn't understand its tail was gone; Arashi felt another rush of intense pity for the creature. It was a poor dumb animal that just wanted to go home and baffled as to why every time it came up out of the ground, even more people were trying to kill it.

In a better world, things would be a lot different, Arashi thought, but here they all were in this one and luckily for them, Ultraman was in it with them. He kicked the monster's stump of tail, then jumped on its back as it fell forward, grabbed its horns, and slammed its head against the ground.

The Gomorasaurus's bellows took on a wailing quality but it managed to heave Ultraman off itself, then got to its feet and rushed at him, using its horns to flip him up and over its head. Before Ultraman could get up, it turned and came at him again, raising one foot to stomp on him. Ultraman swept its other leg out from under it and the monster fell heavily on its back.

It rolled over and sprang to its feet but before it could rush him again, Ultraman grabbed its head and threw the monster over his shoulder with almost perfect form. Roaring furiously, the Gomorasaurus pushed itself upright for another attack and Ultraman threw it a second time, and then a third.

As the monster lumbered toward him again, Ultraman took hold of its horns and yanked downward. Arashi heard a loud *crack!* and both he and Ide gasped as they saw that one of the horns had come off in Ultraman's hand, leaving a large bloody hole where it had been.

Wailing and trumpeting, the Gomorasaurus staggered around in a clumsy circle, swiping at the wound. Then it dropped down on the wreckage from the tower and started clawing through the debris, its movements even more labored.

Please, Ultraman, put it out of its misery, Arashi begged silently.

Ultraman turned toward him as if he'd heard Arashi's thoughts before he yanked the monster away from the rubble and threw it to one side. The Gomorasaurus pushed itself to its feet in the same moment that Ultraman positioned his arms to send a strong, white energy beam at it, blasting the creature right between the eyes.

Wailing, the Gomorasaurus went down on one knee, wavered, and pushed itself to stand… for all of a second. Then it toppled over onto its back. Arashi felt another rush of pity for the thing. It would have torn down the rest of the tower and gone on to level every other structure in the park before tunneling away to emerge somewhere else where it would wreak even more havoc, maybe adding a few thousand human casualties. Still, seeing it dead on the ground beside the partially demolished tower gave Arashi a profound sense of sadness.

As Ultraman took to the air, he saw the light in the center of his chest had gone from bright, steady blue to flashing red. Arashi stared after him, barely aware of Ide telling him he still couldn't raise Hayata.

* * *

'Agent Hayata!'

Osamu's voice cut through the cacophony of people cheering, laughing, and crying at Ultraman's latest victory.

Hayata was surprised to see the kid, but only a little. In fact, it felt right the kid would still be there, because he should be the one to bring Osamu home. Ultraman would want it that way. Although he was a little surprised Arashi volunteered to drive them.

'You know, Osamu,' Hayata said as they rode in the backseat together, 'Ultraman was able to defeat the Gomorasaurus because you helped him.'

'Is that true?' The kid's face lit up with pure joy. 'I really did help Ultraman?'

'Yes, you really did. But you have to keep that between you and him. It's your secret, yours and Ultraman's.' Hayata removed the comm unit from his lapel, adjusted it to send and receive on only one private channel, and pinned it to the kid's shirt. 'This is a special present from me. Now, whenever I need help from a monster expert, I can call you. And you can check in with me, although I won't always be able to answer right away.'

'I understand. I have a secret with Ultraman and this'— the boy tapped the comm unit with one finger—'is a secret between us—you and me.'

'But you have to promise me something,' Hayata added. 'And this is very serious. You must promise you won't just focus on monsters all the time, you'll work just as hard on all your other subjects at school. Okay?'

'I promise,' the kid said, looking from him to the comm unit and back again with an expression of joyful wonder.

'How'd it go?' Arashi asked him as he climbed into the front passenger seat after delivering the boy to his parents.

Hayata chuckled. 'Pretty well, considering. His parents are a lot more traumatized than he is. They didn't even know he was gone until they saw him on the news. A camera crew covering Ultraman's latest triumph managed to catch him sitting in the back of an ambulance, and then again when he ambushed me as I was coming out of the park. Apparently he's never sneaked out of the house before and they never thought he would. So that's gonna cost him.' He laughed some more. 'But I'll say this for him—he didn't try to sell them a tall tale about having to help us fight a monster.'

'Maybe because he knew they'd never buy it,' Arashi said as he started the car and pulled away. 'I think most kids know better than to try putting something like that over on their parents.'

'I'm sure you're right,' said Hayata. 'If he were my kid, I'd probably ground him till his wedding day.'

Arashi burst into hearty laughter; Hayata realized it was the first time he had heard him laugh in quite a while.

'Anything else on your mind?' he asked Arashi after a bit.

'The Gomorasaurus—' Arashi took a breath and let it out, keeping his eyes on the road ahead. 'It didn't come here on its own. We drugged it and hauled it out of its natural habitat just so a university professor could show it off at the International Expo. But he won't be doing that because the creature got loose and destroyed a park and a lot of property around it. And for an encore, it went on to damage a five-hundred-year-old landmark so badly that it might not be salvageable. All of that's on *us*—it's *our* fault. That creature wasn't a monster till we brought it here.'

Hayata shifted in his seat. 'I had no idea you felt so strongly about this,' he said. 'And to be honest, I didn't feel like celebrating when Ultraman finally put the Gomorasaurus down. I just felt sad.'

'This isn't the kind of thing the Science Patrol should be doing.' Arashi signaled a turn onto a street with a police roadblock; as soon as the officers saw their uniforms, they waved them through.

'Are you going to share your thoughts with Cap?' Hayata asked.

'Thought I would, now that it's all over.' Arashi made another turn at the end of the block and headed toward the Osaka HQ two blocks ahead of them. 'I just have to pick the right words.'

Hayata chuckled. 'It'll probably surprise the hell out of him.'

'Why?' Arashi glanced at him. 'Because I'm such a tough guy?'

'Well… aren't you?' Hayata said.

Arashi gave him another glance. 'Tough. Not heartless.'

Hope you heard that, Hayata thought at the Being of Light somewhere inside of him.

CHAPTER
SIX

The weeks following the events in Osaka found the whole country in the grip of Ultraman Mania. People were posting videos online of Ultraman in action, news programs were full of speculation as to where he had come from and how a superhero forty meters tall could manage to stay out of sight when he wasn't doing something Ultra-heroic. And it wasn't just Japan. The Science Patrol had been bombarded with interview requests from as far away as the US and the UK; Muramatsu had granted only a very few and referred the rest to the PR department.

The general mood at HQ, however, had been more subdued. Even Ide seemed to be less high-spirited than usual. But Muramatsu thought that was only to be expected. At his suggestion, Arashi had shared his feelings about the Gomorasaurus with the others. If a team was going to work together successfully, the members had to be aware of each other's state of mind and how each of them was affected by the job.

Muramatsu figured—hoped—the upcoming Aviation Show would lighten everyone's mood but Arashi and Ide surprised him by asking if they could skip it. Arashi wanted to get in some sharpshooting practice with the help of a simulation program that Ide had upgraded. Ide himself was hard at work on the space-flight simulator, adding emergency situations that, in the past, Muramatsu would have called far-fetched. These days, however, the bar for far-fetched was a lot higher than before.

The fact that they were acting on their own initiative made Muramatsu decide he would let them continue working uninterrupted. Instead, he sent Hayata and Fuji to be the Science Patrol's presence. Both of them were more than amenable and Fuji asked permission to bring her youngest brother, Satoru, with them.

Fuji had brought Satoru to HQ a few times because he wanted to join the Science Patrol when he grew up. Muramatsu had been impressed by the caliber of the boy's questions, and by the way he listened more than he talked, a quality Muramatsu associated with highly intelligent people. In any case, he was more than happy to grant Fuji's request. The Aviation Show had gone off without incident for over two decades. Afterward, he'd have Hayata fly the kid home and Satoru could go to sleep while visions of VTOLs danced in his head.

Muramatsu thought it would also do Hayata some good to be around the kid, to remember what it was like to see the world through young eyes. While everybody, himself included, had been affected by what had happened to the Gomorasaurus, Hayata had been different ever since the events at Lake Ryugamori.

At first, Muramatsu had thought it was all to do with the after-effects of physical trauma. Hayata had crashed first in an aircraft, and then only a few hours later in a submarine— who *wouldn't* need time to recover from something like that? But after Osaka, Muramatsu had begun to observe him a little more closely. It became plain to him his second-in-command had more on his mind than the rest of the team and, although he wasn't withdrawn or closed off, he wouldn't, or couldn't, talk about it. Not yet, anyway.

Well, whatever it was hadn't had an adverse effect on how Hayata did his job; in truth, he seemed to be improving all the time. Anything that didn't interfere with the job was technically none of Muramatsu's concern, which made him decide to leave well enough alone.

All he could do was trust that Hayata would reach out to him if he needed to.

Getting to watch the Aviation Show with his sister and Hayata was the best thing ever, Satoru thought as four jets executed a tricky turn and change in altitude. Instead of sitting in the stands with everyone else, he got to perch on the Science Patrol car like he actually belonged there, with no one crowding him or blocking his view or stepping on his feet as they went back and forth to the concession stand.

It made the whole day extra special. Even the popcorn tasted better.

Now he sighed happily as the four jets flying in formation finished their routine with a perfect series of loop-the-loops, their contrails leaving white circles in the blue sky.

'They're *amazing*,' he said.

'What's amazing is how much popcorn you can eat,' his sister said, laughing. 'I don't suppose I could have some?'

Satoru pretended not to hear and pointed at a very large passenger plane with an enormous wingspan. The tip of its right wing cut through the slowly dissipating rings left by the jets. As it flew in a wide circle above the spectators, it wiggled its nose and tail up and down, then did the same with its wings, and finally wagged its nose and tail from side to side, while the guy on the PA system explained to the crowd about pitch, roll, and yaw.

It was a demonstration Satoru had seen more times than he could count but watching such an enormous aircraft do it made it so much more exciting. He was definitely going to be a Science Patrol pilot when he grew up, he thought, as he scooped up another handful of popcorn.

How can someone who knows
so much
about these flying machines
be amazed by something
so ordinary?

Startled, Satoru jumped a little and looked around for

whomever had sneaked up on him but there was no one nearby except Akiko and Hayata. It had been a male voice, so it couldn't have been his sister. But it didn't sound anything like Hayata, either. Besides, he was standing on Akiko's other side—he'd have had to move to get so close. Satoru leaned forward to look at Hayata anyway. The man was watching the big passenger plane and he didn't look like he thought it was ordinary, or like he'd heard anyone say it was. Neither did Akiko. Why not?

Maybe they were ignoring it because it was just some guy acting like he was too cool to enjoy the show. Some people were like that, his mother had said. When they saw someone demonstrate a skill or a talent they didn't have, they'd disparage it ('disparage' was one of his new words for the week) because it made them feel small or because they hated not being the center of attention.

> Aircraft flying in the sky is nothing special—
> that's what they're supposed to do.
> It's all so dreadfully mundane, so normal.
> I can show you something
> a lot more interesting.

Satoru looked over his right shoulder, then his left as quickly as he could but still saw no one.

'What's wrong?' Akiko asked him. 'Did something sting you?'

'No, it's just—' He cut off, unsure. He'd never lied to Akiko or anyone else in the family and this didn't seem like a good time to start. But what if she didn't believe him? 'I heard a voice,' he said finally. 'But I don't know where it's coming from.'

'Ah.' Akiko nodded at him with a solemn expression. 'I know what that is.'

'You do?' said Satoru, amazed.

'Sure. It's popcorn overload. Makes the ears go wonky. You'd better let me eat the rest.' She giggled as she reached for the bag in his hands but then Hayata grabbed her arm.

'Look!' He pointed at something high in the sky.

For a few seconds, Satoru couldn't make out what Hayata was pointing at. As it came closer, he saw it had a long body, numbers on its side, and no wings at all.

'That's a *boat*!' he blurted. 'That's a *flying boat!*'

'An oil tanker,' Hayata added, sounding as shocked as Satoru. 'Everybody, in the car *now*.'

Satoru jumped into the backseat as his sister and Hayata took the front and watched open-mouthed as the tanker moved across the sky in no particular hurry, like this was something oil tankers did all the time. He could hear the engines now and wondered about the captain and crew. Were they still aboard? Did they know they were flying? Had they passed out from shock—or maybe lack of oxygen? The tanker didn't seem to be *that* high, but—

He heard the sound of jets approaching; the same ones that had performed in the air show were now chasing the oil tanker. Only the sky wasn't completely clear anymore. The rings the jets had made earlier hadn't disappeared completely, the remnants were clumping together, thickening into a big, shapeless cloud that swallowed up the jets as soon as they flew into them.

Now, isn't my power impressive, Satoru?

No, Satoru thought at the voice. *You're screwing up a great day for everyone here. I'm not impressed by anyone who would do something like that.*

The oil tanker exploded.

All three of them cried out in horror as fragments of machinery, metal debris, and crude oil flew in all directions. Satoru could hear the terrified screams of the people in the stands and the guy on the PA telling them not to panic, they were out of range and nothing would fall on them. That was obvious, Satoru thought; maybe the guy didn't understand how freaked out people were. He leaned forward to say something to Akiko about it but she shushed him because Hayata was on the car comm with Captain Muramatsu.

'Yes, it really was a flying oil tanker,' Hayata was saying, 'and it really blew up. You might as well let Fuji and me investigate before the rest of you come out here. There's a full disaster team onsite like always, they can handle procedure for now. I'll contact you when we know more, Cap. Hayata out.'

He turned to look at Satoru. 'I'm going to find a police officer to take you home. Your parents are probably already worried sick about you. And please, don't argue,' he added as Satoru opened his mouth to do just that. 'Okay?'

Satoru nodded reluctantly, sat back, and put on his seatbelt as Hayata started the car. But instead of moving forward, the car rose into the air, and kept rising.

I guess I should have said I was impressed, he thought.

* * *

'The tanker "fell up"?' Muramatsu said to Professor Iwamoto in the Operations Center.

'That was how all the witnesses described it,' Iwamoto said. The co-founder of the Science Patrol was a bit older than Muramatsu and even taller than Ide, and as far as Muramatsu could tell, completely unflappable.

'Eyewitnesses aren't always reliable, particularly in extreme situations,' the professor went on. 'But most of these eyewitnesses happen to be the tanker's crew. Now, I'm sure some of them were disoriented by their instantaneous relocation to the dock from the tanker. But all of them, without exception, described the tanker as falling up—not floating or levitating or flying, but falling.'

'What do you think that means?' Ide asked, looking fascinated.

'Well, what it tells me is, someone—some entity—was showing off with intent to intimidate,' Professor Iwamoto replied. 'But whoever's behind this stopped short of injuring or killing the crew. Whatever it wants with us—or from us—isn't something it's willing to kill for. At least, not yet.'

'What do you think that is?' Arashi asked.

'That's the question of the hour, isn't it?' Muramatsu said.

Ide gave a small, nervous laugh. 'Just guessing, I'd say it's not oil tankers. Have Hayata and Fuji reported in yet?'

Muramatsu shook his head. 'I tried them earlier but couldn't get through. There was a storm of interference, probably from emergency services and investigators from every government agency there is. As well as all the spectators trying to call their families and let them know they're okay.' Pause. 'We should get over there and see what they found out.'

'Before we do that, I have a better idea,' the professor said. 'One of our satellites has picked up on something that hasn't registered on any others yet...'

An hour later, Arashi and Ide had achieved escape velocity and had settled into orbit.

'I'm not so sure I'd call this idea of Professor Iwamoto's a "better one,"' Ide said, looking out at the void with apprehension.

'It's better than doing nothing,' Arashi said staunchly. 'And if there's something out here that our instruments can only detect from space, we'd better investigate.'

'I was just thinking that Hayata and Fuji might need our help,' Ide said.

'If they needed us, they'd have found some way to contact us,' Arashi replied.

'Okay, then maybe *we* need *them*,' Ide said nervously. 'Something really weird at twelve o'clock.'

'I see it,' said Arashi. 'It looks like a black cloud or blob.'

Ide looked from the amorphous darkness ahead of them to the scanner on the control panel. 'I really hope that's not a black hole.'

'Don't be ridiculous,' Arashi said, almost snapping at him. 'If it were, we'd have already been spaghetti-fied and sucked in along with the rest of the solar system, sun and all, and we wouldn't be having this conversation.'

'I know,' Ide told him, 'but hearing you say it makes me feel better.'

'Happy to be of service,' Arashi said gruffly, preparing to maneuver around the blob. 'Now *you* be of service and scan that thing, will you?'

'Already on it,' Ide replied. 'I think we found the missing jets from the Aviation Show, and more besides.'

'More?' Arashi looked at him, startled.

'A lot more.' Ide swiveled the screen toward Arashi so he could see the collection of jets and other aircraft hanging in the black as if they'd been glued there, then turned it back toward himself. 'I'm scanning them all but there are no signs of life in any of them. But no signs of death, either—no remains, no organic material present at all.'

'I want to think that's a good sign,' Arashi said, 'but I'd rather know where the pilots went, and if there's anything else in there besides aircraft, like another oil tanker or even some celebrity's yacht.'

'No. Something much worse.' Ide's voice trembled slightly.

Arashi made an impatient noise. 'What are you talking about?'

'See for yourself.' Ide enlarged the image on the screen and turned it back toward Arashi again.

What he was looking at was so out of place that at first Arashi wasn't even sure what it was. A second later, his brain resolved it as if it were an optical illusion and not an automobile with markings clearly indicating it belonged to the Science Patrol.

'Are you kidding me?' Arashi snapped. 'If this is your idea of a joke, Ide, I swear—'

'I don't joke in orbit.' Ide's voice was shaky now. 'That's really the car Hayata requisitioned for the air show this morning. And no, nobody's in it, alive or, uh, not.'

The damned car floated past like it was supposed to be there. Convenient orbital parking, daily/weekly rates available on request, oil tankers and other commercial vehicles extra. Arashi shook the thought away, changed course, and began preparing for re-entry.

'Don't you think we ought to scan for some kind of alien spacecraft?' Ide asked him. 'It's got to be nearby—'

'Nope,' Arashi said. 'I'm taking us home before we get added to the collection.'

'You think an alien's collecting humans?' Ide said.

'I don't know,' Arashi said, 'and I don't want to find out the hard way.'

'There was no organic matter of any kind in any of the aircraft,' Ide said to Professor Iwamoto and Muramatsu. 'No remains, not even trace matter on things the people aboard would have used or handled. It's like no humans were ever there. It's all… untouched.'

Muramatsu and Iwamoto exchanged looks.

'Do you think that's because everybody in them was vaporized?' Ide asked.

'That would still leave some residue,' Iwamoto said. 'Very little, but enough that the scanners would have picked it up.'

Ide opened his mouth to ask another question when the phone rang. The sound was so incongruous that for a moment, all four men just stared at it, as if the phone were a strange machine none of them had ever seen before. Then Ide answered it.

'What?' he shouted. 'Where?' He turned to the others. 'The Defense Force is mobilizing! Fuji's back! She's downtown and she's—' He looked at the receiver in his hand and hung up. 'She's got a big problem. *Really* big.'

Muramatsu made a mental note to take Ide aside when things quieted down and discourage him from making any more jokes at Fuji's expense. Then they arrived at the perimeter set up by the police where the Defense Force was assembling and Muramatsu could think of nothing except the cold hard lump of dread forming in the center of his chest. He jumped out of the car and ran through the ranks of the police and the Defense Force soldiers in the street, turned the corner and then stopped short, dumbfounded.

'Oh my God,' Arashi said from behind him. 'She's the size of Ultraman!'

'Is that who she is now?' Ide said in a plaintive voice. 'Is she Ultra Fuji?'

Giant Fuji stood at the end of the street staring straight ahead with a blank expression, seemingly oblivious to everything around her. Then she took a step forward and

Muramatsu heard the sound of weapons cocking or powering up as police and soldiers prepared to fire on her.

He turned around and waved his arms at them frantically. '*No!* Hold your fire! Do *not* fire on her, she's *not* a monster!'

The Defense Force commanding officer signaled them to obey as he moved to Muramatsu's side. 'Are you sure about that, Captain?' he asked quietly. 'I recognize her but maybe she only looks like your agent. It could be an alien trick.'

'It *could* be but it's *not*,' Muramatsu told him. 'I *know* her. The look in her eyes—'

'Oh, really now, Captain—' the commander started.

'I know what that sounds like,' Muramatsu said. 'I don't mean her appearance. I'm talking about how she *looks*—the way she *sees* the world. That's Akiko Fuji's gaze—I can tell.'

'It's true, Commander,' Ide added. 'That's not a robot or a simulation. I would know if it was. We all would.'

'Commander, can you fast-lift us up to the nearest rooftop?' Muramatsu asked before the other man could respond.

The commander nodded at a couple of his men. Two minutes later, Muramatsu, Arashi, Ide, and Iwamoto stepped onto the round platform of a fast-lifter and held onto the pole in the center as it rose eight stories. It deposited them on the roof of a building close to Fuji while Muramatsu prayed to the universe in general that she wouldn't choose that moment to turn her back and walk away—or worse, walk over the assembled armed police and soldiers. He hadn't expected Iwamoto to go with them and the professor looked more unsettled by the ride on the fast-lifter than he was by the sight of giant Fuji. Maybe this was his first time. If so, Iwamoto's inner ear was going to like the ride down even less.

Now that they were closer to her giant face, Muramatsu was even more certain this was the real Akiko Fuji. He couldn't imagine what could have done this to her and she was obviously in some kind of trance—hypnotized or possibly drugged—but there was no doubt in his mind that he was looking at the young woman who had joined the team three years earlier.

'Fuji!' he shouted. 'Fuji, it's Muramatsu! Can you hear me?'

She turned toward him but still stared straight ahead, silent and expressionless.

'Oh, come *on*, Fuji!' Ide waved his arms at her. 'It's me, Ide! You haven't forgotten me already, have you?'

Muramatsu thought he saw something in her gaze change when she heard Ide's voice but there was still no direct response.

'Why would someone do this to her?' Arashi said to no one in particular.

'Because this alien show-off isn't done showing off,' Iwamoto said, startling Muramatsu, who had all but forgotten about him. 'This is more intimidation.'

'But to what end?' Muramatsu asked.

Iwamoto's face hardened. 'It's showing us what it can do so that when it finally does get around to telling us what it wants, we'll gladly hand it over without a fight.'

'I'd like to know what it's done with Hayata,' Arashi said darkly. 'And Fuji's little brother.'

* * *

Satoru came to on a hard metal floor, to the sound of a deep male voice calling his name, telling him to wake up.

He pushed himself up to a sitting position and looked around. The whole dimly lit room was metal and empty, except for himself and some kind of console or control panel, where the voice was coming from.

'Who's there?' he asked. It was that same voice from before, not quite as distorted and no longer just in his head.

'Wake up, Satoru.'

'I *am* awake,' he said, slightly impatient.

'Well, then, stand up. Let me get a good look at you.'

Grown-ups were always doing that, saying they wanted to get a good look at you, he thought as he got to his feet, glancing around the metal room nervously, wondering what was going to step out of the shadows next. Where were Akiko and Hayata?

'Who's talking?' he said.

'I am.'

A silhouette melted into existence behind the control panel, a completely black shadow with two glowing blue lights that he knew were eyes, even if they were nothing like human eyes. This wasn't a human at all.

More light came up in the room and Satoru couldn't help gasping at the sight of the creature. It had odd silver and black markings on what seemed to be its face, and something like fins on either side of its head. Satoru backed away from it until he was up against the metal wall behind him.

'Is my appearance really so shocking to you?' the alien asked. Where its mouth would have been was a yellow light that flashed on each syllable. 'I've grown quite accustomed to yours.'

Satoru kept one hand on the wall, waiting to see what it would do with the control panel. Was this a spaceship, he wondered; were they in space? It didn't feel like that, it felt like they were on the ground. But where?

'My people are called Mefilas,' the alien went on, 'and we live far away, on the other side of the universe. From there, we can see just about every other inhabited world. We have technology you Earthlings haven't even imagined yet, which allows us to do so many things you cannot.'

Satoru didn't answer. The creature was about the strangest thing he'd ever seen but it sounded awfully familiar—i.e., like a grown-up who wanted something from him and expected him to cooperate.

'I've grown so accustomed to your appearance because I've been observing the Earth for a long time,' it was saying. 'You humans in general and you, Satoru, in particular. And as I watched this beautiful blue world—so much water!—I grew to want it.'

He straightened up, wishing Akiko were with him so he wouldn't have to face this creature all by himself.

'If I wanted to, I could take this world by force,' the alien continued. 'It would be easy for me to do so. But that would also be a contradiction of my most deeply held principles. I detest violence. However, you can help me avoid violence and the destruction and loss of life that comes with it. All you have to do is agree to just give me the Earth.'

So it was one of *those*, Satoru thought; greedy, selfish, and didn't care about what anyone else wanted or needed. It may have been an alien from another world but it was really nothing special at all. He sighed; the first time he'd ever met an alien and it was nothing but a big let-down.

'Surely you must see the wisdom in this,' the alien said. Its deep voice still sounded distorted and inhuman, like it was using a machine to talk but Satoru could tell it thought it was superior to him and every other human. 'After observing you for as long as I have, I know that you're a good Earthling, a wonderful human being who would never deliberately cause pain and suffering. All you have to do is say the right words and this world will be mine.'

The alien fell silent. Satoru said nothing, waiting for the alien to go on. The silence stretched and he realized the alien expected him to talk now, to be a 'good boy' and do as he was told. Some adults were like that (too many, actually)— would-be martinets who thought children were supposed to obey without ever thinking for themselves ('martinet' had been last week's new word). Instead, he pressed his lips together.

'Well, will you say the words for me?' the alien said finally. 'That's all you have to do. You say, "I will give you the Earth" and I'll take care of the rest.'

'Are you for real?' Satoru said.

'"For real"?' The alien sounded bewildered now. 'If you're asking if this is really happening, then yes, it is. It's not what you people call a "dream" or a "movie."'

'Yeah, I figured out that much,' Satoru said. 'And that's

why I'm *not* gonna say what you want. I'll *never* say that, not to you, or anybody else.'

He braced himself, thinking the alien was going to yell at him, make threats. But to his surprise, it remained calm, even friendly, which was actually scarier.

'Of course, I understand how you feel,' the alien said soothingly. 'No one wants to just hand over their home. But here—let me show you something.'

The room darkened except for a bright area directly in front of him, where he saw a 3D image of countless stars in amazing, vivid colors.

'The universe is infinitely vast and wonderful, with worlds that are full of beauty and wonder,' the alien told him. 'There are planets where, unlike here, there are no wars, no sickness or suffering, no pain of any kind. Where you can live for hundreds, even thousands of years and never fall victim to disease or want, never grow old, never die. You can leave Earth behind and live forever on such a world. It would be like going to heaven without having to die. Don't you want that? Doesn't that sound wonderful?'

If something sounds too good to be true, you can be sure that it is. Akiko had told him that and Satoru knew she was right.

'I'm just a kid,' Satoru said, 'but do you *really* think I'm *that* stupid? If those planets are so great, *you* go live on them. I'm staying here.'

Even before it spoke, Satoru felt the alien's anger pouring out of it in waves like heat, but it didn't frighten him as much as he'd have thought it would.

'You stubborn child! What's wrong with you? Why can't you just say, "I will give you the Earth" and be done with it? Don't you understand I'm offering you a life infinitely better than anything you could ever have here?'

'If that's true, why don't you go live on one of those better worlds yourself?' Satoru retorted. 'Why would you want the Earth instead? You've got nothing I want, and I'm not giving you *anything*, let alone a whole world. Especially not this *one*!'

Satoru felt a sort of jumping sensation and all at once he was in a different metal room. It was darker here and there was no gravity so he was floating in midair but now he seemed to have invisible cuffs gripping his wrists and ankles, keeping him in one place and forcing his arms and legs into awkward motions, like he was simultaneously swimming and riding a bike. His shoulders were uncomfortable after only a few minutes but they didn't hurt… yet.

The memory of when his sister had first joined the Science Patrol popped into his head. Their parents had worried for her safety, and they still did. *The situations you face as a Science Patrol agent can turn violent at any moment*, their mother had said.

Oh, Mummy, Akiko had replied, *situations don't have to be violent to be dangerous, and violence isn't the only way people can be hurt.*

Satoru hadn't understood what she'd meant at the time but he did now. No wonder his parents worried so much.

* * *

Hayata wasn't sure how long he'd been unconscious. He'd awakened to find himself in the dark, immobilized and unable to speak, or even make a sound. After a bit, the darkness had receded a bit, and an image of Satoru had appeared in front of him. The boy had been lying on the floor in a metal chamber. Still unable to move or call out to him, Hayata had been forced to watch as the boy woke up and the alien appeared.

What had happened next was completely unexpected. Hayata could hardly believe the arrogance of the creature but the way Satoru had stood up to it made him want to laugh in the alien's face. And then all at once, he was standing in front of the alien doing exactly that.

'Laughter?' the alien said, astonished. 'What do *you* have to laugh about, Ultraman?'

'The joke's on you, Mefilas,' Hayata said, hiding his surprise that it knew he was Ultraman with a contemptuous laugh. 'You thought you could get a child to give you the Earth—literally—just by promising him the equivalent of toys and candy. Well, you thought wrong—so very, very wrong!'

'What *are* you?' the alien demanded. 'Are you a human or an alien?'

'I'm both,' Hayata said, reaching into his jacket for the Beta Capsule. 'I was put here to protect humans from those like you, who think they can just take whatever they want from the innocent and the good.'

Hayata raised his arm but before he could touch his thumb to the button, he *stopped*.

He tried to will his thumb to move a centimeter, even just a millimeter, but he was cut off from any and all physical control of himself, as if he were both locked in and locked out at the same time. He could still feel his body, the position of his arms and legs, the hard metal floor under his feet, even the air on his face and hands, but that was all. His access to motion had been canceled.

'Something wrong, Ultraman?' The alien laughed at him. 'This joke's on *you*.' It did something to the control panel in front of it. 'How do you feel now, Satoru? Do you really want to spend the rest of your life flailing in this weightless chamber? Is the Earth really worth that much to you?'

Only the alien heard Satoru's answer and Hayata could tell it wasn't what it wanted to hear. 'What a horrible, stubborn child!' it fumed and touched the control panel again. 'Akiko Fuji—rampage!'

To Muramatsu's horror, Fuji raised her fist over the building opposite and then brought it down hard, smashing through concrete, steel, and glass. Had the police had enough time to evacuate that building?

Her expression still blank, Fuji brushed away the top three stories as if they were crumbs on a table. Something inside the structure burst into flames and thick black smoke poured into the air. Muramatsu caught a whiff of burning carpet that made him wince but Fuji seemed oblivious to it as the noxious clouds roiled into her face. Raising her fist again, she turned toward Muramatsu.

The horror was in how peaceful she looked, Muramatsu thought, as if she were doing some mundane chore while she thought about something else, like a book she'd read or what she was going to have for dinner or how she planned to spend her day off.

Where does a forty-meter-tall Science Patrol agent shop on her day off?

Anywhere she wants.

Muramatsu told himself to get a grip.

'No, Fuji, *stop*!' Ide was yelling in a high desperate tone. 'Wake *up*! I know you're in there, you'd *never* hurt *us*, I *know* you wouldn't!'

Ide's voice pulled Muramatsu back to the moment and as it did, he saw he wasn't the only one who had responded to it. Fuji's face remained impassive but Muramatsu could tell she had heard him, too. Something in her eyes changed and her fist stopped its downward motion three meters directly above Muramatsu's head.

Then they heard weapons fire from the street.

Muramatsu tapped his comm unit twice to access the Defense Force channel. 'Commander! Cease fire, *cease fire!* That's Agent Akiko Fuji, she's *not* an enemy!'

'She's not acting like a friendly,' the commander replied. 'She could take out every building on the block and start on the next before emergency services get here.'

'She could but she won't,' Muramatsu said earnestly. 'Tell your men to stand by and *hold their fire!*' He turned to look up at Fuji again. 'Fuji, please. You know who we are. *See us.*'

Fuji blinked and her expression suddenly shifted from

blank to bewildered. She had heard him, Muramatsu thought, practically giddy with relief. He started to say something else to her and then saw only billowing clouds of black smoke where she had been standing.

'What the hell?' Ide said as they all looked around. 'Where'd she go?'

'Whatever put her here took her away,' said Professor Iwamoto. 'But you were starting to get through to her, Captain. I suggest we get down to ground level.'

'I agree,' Muramatsu said. They boarded the fast-lifter again and, as Muramatsu expected, the professor enjoyed the trip down even less than the trip up. As they stepped off the platform onto the street, the air was filled with the sound of deep, contemptuous laughter. The police and the Defense Force soldiers hit the ground, clutching their weapons. Muramatsu motioned for Ide, Arashi, and Iwamoto to get low as well, though he remained standing.

'Who's there? Show yourself!' Muramatsu demanded.

The giant figure that appeared wasn't human but Muramatsu recognized the V-shaped head, the unblinking eyes, and the claw-like weapons grafted to its arms. They all did.

'A Baltan!' Arashi exclaimed and for the first time ever, Muramatsu could see how frightened he was at the prospect of having an alien take him over again, forcing him to move at its will, speak its words, think its thoughts. A few moments later, he covered it with a scowl and started to stand up. 'Back for a rematch, eh? Okay, let's go right now, you and me—'

'Oh, stop, Arashi,' said the disembodied voice. 'There's no need for us to fight. But if there were—'

Another giant alien was looming over them now with a single eye at the front of its head; it glared down at them from a lumpy but otherwise featureless head. A moment later, a third alien giant appeared, this one with a wide, flattened head and tiny features in the center of its silvery face. None of them spoke or moved. They didn't have to.

'All right, how about *you*?' Muramatsu hollered, hoping he didn't look as shaky as he felt. 'How about *you* show *your*self!'

'There's no need for you to see me, Captain Muramatsu,' said the voice. '*I* can see *you*. So can the Baltan, the Zarab, and the Kemur. You know only one of them but they are all under my command. If I really wanted to fight, I could simply order them to attack and they would not hesitate. It would end very badly for you and your so-called Defense Force.'

'Oh, yeah?' Arashi said, moving to stand beside Muramatsu. 'We've kicked alien ass before, we can kick theirs!'

'And we can kick *your* ass, too!' Ide added, standing up on Muramatsu's other side. 'All day long!'

Muramatsu swallowed hard, hoping his agents' bravado wouldn't goad the alien into acting on its threats.

But the alien only laughed again. 'You humans—you're ants who believe your small garden is the whole world. Don't overestimate yourselves.'

Ide opened his mouth to respond and Muramatsu elbowed him in the ribs, hard.

'Unlike you, I abhor violence,' the alien went on. 'I'm

not here to challenge your might—I'm here to challenge the human spirit.'

'Huh?' said Ide, rubbing his ribs.

'What do you mean?' Arashi asked.

'You'll see,' the disembodied voice assured them. 'Very soon, Satoru will accede to my request.'

One by one the giant alien figures disappeared and Muramatsu realized they'd been looking at holograms. It made him even angrier. 'Wait!' he yelled. 'Where *is* Satoru? *What* request? Tell us—*what request?*'

No answer now, not even laughter. The cold hard dread was back in the center of Muramatsu's chest, larger, colder, and heavier.

'Cap.' Ide put a hand on Muramatsu's shoulder. 'Whatever's going on here, remember—Satoru isn't just any random kid, he's *Fuji's* brother. That counts for something.'

Muramatsu nodded, even though none of them had any idea what the alien wanted with the boy. What was this request it was making of him? What had happened to Fuji? And Hayata—if he was still alive, where on Earth was he? Was he even on Earth at all?

Were any of them?

'Captain Muramatsu!' The Defense Force commander materialized beside him. 'Our satellites have picked up an alien signal in the mountains in Takizawa and preliminary scans show the presence of a previously unknown underground structure with numerous live humans inside. I'm betting those are your agents and the missing pilots of the planes your people found in orbit. I've already sent out an airborne squad for recon and, I hope in cooperation with you, a rescue op.'

'Cap, we definitely don't want to miss this party,' Arashi said.

'Contact the hangar staff,' Muramatsu said to Ide. 'I want our two fastest VTOLs prepped and flight-ready by the time we get back to HQ.'

Satoru was covered with cold sweat, and his muscles and joints ached like never before. He'd thought if he could relax and not resist the invisible wrist- and ankle-bonds that were forcing his limbs to move, his shoulders and knees and back wouldn't hurt so much. But even weightless, he couldn't seem to manage it.

If he got out of this, Satoru thought, he was going to be a lot more sympathetic to his parents when they complained about aches and pains. If he got out of this, listening to his parents complain about anything would be like the most beautiful music ever. If he got out of this. *If.*

'Tell me, Satoru, how do you feel now?' asked the hateful alien voice. 'You can make this stop. You could be the ruler of an entire planet a hundred times more wonderful than Earth instead of being a puppet in pain. All you have to do is say the words. Just say them. *Say* them. Say them *now!*'

A number of extremely rude answers occurred to him, in the kind of language his parents would have punished him for. Somehow it seemed almost as important not to resort to that as it was for him to refuse to give the Earth to the alien.

And what could have made the alien think *he* could give him the Earth, anyway? He was just a *kid*, for crying out loud, he didn't own the Earth or any part of it, not even his own backyard. Grown-ups owned land, that was one of the grown-up things they did. Why didn't the alien just go ask them for the Earth?

This had to be a trick, a con game. People could lose their life savings by getting tricked into visiting a fake website or even just saying the wrong thing to a scammer on the phone. Only, this was an alien con game, so it was a whole planet up for grabs.

'Satoru! I know you're awake and you can hear me. Will you give me this world? Answer me now!'

'No!' He could hear his breath coming in loud gasps, almost like sobs. 'This world belongs to all the humans on it. And it belongs to the animals—mammals and reptiles, the birds and the fish, even the bugs! You're *none* of those things! That means you're *nothing* on this world, not even a *bug*!'

The alien didn't respond but he knew he must have made it even angrier; he felt the invisible cuffs around his wrists and ankles tighten.

After Iwamoto's experience with the fast-lift, Muramatsu hadn't expected the professor would want to join them for the assault on the alien presence in the mountains but he did. Arashi volunteered to take him; Muramatsu and Ide would partner up in the other VTOL. Ide looked a bit surprised and Muramatsu realized he'd thought he'd be flying a third aircraft.

'I need you on instruments and weapons,' Muramatsu told him. 'We want to avoid destroying the alien's spacecraft before we can get all the humans out safely and the best way to do that is to force it out into the open somehow. There's no way I can do that and fly at the same time.'

'You got it, Cap,' Ide said, looking mollified.

The Defense Force was circling the location of the alien vessel when Muramatsu and Arashi caught up with them. The guy flying point had managed to scan it thoroughly enough to find the spacecraft's exact location in one of the more scenic valleys.

'Ide, tell me there aren't any climbing expeditions in the vicinity compounding our problems,' Muramatsu said as they neared the target.

'It's our lucky day, Cap,' Ide said, peering through the binocular eyepiece of a newly upgraded scanner built into the cockpit controls. 'Well, *relatively* lucky. No innocent bystanders. Or by-climbers. Even the animals are giving the place a wide berth. I guess they can sense something there that doesn't belong.'

'I know how they feel,' Muramatsu said wryly. He opened a channel to the Defense Force mission commander to confirm their arrival.

'We'll try targeting the area around the alien ship,' Commander Okada told Muramatsu. 'If we shake things up enough, we might get it to pop itself right out of the ground. But if it fires on us, we'll have to answer in kind.'

'Just keep in mind there are Defense Force pilots being held prisoner inside along with a number of civilian flyers and crew members. And the one minor among them is a Science Patrol agent's brother, which means he's family to us as well. We want to handle them all with care and bring everybody home alive and unhurt.'

'We'll do everything we can to avoid casualties, Captain, but this is one twisted alien. Claims to hate violence but there's at least one former building downtown that serves as evidence to the contrary. And if that giant lady shows up and goes all King Kong on us, we're gonna have to take her out.'

'There's no giant lady swatting at planes yet, Commander,' Muramatsu said sharply, praying the alien wouldn't decide to make that its next move. 'If we're going to come out of this with all our people safe and alive, we can't be getting ahead of ourselves. One crisis at a time, okay?'

'Copy that, Captain. Okada out.'

The reply made Muramatsu think of Hayata, still conspicuous by his absence. The alien hadn't even mentioned him, as if Hayata hadn't been with Fuji and Satoru when it had taken them. Maybe the alien had decided everything would be easier if it got rid of him first. Then it could do whatever it wanted to Fuji and her brother without Hayata putting up a fight. It was a horrible, unwanted idea that made horrible, unwanted sense.

No, Muramatsu told himself firmly. Until a body turned up, the only thing he could say with any certainty was that Hayata was missing, period, end of, nothing more. His own words came back to him: *One crisis at a time, okay?* He sighed.

'Problem, Cap?' Ide asked, looking up from the eyepiece.

'Just a thought I can't un-think, but nothing we're not already dealing with,' Muramatsu said. 'Find us a spot clear enough to serve as a landing zone. I'd like to be on the ground and ready to breach as soon as that alien tin can shows itself.'

'Your wish equals my command,' Ide said. 'Feeding LZ coordinates to the control panel in three... two... *there* it is.'

The top of the alien spacecraft broke through the surface just as Muramatsu set the VTOL down. In the next moment, the first Defense Force harrier jet exploded.

Ide wanted to disembark immediately and head for the alien vessel with weapons blazing but Muramatsu made him wait. Moments later, they saw the spacecraft shudder up out of the ground completely.

At first, Muramatsu was afraid the alien had decided to take to the air for an old-school dogfight. But it stayed where it was and when scans showed its engines had shut down altogether, Muramatsu and Ide armed themselves with Spider Shots and plasma rifles and disembarked. By then, two more Defense Force harriers had been lost but Arashi was doing his best to draw the alien's fire and keep it distracted.

'I think that's the fanciest flying I've ever seen Arashi do,' Ide said to Muramatsu as they sheltered under a large tree and watched their teammate elude a fiery energy beam from the saucer. 'And I bet he's never had more fun.'

Muramatsu nodded absently, thinking the professor had probably used up the onboard supply of airsickness bags. He tapped his comm unit. 'Muramatsu to Arashi. Can you draw fire to the west-south-west?'

'Sure thing, Cap,' Arashi said lightly, as if Muramatsu had asked him for a cup of tea. 'What's the plan?'

'Ide and I are about to breach from the other side. It'd be good to keep the attention of whatever's on defense away from us.'

'No problem, Cap. The professor says there are four possible ways in and you're nearest the easiest one—the exterior airlock door's gone, you can probably break in with a crowbar.'

'Thanks for the tip, Arashi,' Muramatsu said. 'Don't get your ass shot off—that's an order.'

'Copy that. Arashi out.'

'Did you hear all that?' Muramatsu asked Ide.

'Every word,' Ide replied. 'Let me go first and see if I can jimmy the door or pick the lock or pry the hinges or whatever it takes to jack an alien's ride.'

In spite of everything, Muramatsu chuckled. 'If you can't do it in thirty seconds, come back and we'll go to Plan B.'

'There's a Plan B?' Ide asked innocently, then dashed away, zigzagging across the thirty meters from the tree to the airlock in a demonstration of broken-field running worthy of an American footballer hell-bent on winning the Super Bowl. Muramatsu half expected him to do a victory dance when he reached the featureless airlock door. Instead, he put his hands all over it, feeling for something that might be a lock or even just a handle. After thirty seconds, he stood back, put his plasma rifle on a lower setting, and gave each corner a short blast.

For a moment, nothing happened; the plasma blasts hadn't even left scorch marks. But just as Muramatsu was about to order Ide to come back, the door suddenly fell inward. Ide gave him a thumbs-up and stepped inside.

Muramatsu ran a different zigzag to the vessel and caught up with Ide in a narrow, dimly lit corridor that apparently ran the circumference of the spacecraft. The inner walls were festooned with piping in complex coils that Muramatsu first took for metal but discovered had a texture like stiffened fabric. Part of the life-support system, he wondered, or just the alien equivalent of spinning rims?

'Cap, in here!' Ide beckoned from an open doorway a few meters farther on. Muramatsu joined him to find Hayata standing motionless in the middle of a metal chamber, one arm raised, and his face set in an expression of resolute determination Muramatsu was more than a little familiar with. Nearby was something that looked like a control panel, possibly a navigation console. Muramatsu had a quick look at it; whatever it was, it didn't look like it was for piloting or navigating. But then, this was alien technology; all bets were off. For all he knew, it was making the alien's dinner.

'Cap, he's frozen or something,' Ide said, waving one hand in front of Hayata's face.

Muramatsu looked over at him. 'Suspended animation, maybe.'

'But why?'

'Maybe the alien was planning to take Hayata with him when he left.' He hurried over and stopped Ide as he was about to try picking Hayata up. 'If that even is Hayata. It might not be—it could be a decoy or it could be booby-trapped. For now, don't touch him.'

Ide looked from Hayata to Muramatsu and back again. 'Cap, I know that face. That expression, I mean—it's totally Hayata.' Before he could say anything else, something hit the spacecraft, making everything shake including Hayata, who might have fallen over if Ide hadn't held him upright.

'Captain! Ide!' The voice was muffled but they both recognized it. 'We're *here*! *In here*!'

'Fuji!' they said in unison and started looking around frantically. Muramatsu went back to the control panel. The array of buttons and switches were unmarked and unlabeled; it was foolish to touch them when he had no idea what any of them might do—

There was another mighty impact that shook the saucer even harder. Again, Ide kept Hayata from falling over while he called out to Fuji. *Desperate times*, Muramatsu thought and began pressing buttons, hoping none of them triggered the spacecraft to launch or, worse, self-destruct.

Abruptly an image appeared overhead showing Satoru and Fuji floating side by side in midair, their arms and legs flailing in awkward movements.

'Can you hear me?' Muramatsu shouted. 'Where are you?'

'There's a switch *under* the console,' Fuji panted breathlessly. 'Find it, help us!'

Muramatsu felt around under the control panel and found something that felt like a switch. Hoping it was the right one, he flipped it. He heard an electronic *ping!* and suddenly Fuji and her brother were standing beside the still-unmoving Hayata.

Fuji ran to the control panel and looked it over, one hand hovering above the buttons. Then she pressed several of them quickly. 'If that doesn't release the door, you'll have to shoot out the controls.'

'What door?' Muramatsu asked as she grabbed her brother by one arm and headed for the doorway.

'To where the pilots are being held,' she said. 'Come on, we have to hurry, some of them are injured!'

'What about Hayata?' Ide asked, still holding Hayata upright by his shoulders.

Fuji stopped short, looking devastated. 'I don't know what to do about him,' she said unhappily. 'I watched the alien use that console a bunch of times for different things. Maybe it thought that just because it could turn me into a giant zombie, I wasn't smart enough to figure out what it was doing. Not the first time some jerk underestimated me.' She gave a short, humorless laugh. 'But it never unfroze Hayata so I can't, either.'

Ide was horrified. 'Cap, we can't just *leave* him here! We never leave *anyone* behind!'

'We've got injured people we need to get out first, then we can come back for him,' Muramatsu said. *I hope*, he added silently, glancing back at the motionless figure as he shoved Ide ahead of him into the corridor after Fuji. To date, he'd never been forced to leave anyone behind and he wasn't sure he could live with himself if he did.

But that wasn't the question of *this* hour. Right now, he had to follow his own advice: one crisis at a time.

At last, Hayata thought as they all disappeared into the corridor. He waited to see if they would come back the other way but they didn't. *Please, let it be because they found a different way out and not because the alien caught them.* Fuji had told Satoru she'd seen something like twenty pilots crammed into a metal cell only a little bit larger than a walk-in closet and the alien had shown no particular concern for their comfort or needs. Four of the Defense Force pilots had been injured when the alien had popped them out of their cockpits; none was critical but if they didn't get treatment soon, they would be. And that would be *his* fault.

Well, not exactly. Once the alien had realized he was Ultraman, it seemed to lose all interest in the other humans, except for Fuji and her brother. The hell of it was, he'd already have rescued all of them if Ide had not kept him from falling over.

On the other hand, if he had fallen over with Ide and Muramatsu in the chamber with him, Ultraman's secret would have been revealed. Which was actually a lot less important than the fact that they and all the other humans would probably have been badly injured or worse when his transformation blew the spacecraft to pieces. As soon as they all got clear, he could fall over freely, without misguided interference from Ide or anyone else.

Another blast hit the spacecraft, followed by two more in quick succession. Hayata felt the floor tilting under him. This was it, and not a moment too soon. The Being of Light within him was sure now that all the humans were safely out; Hayata could only hope it was true.

Still, it seemed to take forever before he was finally, finally, finally toppling forward, watching the floor rush up to meet him.

Muramatsu and Ide moved everyone to a safe distance from the spacecraft before starting back for Hayata. But they'd barely taken a step when the spacecraft exploded into fragments with a force that knocked them all down. As the Science Patrol members checked themselves and everyone else for any additional injuries, Muramatsu flashed on another group of people in a different forest. Ide caught his eye and he knew from his expression the younger man had remembered Lake Ryugamori, too.'

'We thought Hayata was dead back then,' Ide said in a low voice. 'But he wasn't. So maybe—just maybe—maybe…' His voice trailed off.

Muramatsu swallowed hard. 'Maybe his run of fantastically good luck isn't over yet.'

Ide's expression said he wanted Muramatsu to say it again with more confidence. Then suddenly his face lit up. Muramatsu turned to follow his gaze and saw Ultraman launching himself straight up out of the crater where the spacecraft had been.

'How does he—' Ide started.

'Because he's Ultraman,' Fuji said, hugging her little brother. 'Did you forget already?'

'No, I just like hearing it,' Ide said happily, as the rest of the captives cheered and shouted with joy.

Later, Hayata thought, he could tell his teammates that once again, Ultraman had showed up just in time to save him. Right now, however, he had to have a few words with Mefilas and they weren't going to be the ones it wanted to hear.

He found the alien waiting in a rocky area well away from the burning wreckage. The Being of Light within Hayata knew it had used the last of its ship's energy to enlarge itself to Ultraman's size. Had the alien done that because it was absolutely convinced Satoru would give the Earth over to it, he wondered, or was it trying one last desperate trick?

'Hello, Mefilas,' he said, landing lightly in front of it.

'Are you going to fight me for this world?' the alien asked him with open belligerence, as if it were hoping for exactly that. Underneath, however, Hayata could sense its apprehension.

'Not if you just pack up and go home,' Hayata replied. 'Would you like me to fling you across the universe or do you have an escape pod hidden nearby?'

'My escape pod is waiting in orbit,' said the alien. 'Have

you been spying on me, Ultraman? That's not worthy of either of us.'

'I don't have to spy on you. I know all about you and your plans for the Earth,' Hayata told it. 'There's nothing wrong with your world, and even if there were, you still wouldn't have the right to take this one.'

'But I like this world better. I *want* it.'

'Only because you can't have it.' Hayata chuckled.

'I can have any planet I want,' said the alien and Hayata could feel anger emanating from it in waves. 'No one can stop me, not the Earthlings and not you.'

'Are you sure?' Hayata felt the Being of Light's sense memory take hold, moving his arms to let the Spacium running through his body gather in his fingertips. He drew his arm back and hurled the whirling circle of the Ultra Slash at the alien.

The alien thrust both fists forward and ropes of white energy snaked through the air to collide with the Ultra Slash in an explosion that left only a few fast-fading sparks in the air.

A memory from the Ultra came to him: *A cowardly opponent is often quite resourceful, and thus very dangerous.*

Was this alien cowardly? Was it claiming to hate violence simply because it was afraid of any lifeform it couldn't bully? If so, he couldn't let it find out that his powers had a time limit.

Seeing that the alien could assume Ultraman's proportions had been a shock for Muramatsu; finding out it could fly, on the other hand, was practically anti-climactic. Of course it could fly, and he didn't doubt it had a number of other tricks in its repertoire.

But so did Ultraman, Muramatsu thought, watching the giant arms go into a position he recognized as the mirror image of what he'd seen before—this time, the right arm made a horizontal support for his upright left hand. Bright white arrows poured from his arm, flying straight at the alien.

But the alien met them with a jagged bolt of energy, neutralizing them in a blinding explosion that sent Ultraman plunging toward the ground, making Muramatsu and everyone else cry out in horror. Ultraman managed to touch down safely, crushing a tree but not endangering any of the humans. For several moments, he stayed where he was, one hand to his head as if he were waiting for it to clear.

Get up, Muramatsu begged him silently. *Please. Get up.*

Hayata could sense Muramatsu's desperate plea even at a distance. As he started to get up, a wave of dizziness hit him and he had to wait for it to pass.

Pull it together, he ordered himself. *We're on a clock here, remember?*

And now the alien was on the ground again, too, and coming toward him. He tried standing up again and the alien kicked him in the face.

Landing on his back, Hayata rolled over and stood up just as the alien went to throw itself on top of him. It hit the ground a fraction of a second too late and Hayata gave it a hard blow to the back. The alien jumped to its feet and Hayata grabbed its head for a quick throw. It tumbled forward, stood up, grabbed Hayata's arm as he reached to throw it again, and it threw him instead.

Hayata let himself roll with the momentum so that he was out of the alien's reach when he got to his feet. His arms were already moving into position for the Spacium Beam, the power racing through his body toward the point of contact between his left arm and his right hand, so much more forceful than the Ultra Slash. The alien wouldn't be able to counter or neutralize this one. The Spacium Beam was going to cut straight through—

'Stop.'

Still in position, Hayata managed to hold the energy back before it could blast out of him, curious as to what kind of trick the alien was trying now. Whatever it was wouldn't stand up to the Spacium Beam.

'Enough of this, Ultraman,' the alien said. 'We could fight for days and nothing would come of it. We're evenly matched—neither of us would win.'

Now that was an interesting point of view, not to mention unexpected, Hayata thought. Meanwhile the Being of Light within him was remembering that cowards were masters of rationalization. They were especially good at getting out of a fight they knew they were about to lose.

'I wanted the spirit of the Earth,' the alien went on. 'And it was denied me, even by a child.'

'The spirit of the Earth isn't something you get just by asking someone to hand it over. In case you're wondering,'

Hayata said, amused in spite of the situation. 'Your failure to understand this is why the Earth will never be yours.'

'Ah, but I'm not giving up,' the alien said. 'This won't be my last visit. Someday I'll come back and I will find a human to hand the Earth over to me. You'll see.' There was an electronic hum and the alien disappeared as the orbiting escape pod located it and removed it from the surface of the planet to make the long trip home.

'Don't overestimate yourself,' Hayata said as he sensed the escape pod making one last slingshot circuit of the Earth before it zoomed away into the void.

The alien probably would come back, he knew, but that was a problem for another day. For now, it was gone and his Color Timer was still blue. Today was a good day, with good results all around, he thought as he took to the sky.

Satoru was startled when Hayata touched his shoulder but immediately threw both arms around his neck in a joyful stranglehold of a hug. 'Hayata-san! How did you escape from the spaceship?' he asked.

'Ultraman, of course,' he said, laughing a little as he peeled the boy's arms off himself one at a time. 'You must have seen him. He always seems to show up just when we need him the most.'

'Copy *that*,' said Arashi. 'But I don't understand why he just let that alien go. I thought for sure he was going to kick its ass but then—nothing. They just stopped fighting. I've never seen him do anything like that before.'

'You weren't as close to them as I was,' Hayata said. 'Ultraman had an alien-to-alien conversation with it and I guess it decided it would rather go home than keep on fighting. And Ultraman, good guy that he is, decided to let it go. This time.' He clapped a hand on Arashi's shoulder, gesturing at their surroundings with the other. 'And hey, look at all the scenery that didn't get flattened or blown up or burned to a crisp in the big fight they didn't have.'

'Oh, that's definitely a good thing,' Ide said, 'but you have to admit it's kinda strange. Or maybe it only seems that way because I never heard Ultraman talk. What did he sound like?'

Caught by surprise, Hayata hesitated. What did Ultraman sound like? He hadn't thought he sounded any different than when he was in regular human form but they'd probably never believe Ultraman's voice was just like his own.

'A lot of it was in an alien language and I couldn't understand those parts,' he said slowly, trying to come up with something plausible. 'But he sounds very…' He hesitated again. 'Very reasonable. The way you'd expect a good guy to sound, like someone easy to talk to. I could pick that much up in any language.'

Arashi nodded. 'That makes sense.'

Before anyone could think of any more questions, Hayata turned quickly to Satoru and said, 'Ultraman also told me you're the real hero of the day.'

'He did?' Satoru stared at him, open-mouthed.

'Yes, he did, and I agree,' Hayata said. 'You stood up to an alien bully who tried to intimidate you into handing over the whole world. And no matter what that alien did, you stood your ground—even when you couldn't actually stand.'

'Yeah, well, that part was pretty scary,' Satoru said. 'I wasn't sure Fuji and I were going to live through it.' He took a breath. 'I still can't figure out why it thought I could give it even the tiniest little bit of Earth, let alone the whole thing. I don't have that kind of power.'

Yes, you do, Hayata told him silently, *you just can't see it that way. For you, the world is a place to coexist with other people, not some kind of shiny toy or trinket only made for your amusement.*

But he had a strong feeling that the Being of Light inside him would have said this was an understanding Satoru had to come to on his own.

Aloud, Hayata said, 'You'd be surprised.'

'Must be an alien thing,' Ide said.

'No, not really,' said Hayata, chuckling.

Ide was unmoved. 'Okay, then, *some* aliens.'

'How are all the pilots, Cap?' Hayata asked, turning to Muramatsu.

'All alive and accounted for,' Muramatsu replied. 'There's a transport coming to pick them up. As soon as they're all safely aboard and on their way to a hospital, we can go back to Headquarters.'

'You really *did* do well, Satoru,' Arashi told the boy, then looked around at the group. 'And I'm really glad everyone's all right.'

'I'm relieved that everything worked out for all of us,' Ide said. 'Even Fuji's diet worked. She lost *tons* of weight.'

Fuji stared at him in disbelief. 'Seriously, Ide? A *diet* joke? At a time like *this*?'

For a moment, no one dared to speak or even breathe as she glared at him. Hayata didn't know what was going to happen next but he was pretty sure even Ultraman wouldn't be able to get Ide out of it.

Fuji's face suddenly broke into a broad grin. 'Gotcha!' she said, laughing.

Ide let out his breath in a relieved rush. 'Jeez, don't scare me like that,' he moaned.

'Sorry,' Fuji told him, looking smug now, 'but you had that coming!'

Everyone else laughed with her, mostly out of relief.

'Although I've gotta admit, that one was pretty funny,' she added, which made everyone laugh harder.

'Thanks,' Ide said, his face slightly apprehensive. 'I think.'

'You're welcome,' Fuji said primly, then looked up at the sky. 'Hey, everybody, the transport's here. Let's go home!'

CHAPTER

SEVEN

The awareness that he was actively waiting for something came to Hayata so gradually, he had no way to know exactly when it started. He only knew the anticipation had been building steadily, filling him with a nervous energy that never burned off completely, no matter how busy he was. And these days he seemed to be busier all the time.

Every morning he awakened feeling as if his blood were humming in his veins like Spacium when Ultraman called it into action. He would dive into a full day of patrolling, research, consultations (on both sides of the table), paperwork (which was now mostly paperless), and as much vigorous exercise as he could squeeze into his schedule. But when he fell into bed so exhausted that he was asleep as soon as his head hit the pillow, he would still be thrumming with the gut certainty that something was on the way.

Intuition told him it was going to be something highly

personal but at the same time significant, something that would affect not only himself but the people closest to him. It would also be inevitable. He just didn't know what it would be.

There was plenty to keep him and his teammates busy— Science Patrol agents were never at a loss for something to do and the days were never completely predictable, especially now that Ultraman had taken up residence on the planet. There were all kinds of new creatures to learn about, a good many of them as gigantic as Ultraman, and the dangers they posed weren't confined to one area, or even one country.

Ide had wondered if the influx of monsters was somehow connected to Ultraman. *Maybe they followed him here*, he'd suggested. *Or maybe he's actually attracting them somehow.*

Fuji had asked him if he was blaming Ultraman for the various giant creatures that had fallen out of the sky or come up out of the ground or the ocean to menace the population.

I don't mean it that way, Ide had said. *I'm not saying Ultraman's to blame for all the attacks. Remember the Gomorasaurus?*

Yeah, Arashi had said with solemn certainty, *that one's definitely on us. And I don't think the creatures on Tatara Island were bad-tempered tourists whose bus broke down, either.*

But not the Baltans, Fuji had pointed out.

No, they just barged in uninvited and tried to take over, Ide had agreed. *Luckily, Ultraman got here before they did. Otherwise the population of Earth would all have center parts in their heads.*

Very true, Arashi had said. *But I don't think they'd have come here at all if they'd known Ultraman was here to protect* us. *Remember, we had alien visitors before Ultraman got here. That's why the Science Patrol was founded in the first place.*

Yeah, but I don't think aliens visited us as often, said Ide, and they'd all admitted he was probably right about that.

Was *that* what he was sensing, Hayata wondered, the approach of another alien or group of aliens wanting to invade and take over? Or maybe just wanting to make contact?

Wouldn't *that* be nice—to see a fleet of aliens appear in the sky and then discover all they wanted to do was get acquainted. Hayata concentrated but still couldn't sense anything one way or the other. The Earth was part of an unremarkable solar system orbiting an unremarkable star in the galactic boondocks, where visitors were so few and far between that for millennia, most of the inhabitants had believed they were alone at the center of a very small universe revolving around them.

Hayata tried to take time whenever he could to contemplate the question of whether he was sensing the imminent arrival of an invading force but nothing came to him. If past events were any indication, the Earth could expect some kind of alien visit in the near future. It might or might not be hostile but, given their previous encounters with aliens, the odds didn't favor a peaceful visit from happy-friendly lifeforms looking to trade household hints, recipes, or nifty new apps.

Eventually, it occurred to him that the feeling leaking through from his alter ego had to do with something beyond human understanding.

The notion came to him on an afternoon when the subject of aliens was the furthest thing from his mind. All his attention was focused on the Science Patrol's latest acquisition, viz, the brand-new armored heavy-lift helicopter. Professor Iwamoto and Ide had designed it together, in between monster attacks and alien invasions, some of which had delayed production. But here it was at last, off the drawing board and out on the helipad, all done up in Science Patrol orange and white, with the comet logo prominently displayed on either side.

The original idea had been Ide's. He had started talking about it right after the Gomorasaurus had torn up a good part of Osaka. Anyone who held still for longer than a minute risked having to hear about Ide's concept for the world's most wonderful airship, strong enough to lift Ultraman yet maneuverable enough to fly rings around anything else in the sky. He might have still been waxing rhapsodic about it over tea in the break room except Professor Iwamoto had overheard him bending Muramatsu's ear about why they just had to make room in the budget for a new helicopter and it had inspired the professor to join the cause.

Ide and the professor had put their heads together in the lab and for a while, they were practically inseparable. Muramatsu had worked extra time in the lab into Ide's schedule, after determining that Hayata, Arashi, and Fuji were okay with covering some of his usual duties.

'I figure he'll either get it all out of his system, or he'll ask for a transfer to Research and Development,' Muramatsu had told Hayata as they were preparing for the annual performance evaluations.

'What if he decides he wants to be in R&D full time?' Hayata had asked him.

Muramatsu gave a resigned shrug. 'Then we'll have a vacancy to fill and there's no shortage of candidates among this year's STEM grads. We'll just have to see what happens.'

'You sound like you're pretty sure he'll want to stay with us,' Hayata said.

'I am,' Muramatsu admitted. 'I don't think he'd be happy as a full-time lab rat. He wouldn't have you, Arashi, and Fuji to play with.'

Hayata was jarred out of the memory by the sound of the emergency signal, three short buzzes that meant he had to return to HQ immediately, maintaining radio silence. He'd always thought 'radio silence' was such a quaint term, with a charming retro finish to it like icing or fondant. Now it was just unsettling.

Hayata found the rest of the team along with Professor Iwamoto waiting for him in Operations, and none of them looked happy. If whatever he'd been waiting for was here, he thought, looking at each solemn face in trepidation, it wasn't anything good.

Muramatsu looked at Iwamoto, who cleared his throat. 'For several days, I've been tracking—well, *trying* to keep track of a signal traveling inward through the solar system, toward the sun. The problem was, the signal kept disappearing and reappearing without warning.'

Hayata nodded, wondering if there were any alien signals that *didn't* disappear and reappear.

'I called in some help,' the professor went on, glancing

at Ide. 'Between the two of us, we developed a receiver sensitive enough that we wouldn't keep losing the signal. After we refined the results, I contacted several of the larger observatories to confirm the data but none of them could confirm anything.'

'Because they detected nothing,' Ide put in. 'They all claimed we had overly sensitive equipment picking up on space flotsam.'

Space flotsam? Hayata wondered if that was a standard observatory term or a clever term Ide had come up with. It sounded very much like the latter.

'You would think the events of the last decade or even just the past year would have made certain organizations more open to the possibility of—' Professor Iwamoto cut off, looking peeved. 'Well, never mind. I've asked the captain to bring you all in because there have been a few rather crucial developments. First of all, this isn't actually one signal but at least two dozen, individual but related, possibly more. Almost certainly more, I'd say.' His gaze went to Ide, who took over from there.

'The second one is, we finally got a visual,' Ide said. 'And these things coming at us are all—and I swear to all of you, I'm *not* making this up—they're all flying saucers. Like classic UFO saucers.'

Hayata blinked at him. 'That's so… surreal.'

Arashi hit his forehead with one hand. '*That's* the word I was looking for and couldn't think of till you just now said it. It's surreal. Like Salvador Dalí's melting clocks.'

Everyone stared at him.

'What?' he said. 'I'm a *deep* tough guy and sometimes I can't think of the right word. *Surreal.*'

'It's more than surreal,' Professor Iwamoto said grimly, looking past Fuji to the monitors on the wall behind her. Normally they displayed data or video from various satellites but now they were all dark. 'It's also problematical, several times over.'

Fuji went to the console and started to run diagnostics, only to have them cut off after a few seconds and start the routine over again.

'I've seen them glitch—everything glitches sooner or later,' Fuji said. 'Sometimes one or two of them will go blank for as long as half a day. But I've never seen them all do *that* before.' She glanced back at Professor Iwamoto and Muramatsu. 'Something's knocked out our satellites. We're blind and deaf—and it's not just ours, it's everybody else's, too, all of them, worldwide.'

'Is it permanent?' Arashi asked.

'I hope not,' Fuji replied. 'Because that's *everything*, from weather satellites to spying eyes masquerading as streaming entertainment. And just FYI, it's only the important stuff that's scrambled. Streaming entertainment is the only thing that's still working—everyone can still binge-watch their favorite box sets and movies and the umpteenth reboot of so-called *Real Housewives*, but we're blocked from interrupting those signals or using them to carry extra data. As you can see, I can't even get a diagnostic to run. We're locked out.'

'Is there any way you can hack back in?' Muramatsu asked.

'I can try. But it'll take some time,' Fuji said. 'I'll have to build a super-firewall to counter the alien disruption and I need someone to fend off any new cyberattacks while I work.' She sighed. 'If only Ultraman were an Ultra Hacker.'

Dr. Iwamoto cleared his throat. 'Well, I may not be an Ultra Hacker but back when I was a student, I did a little creative computing here and there. It was a while ago but I think I remember enough to assist you. Just tell me what you need and I'll see what I can still do.'

Fuji beamed at him, grateful and slightly surprised. 'Then grab yourself a terminal, Professor, and log in. We've got a lot to do.'

Just as Muramatsu turned to Arashi, the phone rang. Hayata picked it up. 'The Hawaii Observatory has confirmed thirty unknown spacecraft have entered our atmosphere about a hundred kilometers north of them,' he said as he put the receiver down. 'They're all currently headed our way. ETA, forty-five minutes, probably sooner.'

'Cap, I've got one ear on the Defense Force,' Fuji said. 'They're mobilizing an airborne welcoming committee, to try to keep them over the water and out of our airspace.'

'That's our cue,' Muramatsu said. 'Fuji, you and the professor keep trying to get our satellites back. Everyone else, with me. And yes,' he added to Hayata, 'let's see what our new armored heavy-lifting airship can do.'

Minutes after they were in the air, Fuji contacted both the Science Patrol and the Defense Force commander with a new and rather startling message about the saucers.

'Fuji, are you sure?' Muramatsu asked her, incredulous.

'I'm positive, Cap,' came the slightly breathless reply. 'I've recorded everything so you can see for yourself: except for the largest one, all of those "saucers" are unmanned. They're drones, presumably controlled by an AI.'

'Then the Artificial Intelligence must be in the largest saucer,' Ide said.

'That seems likely, although I can't say for certain,' Fuji said. 'But I *can* tell you the largest saucer is in communication with a third party, which is already on Earth. Lying in wait, I'd say, and cloaked so well, we never knew it was here. It only broke cover when it started communicating with the big saucer.'

The Defense Force was already firing on the saucers, which returned fire, causing one of the DF aircraft to burst into flames as it went into a sharp dive. The pilot was able to eject but barely a second later, there was a blinding light where he had been, leaving only a few rags of parachute material to flutter away on the wind.

'Fuji, we want our satellites back but I want whatever's controlling these things from the ground located five minutes ago,' Muramatsu said grimly as he took out two saucers, one after the other.

'So do I, Cap,' Fuji replied.

In Operations, Fuji had replaced some of the offline satellite feeds with live video from the Science Patrol aircraft, including the new airship, although seeing what had happened to the first pilot who'd ejected made her wonder if there was a little too much visual coverage. Poor Professor Iwamoto still looked like he was going to be sick.

'Professor,' she said, keeping her tone light but brisk and all-business, 'would you mind going down to the break room and bringing me a few packages of seaweed crackers? I need to keep my blood sugar up to concentrate.'

'Of course,' he said, still looking a bit sick but also relieved. 'I'll be as quick as I can.'

'Thanks,' she said. 'I'm on the verge of getting one of these satellites back.'

'Great!' he said and hurried out.

Iwamoto had to pause at the top of the stairs to collect himself. He'd seen much more graphic video but the sight of that lone pilot dangling from a parachute one second and then just *gone* the next had hit him in a way he hadn't expected. Perhaps because he had known it was happening in real time, while he was watching. Or maybe he was just getting old and tired and soft, he thought. Thank heavens Fuji had understood he was in difficulty and given him a reason to leave the room to collect himself. She reminded him of a younger Muramatsu in that way and he decided to put a line-of-duty mid-action attaboy—or in this case, attagirl—in her file.

And while he was at it, he thought, feeling a little better, he should grab the prototype of the weapon he'd been working on. The lab was on the same level as the break room so it wouldn't take but a few extra seconds. He straightened up and trotted down the stairs, reached the bottom, then realized the break room was another floor down. *Should have taken the elevator,* he thought as he rounded the bend for the next flight.

It was his last thought for some time.

Fuji's claim that she was about to restore a satellite link had been deliberately over-optimistic; she had simply wanted to get the professor out of the room so he could maintain his dignity while he pulled himself together. As it turned out, however, she was closer than she had realized to restoring communications with the geostationary satellite directly above HQ. Now she could see she might even have it back online by the time Iwamoto returned with her crackers, or at least very soon after. She could hardly wait to tell him.

Fuji locked her focus on the last bit of resetting and reprogramming, refusing to let herself glance away even briefly until she had it. Touching the comm unit on her lapel, she swiveled around in her chair, intending to call the professor, and nearly jumped out of her skin when she found him standing behind her.

'Oh! I didn't even hear you come in,' she said. 'I did it, Professor! I got one of the satellites—'

He stared down at her stonily and, without a word, started to put his hands around her neck.

'Excuse me!' She tried pushing him away but he was much stronger than he looked. It was as if he didn't even feel her hitting him as he took hold of her throat, pressed his thumbs against her windpipe and squeezed. All the while, his expression never changed from that cold stare, as if she were nothing to him, not even alive.

The next thing she knew, she was lying on the floor, dazed, while he aimed a strange-looking weapon at the console. There was a burst of sparks, and she saw small tongues of flame. The air was starting to turn gray.

She had to get up and call for help, Fuji thought, she had to get up. Then there was nothing.

'Hayata to Captain Muramatsu, private channel.'

'Go ahead, Hayata,' came the reply.

'What do you think the point of all that was?' Hayata asked him as he followed the VTOLs back to the hangar.

'Question of the hour—I was about to ask you the same thing,' Muramatsu said with a grim chuckle. 'Taking out this so-called invading force was too easy. Thirty of these things attack but they don't make much effort to evade fire? What do you suppose that's about?'

'I don't know but the big one got away,' Hayata said. 'I'd like to review the video when we get back to HQ to see where it went.'

Ide broke in on the general channel. 'I can't raise Fuji or Professor Iwamoto. HQ comms are offline.' Before anyone could respond, an emergency alert went off, indicating a fire in the Operations Room.

'Okay, I'm pretty sure we now know why we were inveigled

into fighting an invasion by a bunch of drones,' Hayata said wryly. 'But I guess they didn't expect us to shoot them all down this quickly.'

'Arashi, Ide, you two get back to HQ and find Fuji and Iwamoto—'

'Copy that, Cap,' Arashi said, on edge as well as gruff.

Ignoring the smoke-filled air, Ide and Arashi took the stairs two at a time up to Operations, where they found Fuji on the floor near the burning console. Ide picked her up and he and Arashi dragged her out of the room toward the stairs.

'Fire suppression should have kicked in already!' Arashi said, looking around. 'I don't know what's wrong with it.'

Fuji coughed a few times and opened her eyes. 'Iwamoto,' she said weakly. 'He tried to strangle me. He destroyed the console—' She began coughing again.

'We've got to get her out of here,' Ide said and bent to sling her across his shoulders in a fireman's carry.

'You take care of Fuji. I'm going to kick the science out of Iwamoto's ass.' Arashi ran down the steps ahead of them.

Hayata and Muramatsu reached the front entrance just as Arashi burst out of the door in a cloud of smoke.

'Iwamoto's a saboteur!' he called to them as he raced past. 'We've got to stop him!'

'Where's Fuji?' Muramatsu shouted after him.

'I've got her,' said Ide from behind him, coming out of a

swirl of gray smoke with Fuji across his shoulders. They all moved away from the building so Ide could put her down on the lawn and bring her to, cradling her head gently in his arms as she started to cough.

'Iwamoto did this?' Hayata said, staring in horror at the darkening bruises on Fuji's neck.

Ide nodded. 'She's going to be okay,' he said, 'but he could have killed her.'

'And if Arashi catches up with Iwamoto, he'll kill him,' Muramatsu said grimly. He stood up to look around.

'You two better find him first,' Ide said. 'We'll be okay here.'

Hayata and Muramatsu ran after Arashi, spreading out to flank him where he stood on a grassy hillock, turning around and around in angry bewilderment.

'I could've sworn he came this way,' Arashi said to Hayata. 'He couldn't just disap—' Something caught his eye and he rushed down the hill to a newly paved footpath. Hayata and Muramatsu followed at a run as Arashi tore across a flat stretch of lawn in pursuit of Iwamoto, who had burst from cover behind a low hedge. The professor was heading toward an open field of uncut grass next to the engineering annex at a speed no one would have believed he was capable of, his suit coat and shirt tail flapping wildly behind him.

Because that wasn't Iwamoto, Hayata realized, pushing himself to run faster in the hope of reaching the impostor first. But anger had turbocharged Arashi; before Hayata could close the distance between them, Arashi sprang forward in a wild, flying tackle, landing on top of the professor.

Arashi scrambled to his feet, yanked Iwamoto up by the

front of his shirt, and gave him a right cross hard enough to put him face down on the grass. Muramatsu caught Arashi's arm before he could haul the professor back up and do it again, and pushed him at Hayata, who restrained him so he couldn't throw any more punches.

'That's enough!' said Muramatsu.

'He tried to kill Fuji!' Arashi shouted angrily, struggling to get away from Hayata so he could hit Iwamoto again.

Muramatsu paid no attention. 'Professor, are you all right?' He rolled the man over. 'I'm so—' He cut off as he saw what was really lying on the grass.

The creature pushed him away with a rubbery thick-fingered hand and stood up. The irregular blob of a head sticking out of Iwamoto's suit had a single eye in front and another on its right side. It should have looked ridiculous—the anatomy made no sense to Hayata but he supposed any creature with shapeshifting abilities didn't need a body that made sense—it could just morph into one that did.

As it reached for Muramatsu with its chunk of a hand, Hayata drew his sidearm and fired an energy blast at the middle of its head, just below its single eye.

'*Zetton*,' it said in a low, inhuman growl.

'What?' demanded Muramatsu. 'What did you say?'

'*Zetton!*' it growled again, and then vanished.

'What do you think *that* meant?' Arashi asked tensely. Before anyone could answer, they all felt the earth under them begin to tremble.

'I guess we're about to find out,' Hayata said, nodding at the open field ahead of them. Part of the ground was rising up in an enormous hump. After a few moments, the soil broke apart, revealing the large saucer-shaped spacecraft tearing through the long grass and uprooting a couple of small trees as it emerged from the ground.

A hatch on the top of the saucer opened and a blue-green sphere began to form. Hayata raised his weapon and took aim, watching as the sphere grew larger and more substantial. But before he could squeeze the trigger, the sphere exploded in a burst of blinding light.

'Zetton.'

The word rolled through the air like thunder while Hayata blinked up at the gigantic alien that stood in front of the spacecraft. The creature had yellow markings on its deep gray body, thick limbs, paddle-like hands, and what looked like antlers atop its head. Where its face should have been was a long vertical split showing a gelatinous blob of yellow. Was that some kind of sensory organ, Hayata wondered, or possibly even a weapon?

He fired on it. The energy beam managed to burn the monster's thick hide, but only a little, not nearly enough to do any real damage.

'Give me that,' Muramatsu said, taking his sidearm from him. 'Iwamoto just contacted me—the *real* Iwamoto. He's still inside HQ and he says he's got a new weapon—'

Suddenly Hayata flashed back to Lake Ryugamori, with Ide asking him, *Are you the* real *Hayata?*

There's no real or fake. There's only one me.

Then he heard Arashi say, 'I'll get him,' as he turned to run back into the burning building.

'Go with him,' Muramatsu told Hayata and turned to take aim at the giant alien.

Hayata trotted after Arashi, letting him enter the building before ducking around a corner and grabbing the Beta Capsule from his jacket. Arashi could handle rescuing a man from a burning building but Muramatsu was badly outmatched. So was the rest of Japan.

No more humans would be injured today, Hayata promised his teammates silently as he soared into the bright blue sky. By the time Fire and Rescue arrived, he would have this monster down for good, so they could determine how much of the Science Patrol complex they could salvage and how much had to be rebuilt. With any luck, they'd get most of it finished before some new menace dropped in from outer space or popped up from underground or congealed in some mad scientist's secret laboratory.

As he descended behind the alien, his Ultra instincts told him to spin and his Ultra vision let him see the Catch Rings forming above the alien's head. They sank down, pinning its upper limbs to its body in a way that reminded Hayata of a straitjacket. He could sense the way the alien was resisting, not knowing that pushing against the rings would only make them tighten even more. After it used up all its energy trying to free itself, he could stuff it back into its saucer and hurl it back into space—

Abruptly, there were several fiery red flashes and he had a glimpse of energy blasts coming from the creature one after another. In the next moment, Hayata found himself on the ground, enveloped in a noxious red cloud while the alien came toward him, now free of the rings.

Fuji felt as if her neck was one big bruise. Now she knew what it was like to get strangled, she thought. Not that she'd ever wanted to know, nor was it a sensation she cared to endure again. Tomorrow, she'd have a Technicolor neck and she'd have to cover it up with scarves for a while. At the moment, however, she was less concerned with her own pain and discomfort than she was with Ultraman. Seeing him produce energy rings to trap the alien and immobilize it had made her want to cheer, sore throat notwithstanding.

But any joyful noises she might have made had been stifled by the sight of the alien blasting Ultraman with bolts of energy the color of blood and fire. When the red cloud had enveloped him, he'd actually disappeared and she'd been afraid that he had disintegrated and the 'cloud' had been all that was left of him. But seconds later, he'd reappeared, confronting the alien in a combat stance—of course. Because Ultraman never failed them. Never.

Unconsciously holding one hand protectively over her neck, she watched the alien take a few steps toward him, its arms raised menacingly.

In the next moment, it popped out of existence.

Fuji jumped, letting out a startled cry. Before she could panic, however, the alien reappeared several meters behind

Ultraman. But if its plan had been to sneak up behind him, it was out of luck—Ultraman sensed it and turned to face it as it sent a series of concentrated energy bolts at him.

Ultraman sidestepped the blasts easily and responded with a gesture that hurled a brilliant white circle at the alien's antlered head. The alien held its position and Fuji braced herself, sure the circle would reduce it to a pile of parts. Instead, it was suddenly encased in a strange shimmer, mostly transparent and barely visible. Ultraman's bright white circle fetched up against it, bounced off, burst into millions of tiny sparks, and disappeared.

'Uh-oh,' Ide said, his arm tightening around her waist a little.

'Ultraman can—' she started as Ultraman rushed forward. Her voice died in her sore throat as Ultraman seemed to bounce off the alien and tumbled backward in an awkward somersault.

The creature pounced on him, grabbed his neck with both of its thick, rubbery hands, and squeezed. Fuji drew back, unconsciously shielding her own neck as she tried to will Ultraman to break the alien's grip and get up.

Except he didn't. The alien was kneeling on his chest, its rubbery hands still gripping Ultraman's neck while Ultraman twisted and squirmed, trying without success to break its hold on him.

Please, Ultraman, please, she thought at him. Tears were running down her cheeks; she smeared them away with the side of one hand, not caring if the rest of the team saw. *Ultraman, please, get up—*

The light in the middle of Ultraman's chest was flashing red now.

Hayata finally broke the alien's hold and shoved it away. Moving quickly, he rolled to his feet, his arms slipping into position for the Spacium Beam. As the energy rushed through him, he could feel it amplifying his life-force. The world around him became *more*, better and brighter as the Spacium Beam burst from his crossed hands with every bit of Ultra strength he had.

And... nothing.

Unharmed, the alien extended both arms toward Hayata, sending waves of power at him. They crashed into him, one after another after another after another, sapping his strength with every blow until he heard something crack. It was a very small sound but at the same time, it was fiercely, painfully, shockingly loud, earsplitting, unbearable. Something deep within him gave way.

When his vision cleared, he was lying on the ground, looking up at the alien looming over him. The sunlight started to dim and while he could still sense his friends, they seemed to be almost as far away as the Land of Light.

'Did that monster just *kill* Ultraman?' Fuji asked incredulously.

'I don't know but I'm gonna kill it right back,' Arashi promised, drawing his sidearm.

'Here. Attach this to the end of the barrel.' Professor

Iwamoto held out something that looked like an oversized dart. 'Aim for dead-center mass.'

Arashi looked at it dubiously.

'It's only a prototype,' the professor added, 'but what have we got to lose?'

Arashi took the device from him and clicked it onto his weapon. Keeping low, he approached the alien still towering over Ultraman's motionless form. *It must believe it won*, he thought and then jumped a little when he felt a hand on his shoulder. He turned to see Ide beside him; he gave Arashi a nod of encouragement.

Taking a breath, Arashi turned back to the alien, aimed at its center, and squeezed the trigger.

Professor Iwamoto's prototype disappeared into its body and for one terrible moment, Arashi was afraid it had passed all the way through the creature without it even feeling it. But a fraction of a second later, the alien began to rise into the air. Six meters above the ground, it stopped, shuddering, and he could hear it gasping for breath.

He was wondering if he should try the Spider Shot as well when the alien exploded.

Crouching on the grass, he and Ide watched in astonishment as chunks of its body rained down all around them.

'You *did* it! You saved us!' Ide crowed, alternately shaking him and hugging him.

Arashi managed to push him away so he could stand up and the solemn expression on his face cut Ide's celebration short. 'Not quite all of us.' He turned to look at Ultraman, still lying motionless across the field.

* * *

If this was what he'd been actively waiting for, Hayata thought, it was one hell of a disappointment. In fact, it was *the* biggest let-down of his young life, which he could feel fading out with the light from his broken Color Timer. And this time there wasn't a thing that *anyone* could do to save him. Both he and the Being of Light within him had gone down for the count together and there was no possibility that either of them would be getting up again.

Dammit. Why had the big moment he'd been anticipating so intensely turned out to be the last day of his life? How the hell could this have happened?

He waited but there was no answer. Of course not. He was only human and humans didn't get answers like that.

Still, wouldn't the Being of Light merged with him have known what was coming even if he hadn't? But then, after a lifetime lasting thousands of years, wouldn't you feel like you'd had one hell of a ride that had fulfilled every last bit of your potential? That would make the last day of your entire life no big deal, just the end.

Hayata couldn't say the same. The last day of his entire life was a very big deal indeed. The day he'd originally thought was his last had turned out to be the first day of his brand-new life. It had started with his vanquishing a demon-like monster who disrupted peace and harmony in the universe and continued on a high-energy trajectory of monsters, alien invasions, and giant rampaging beasts that had never eased off.

But then, he had understood the gift of life had not been simply for his benefit. Without his alter ego, the human race might have survived but its numbers would have been greatly reduced, and the planet itself might have been a desolate, smoking ruin. This was why he had done his best to be worthy of this extraordinary second chance. Still, he was also who he had always been: Shin Hayata, and as such, he was only human. He couldn't help wishing his time on Earth had lasted a little longer—no, truth to tell, a lot longer.

The voices of his Science Patrol teammates came to him then, seemingly from very far away but as clear as a starry winter night.

'Look!' said Muramatsu, and Hayata pictured him in the sunlight, a safe distance from HQ, the fire dying now that Arashi and Ide had activated the exterior controls for the fire-suppression system. 'It's Ultraman!'

'Another one?' Fuji said incredulously. 'How many are there?'

In his mind's eye, Hayata could see her shading her eyes from the sun, wisps of her shoulder-length hair blowing a little in the breeze, partially obscuring the marks on her neck, which were starting to become darker. Arashi and Ide were standing on either side of her, closing ranks protectively. He could also see the bruises on Arashi's knuckles after he'd punched out the fake Professor Iwamoto for hurting Fuji, while Ide still kept one arm around her, ready to hold her up if she felt weak, with no thought of any more jokes. It gave him an intense longing to be back among them.

There are many more Ultras, Hayata told Fuji silently, even though he knew she couldn't possibly hear him. *They live in Nebula M78, on a world of light. And now one of them has come to take Ultraman home.*

This was it, *this* was the thing he had sensed was on its way to him, Hayata realized—another light being, here to save the one merged with him. They would be going back to their life in Nebula M78, while he… wouldn't.

Well, it had been borrowed time the Being of Light had given him and now it had to be repaid. But any disappointment he felt was tempered by a rush of gratitude for the experience of being Ultraman, of being able to save his friends, to help people in ways beyond anything he'd ever imagined.

The Being of Light within him enhanced his senses even more, allowing him to see the Ultra who had come for him as it generated a red sphere very much like the one from Lake Ryugamori. For a moment, he wondered again if this were just a wish-fulfillment dream, a last gasp from his dying, addled brain. Then he felt himself being lifted up and it was exactly like that night, when the Being of Light had merged with him.

Ultraman. Open your senses to me. See me as I am.

Ultraman saw and Hayata saw with him.

I am Intergalactic Defense Force member Zoffy of Nebula M78, and I have come to bring you home with me.

The voice was more than a voice and Hayata could feel the Being of Light within him answer in kind.

Zoffy, I'm glad to see you but my life isn't just mine alone. If I leave this world, a human will die.

Mild bewilderment emanated from the Ultra. *But have*

you not fought enough for this world? Surely the human will forgive you.

It was true; Hayata *would* have forgiven him without hesitation—if there had been something to forgive. But the new life he'd been given had been filled with purpose and the power to turn good intentions into reality, and all while remaining himself, Shin Hayata. That wasn't something to forgive, that was a *raison d'être,* a cosmic win, an actual state of grace. He couldn't believe he'd been so lucky.

Which is why I cannot sacrifice him, replied the Being of Light. *Honor demands that I remain here on Earth and continue to work for peace, and enlightenment.*

Hayata sensed resistance from the newcomer. *Peace on any world has value only if its people come to understand it for themselves. And they can only achieve enlightenment by their own efforts—no one can do it for them. You can't remain here forever.*

If this turned out to be just a dream after all, Hayata thought, he hoped he could remember every detail after he woke up. He wanted to remember how it felt to be part of something far greater and even more wonderful than the world he knew.

So be it, Zoffy. I give Hayata my life. Let him go on living.

Astonished bewilderment came from Zoffy in waves, strongly enough that Hayata felt their turbulence like an incoming storm-tide. *But that means your life will end. Does it not matter to you that you will die?*

Zoffy, I have lived for millennia. But these humans—their lives are so short, not even the blink of an eye on the world

275

of light, and Hayata is still very young. He has barely had a chance to live and I will not sacrifice him.

You will not have to, Ultraman. I have life enough for both of you.

Hayata felt an outpouring of gratitude from himself and the Being of Light.

Prepare now to separate from—

There was a fleeting but intense sensation that was very much like an embrace, but was much more, something he thought must be what it was like to feel blessed—as if some powerful force had looked on him and found him worthy in all the ways he had ever aspired to be.

And then he was standing alone, one arm raised high in the air.

Several meters away, he saw Muramatsu, Fuji, Ide, and Arashi standing with Professor Iwamoto in front of their partially destroyed HQ. All of them were gazing up intently at something in the sky. He turned to see what it was and his heart leaped at the sight of the red sphere.

'Hey, Cap!' he yelled excitedly. 'That's it, that's the red thing that crashed into me over Lake Ryugamori and—' He cut off. Something had happened after that, something incredible and impossible, more wonderfully wondrous and intensely extraordinary than the best dream he'd ever had. But it hadn't been a dream, it had most definitely happened and it had changed his life and his world and everything else. And just a minute ago, he had known what it was but now it was gone, leaving only a great big blank in his memory.

Hayata squinted up at the sphere and the red and silver

figure flying upward with it and he had another fleeting sensation, of how it had felt to have been part of something greater than himself before he'd been restored to the life he knew. He put a hand on his chest but what he'd expected to find wasn't there. Not that he actually knew what that could have been, only that it was something important, crucial, a matter of life and death.

But never mind, here he was alive. Whatever had been in the great big blank of his memory hadn't been his to keep, and that was actually a good thing because it meant his life was his own again. And life was good; not easy, but then, what fun would that be?

'Hayata, are you all right?' Muramatsu asked as his teammates gathered around him. 'You look dazed.'

'That big red sphere,' Hayata said. 'It crashed into me at Lake Ryugamori. But—' He looked around at Fuji, Ide, Arashi, and then back to Muramatsu. 'I don't remember anything after that. I try but there's—' He shook his head. 'There's nothing. It's all just… blank.'

'Seriously?' Ide said, looking as if he didn't know whether to laugh or cry. Arashi and Fuji were staring at him in astonished bewilderment. Muramatsu, however, was smiling like a man who had just had all his questions answered.

'Hayata,' he said warmly, 'we have a great deal to talk about.'

'Fine with me, Cap, I'm—' Hayata cut off. He'd been about to say invincible and for the life of him, he couldn't imagine why. 'I'm all ears.'

There were sirens in the distance as Muramatsu herded them away from Headquarters.

Epilogue

Elsewhere in the Milky Way, some three million light-years from Earth, a Being of Light approached a bright formation known as the Nebula M78 with a Travel Sphere in his arms. He was still a few parsecs from the nebula's edge when the sphere could no longer contain the joy its passenger felt at coming home again and gave way to reveal another Being of Light.

The happiness of both combined and increased until it was so bright, its light poured out across space and illuminated every part of their world, telling all who were waiting that Zoffy's mission had been successful.

The lost one had been found and once again, the company of Ultras was complete.

NOW it's THE END

ACKNOWLEDGEMENTS

Many, many, many thanks to my Ultra editor, Fenton Coulthurst, whose acumen, support, and nerves of titanium kept us on course, and to George Sandison for guidance and back-up.

Thanks also to Jeff Gomez at Starlight Runner and Danny Simon at the Licensing Group, who really know their stuff.

And of course, to Eiji Tsuburaya, for giving us Ultraman, a wonderful creation that fascinated a thirteen-year-old American girl so much in the 1960s, she ran home from school every day to watch all thirty-nine episodes on a snowy UHF TV station.

ABOUT THE AUTHOR

PAT CADIGAN is a science fiction, fantasy and horror writer, three-time winner of the Locus Award, twice winner of the Arthur C. Clarke Award and one-time winner of the Hugo Award. She wrote the novelization of *Alita: Battle Angel,* and a prequel novel to the highly anticipated film, *Iron City.* She also wrote *Lost in Space: Promised Land,* novelizations of two episodes of *The Twilight Zone,* the *Cellular* novelization, and the novelization and sequel to *Jason X.*

For more fantastic fiction, author events,
exclusive excerpts, competitions, limited editions and more

VISIT OUR WEBSITE
titanbooks.com

LIKE US ON FACEBOOK
facebook.com/titanbooks

FOLLOW US ON TWITTER AND INSTAGRAM
@TitanBooks

EMAIL US
readerfeedback@titanemail.com